Pagan Spring

Pagan Spring

A MAX TUDOR NOVEL

G. M. MALLIET

MINOTAUR BOOKS

A THOMAS DUNNE BOOK

NEW YORK

A THOMAS DUNNE BOOK FOR MINOTAUR BOOKS.
An imprint of St. Martin's Publishing Group.

PAGAN SPRING. Copyright © 2013 by G. M. Malliet. All rights reserved. Printed in the United States of America. For information, address St. Martin's Press, 175 Fifth Avenue, New York, N.Y. 10010.

www.thomasdunnebooks.com
www.minotaurbooks.com

Design by Omar Chapa

Endpaper maps design by Rhys Davies

The Library of Congress Cataloging-in-Publication Data is available upon request.

ISBN 978-1-250-02140-3 (hardcover)
ISBN 978-1-250-02139-7 (e-book)

Minotaur books may be purchased for educational, business, or promotional use. For information on bulk purchases, please contact Macmillan Corporate and Premium Sales Department at 1-800-221-7945, extension 5442, or write specialmarkets@macmillan.com.

First Edition: October 2013

10 9 8 7 6 5 4 3 2 1

CONTENTS

ACKNOWLEDGMENTS

My thanks to the Reverend O'Brien and the Reverend Warder for graciously sharing their knowledge of their churches' doctrines and traditions. All mistakes are my own.

In memory of my friend Earl J., rare gentleman

CAST OF CHARACTERS

MAXEN "MAX" TUDOR: A former MI5 agent turned Anglican priest, Max thought he'd found a measure of peace in the idyllic village of Nether Monkslip—until murder began to invade his Garden of Eden.

AWENA OWEN: The owner of Goddessspell, the village's New Age shop, Awena also has come to own Max Tudor's heart.

SUZANNA WINSHIP: Sister of the local doctor, the vampy, ambitious Suzanna often feels restless in the small village. The arrival of Umberto Grimaldi does much to alleviate her boredom.

ELKA GARTH: Owner of the Cavalier Tea Room and Garden.

ANNETTE HEDGEPETH: Proprietress of the Cut and Dried Hair Salon in Nether Monkslip.

GABRIELLE "GABBY" CREW: Hairdresser at the Cut and Dried.

MME. LUCIE CUTHBERT: Proprietress of La Maison Bleue. Lucie hosts a dinner party with her husband to celebrate the move into their new home.

TARA RAINE: A lithe, attractive yoga instructor, she rents studio space at Goddessspell.

FRANK CUTHBERT: Local historian, author (*Wherefore Nether Monkslip*), and husband of Mme. Lucie.

THADDEUS BOTTLE: A playwright and actor most recently appearing in London's West End. In retirement, he returns in triumph to the village of Nether Monkslip.

MELINDA BOTTLE: Thaddeus Bottle's long-suffering wife. Has she finally suffered too much?

BERNADINA STEED: An estate agent operating in the county of Monkslip, she sold the Cuthberts and the Bottles their new homes.

DR. BRUCE WINSHIP: An expert in general ailments, Dr. Winship revels in theories of how the criminal mind operates.

MRS. HOOSER: Max's housekeeper at the vicarage, and the mother of Tildy Ann and Tom.

ADAM BIRCH: Owner of The Online Begetter bookshop, the site of monthly meetings of the Nether Monkslip Writers' Square.

MAJOR BATTON-SMYTHE: An amateur historian.

UMBERTO AND FABIO GRIMALDI: Brothers who own the new restaurant, the White Bean, which is the talk of the village.

DETECTIVE CHIEF INSPECTOR COTTON: The kinetic DCI is again dispatched from Monkslip-super-Mare to investigate a most suspicious death in the placid village of Nether Monkslip.

FARLEY WALKER: An architect with designs on more than buildings.

KAYLA PRINCE: A waitress who waits for her big break. What makes her react so strangely to one table of customers?

THE RIGHT REVEREND BISHOP NIGEL ST. STEPHEN: He wants to know why Max Tudor is once again involved in murder.

HENRY CORK: A theatrical director, he knows where many bodies are buried.

LUCAS COOMBEBRIDGE: A seascape artist in Monkslip Curry, he may hold the clue to a baffling murder.

I am living, I remember you.

—Marie Howe, What the Living Do

You have bewitched me, body and soul, and I love, I love, I love you.
I never wish to be parted from you from this day on.

—Mr. Darcy in Pride and Prejudice

PROLOGUE

The dark was always the time of special danger. Few people ventured from their homes after sundown, as even legitimate business might be questioned.

But to be out on one's daily rounds with a shopping basket, in broad daylight, this was normal, even in these times. Even when food to fill the basket was scarce.

Even when the basket sometimes contained things hidden beneath the false bottom, things dangerous to have in one's possession, with the meager supplies of bread and vegetables piled on top.

All this had to look normal—and today's mission was for her the most important of all. Despite the risks of exposure by daylight, in the end she had decided it was safest to hide in plain sight. To brazen it out. To be just another young wife or daughter on a mission to feed her family.

Still, the risk had had to be mitigated. Nothing could happen to draw attention. There could be no unexpected sound or noise. God would forgive this one necessary thing.

Her burden was as light as a basket of kittens and she had only a short distance to walk. Having tightened her resolve, she opened the door, deliberately not looking around her—that would seem suspicious to anyone watching. She had to look as though she were dropping off supplies, an innocent errand. Once inside the ancient building, she took off her shoes, tiptoeing in her stocking feet. The hard soles of her shoes striking the stone floor might also attract attention before she was ready for it.

She set the basket down behind the door, and loosened the blanket covering its contents, averting her eyes as she did so. This would be easier without the final images. She had learned that much in recent months, to prevent any memory that could be dangerous. She had prepared a note explaining everything, and asking for prayers, and tucked it well inside the basket.

She retrieved her shoes and then rang the bell, one swift pull on the rope, and breathed a silent farewell.

Again hardening her heart, she closed the door behind her and walked down the cold stone steps.

This time, she had been unlucky, for unfriendly eyes had followed her. She didn't know it, but she had just exchanged her last ration of luck.

CHAPTER I
New Moon

Thursday, March 22

The vernal equinox had come and gone, and Easter would soon be upon them. The Reverend Maxen "Max" Tudor was in his vicarage working at his computer, a machine so antiquated, it almost needed foot pedals to operate. He was rather feverishly trying to write a sermon on one of Saint Paul's letters to the Corinthians, a sermon that was beginning to irk even Max. Paul could sound so smug at times. So sure of himself. So holier-than—

Inspired, Max began to write: "Saint Paul at times appears to our modern world as the smug apostle—a man holier-than-thou, a preachy know-it-all full of scoldings and reprimands, chiding others for the way they lived their lives. But the Corinthians . . ."

But the Corinthians, what? There was no *but.* Saint Paul at his worst had always been hard to take—the garrulous, advice-giving uncle no one wanted to sit next to at dinner, the Polonius of his day. The fun-loving Corinthians had probably stampeded in their rush to avoid the old Gloomy Gus missionary.

Max, searching his mind for a more inspiring topic, a more accessible theme, a more man-of-the-people apostle, began playing with the various fonts in his word-processing software. Gothic typeface in deep purple for the stories of the apostles, orange Arial for the words of the angel Gabriel to Mary, and blue Garamond in italics for her replies. Max deliberated some more, then in twenty-point Gothic he typed "Let there be light," and highlighted the words with the yellow text highlight function.

Well, *this* was getting him nowhere. He selected all the text on the page and with a sigh changed everything to boring old twelve-point black Times New Roman. He thought a moment, then keyed in "And darkness was upon the face of the deep."

Backspace, backspace, backspace. He stole a glance at the copy of *Glossamer Living* magazine on his desk, left behind by one of his parishioners—a sort of negative inspiration, since he and his parishioners were living in the season of Lent, a time for setting aside personal indulgences, most of which were featured between the covers of this publication. High fashion and fast cars; pricey houses, restaurants, and vacations. On the cover was a photograph of a castle garden in Normandy, with a bed of Technicolor tulips in the foreground.

How had it gotten to be springtime already? Max, leafing through his desk calendar, blinked with something like wonder, then looked at the watch on his wrist, as if that might confirm what he was seeing. The variable weather of the past few months had been disorienting, for humans as well as for plants and animals. It seemed to him the newborn lambs had arrived earlier this year. Easter, the most important day in the church calendar, would be here before he knew it—or, at this rate, had a sermon ready for it. He noticed the full moon fell on Good Friday this year, which seemed fitting somehow. Awena called it the "Egg Moon"; he had no idea why. Some pagan tradition rolled into the Easter traditions, he thought, enjoying the unintentional pun.

The God Squad would be meeting soon to discuss the "Eat, Pray,

Plan" retreat, and while preparing for these vestry meetings seemed a futile gesture, preparation was necessary to maintain some semblance of order. He also needed to schedule tryouts for instrumentalists for the Sunday services while the organist was away for the summer. Max so far had vetoed the zither and banjo, but that had left him with few options. Awena had offered to play her set of crystal singing bowls, but that was as yet a step too far for St. Edwold's.

And—*oops!* There was the appointment with the bishop coming up in a few days' time. How could he nearly have forgotten? The man's secretary had been most insistent it was important, but she hadn't known what it was about. Max, who could guess, took a red pencil out of the top drawer of his desk and drew a big star on his calendar by the appointment date. Then, still unwilling to return to his sermon, he scrabbled around in the drawer for a pencil sharpener and began honing all his pencils to a fine point.

As he procrastinated in this way, Max glanced out the casement window of the vicarage study. The slice of Nether Monkslip in his view was of a classic village whose roots predated recorded history, a place that had survived centuries of wars and feuds and conspiracies largely because it had managed to go unnoticed. It was a village of stone cottages and thatched roofs, and of timber and brick; of Tudor wattle and daub and Georgian houses and the occasional postwar development—a mix of styles pleasing to the eye and just managing to avoid the chaotic. Max, from his favorite spot up on Hawk Crest, where he would rest with his dog, Thea, from the strenuous climb, found time evaporating as he gazed, trancelike, at the peaceful scene below. The villagers more often than not would be going about their shopping, or be huddled in little groups, often accompanied by a swirl of dogs. He was reminded of a toy village setting for an elaborate train set. Outlying fields were divided by drystone walls kept in perfect repair; on a clear night, he might see in the distance a ferry leaving Monkslip-super-Mare, lights ablaze. Once the weather warmed, there would be a duck race on the River Puddmill, an event to which Max looked forward with as much innocent pleasure as a child.

The eldest villagers of Nether Monkslip, most of whom descended from serfs, were rapidly dying off or selling up, to be replaced by Yuppies from afar. These transplants—many his parishioners—were today carrying bright umbrellas against a mild March drizzle. They often passed down the road fronting the vicarage, headed to or from the High Street, which is why Max had positioned his desk at the window for maximum viewing. Hedges in front of the window provided a bit of a screen for him to hide behind.

He saw Suzanna Winship slink by, in her dolce far niente way, throwing a provocative glance in the direction of the vicarage and metaphorically revving her engines, probably just to keep in practice. He watched Elka Garth of the Cavalier Tea Room and Garden bustle past, carrying supplies, her son loitering empty-handed in her wake. That he was with her at all meant she'd managed to tear him momentarily from the video games he played so obsessively.

Then there came the ironmonger, delivering a roll of chicken wire, followed by the woman who created beaded-jewelry purses she sold over the Internet—Jeanne something. And Annette Hedgepeth, who owned Cut and Dried, the local beauty salon. Annette was with two of her hairdressers, their three shiny well-coiffed heads—one blond, one brown, one white—together in furious discussion under a large blue umbrella. Hairstylists, he supposed they were called now. The eldest of them he knew by name, even though she was not a member of St. Edwold's, but attended a Catholic church in Monkslip-super-Mare. She was Gabrielle "Gabby" Crew—a widowed aunt or some sort of relation to Mme. Lucie Cuthbert—who would be at the dinner party to which he was invited Friday night. He knew little more about this woman with the beautiful white hair than that she was the type of person often to be seen with a yoga mat under her arm: She was a frequent habitué of the yoga classes taught by Tara Raine at the back of Awena's Goddessspell shop.

The party was to be held at the new home of Frank and Lucie Cuthbert, just outside the village proper. The ostensible purpose of the gathering was to formally welcome four relative newcomers to the village; its, in reality, purpose was to showcase both the house and Lucie's expert French cooking. Two of the newcomers were a couple, Thaddeus and Melinda Bottle. Thaddeus Bottle needed no introduction, or so Max had been assured, since Thaddeus was legendary for his roles on London's West End stages as well as for his authorship of several plays. Much like Shakespeare, Thaddeus in retirement had returned to the village of his youth and bought its second-largest house. But there, Max somehow felt certain, all similarities stopped. Apart from the fact of Shakespeare's unrivaled genius, there was his differing taste in architecture: Shakespeare had his timber and brick New Place, and Thaddeus had a remodeled glass and synthetic-wood horror, which stood just past the train station on the road to Staincross Minster. The villagers called it "Bottle Palace."

In addition to the hairstylist Gabby Crew—who was living over Lucie and Frank's shop in the village until she could find other accommodation—there would be the estate agent, Bernadina Steed, who had sold thespian Thaddeus and Melinda their new home. Bernadina had, in fact, lived in the area nearly four years, but like Max she was a newcomer in Village Standard Time. Village doctor Bruce Winship had also been invited, to make an even eight at table.

Max gathered he himself had been included to balance out the male-female ratio, his usual role. He had a suspicion from hints dropped by Mme. Cuthbert that Dr. Winship was intended as a potential match for the "new" estate agent. Somehow—and Max did not yet suspect the reason—the frantic matchmaking efforts aimed at his own eligible and attractively ruffled dark head had ceased. Max's involvement with Goddessspell shop owner Awena Owen, she of the faraway gaze and shiny smile and New Age beliefs, had retired him from the field, after his having defended his "most eligible bachelor" title in several skirmishes with matchmaking members of the Women's Institute—particularly those with daughters, nieces, sisters, and maiden aunts of marriageable age. Bitter as the disappointment had been for many (particularly Dr. Winship's sister, Suzanna), no one seriously questioned Max's choice. Awena was too well liked for that, and the match, if a bit unusual, seemed (in a word) preordained.

Awena might herself have been invited, but she had gone to teach a weeklong residential course on "Cooking and Curing with Herbs" at the Women's Institute's Denman College in Oxfordshire.

Max recalled a conversation he'd had with Awena when the Bottles had first moved into the area.

"Thaddeus doesn't go out of his way to endear himself to the villagers," Awena had said. "Nor did his wife at first, really, although the general trend is to feel sorry for her. It is felt she's made a bad bargain in marrying him and doesn't quite have the wit to know how to get out of it."

"Nor the money."

"Nor the money," Awena had repeated. "It so often comes down to that, doesn't it? There have been rumblings . . . something about a prenuptial agreement."

"How in the world did the villagers learn that so quickly?" Max was genuinely stunned, although on reflection he realized this sort of thing was all in a day's work for the village grapevine, under the command of former schoolmistress Miss Pitchford.

"Melinda drinks," Awena had added. "Quite a bit. Which must cloud her judgment, not to mention drain her energy for leaving him—assuming that's what she wants to do."

"Perhaps I should go and visit them, even though they've not joined St. Edwold's."

"I'll go," said Awena. "I'll visit her when I know the Greatest Star Ever to Shine on the West End is not around. I'm liable to get much further that way. And it's a woman she needs to talk to—that is my sense of things."

"All right," said Max. "You're right. I can see that."

"Besides, I think she's used to trying to manipulate men to get what she wants. It will save you hours if I go, since we'll be able to cut through all that."

And so it was decided. Although Awena kept the details of her conversation with Melinda confidential, Max gathered that Melinda had been grateful for the offer of friendship. Once Awena learned Melinda was a great reader (somewhat to Awena's surprise), she made sure the newcomer was included in the village's book club meetings. Awena also mentioned the local writers' group was always open to new members. Again to Awena's surprise, Melinda expressed an avid interest.

Max, after briefly returning his wandering attention to his sermon, thought how much he welcomed Lucie's dinner invitation as a novelty that would take his mind off Awena's absence. For his mind dwelt on Awena more than he had thought possible: She had quickly become a mainstay in his life. Several times a day, watching something on the telly or reading a book, he would turn in his chair to make some comment or to share a joke with her and be caught up short, realizing she was gone. It all somehow led him to think of what the world—his world—would be like without her in it ever again, and his heart would seize up with despair, his breath caught by the starkness of the vista painted by his imagination. Then he would give himself a mental shake—she was only miles away—and return to the task at hand. But still the shadow would have fallen on his day.

Max again checked his watch. It was not a good time of day to call her. Awena had set times for daily meditation, Max knew—not unlike his own prescribed Anglican practice.

A shaft of sunlight just then broke from behind a cloud, enveloping the village in a haloish spring glow. "From you have I been absent in the spring," thought Max. And he sighed, this time with a sublime happiness that radiated through his heart and his soul. He was as content in his personal life as a man could be without imploding from sheer joy. His concerns, if they could even be labeled as such, were minute. Yes, his sermon for the week would not quite come together, but he'd think of *some*thing—he always did. There was a recurring stain on one wall of the church of St. Edwold's, but that would be corrected by a new roof, paid for out of a wholly unexpected benefice from a wholly unexpected benefactor. A small patch of skin on his right arm stung from a cooking wound he'd dealt himself the evening before. The local writers' group was erupting with the usual skirmishes, and he was fending off requests to join and pour oil on those troubled waters: He had enough to do getting the sermons written. That several of the members were suggesting he, as a former MI5 agent, might write a spy thriller was added inducement for him to stay away. For one thing, he was bound by the Official Secrets Act from disclosing most of what he had done and who he had been during his years with the agency. For another thing, *no*. Just: no.

These were all, however, minor, negligible irritations. He was grateful. He was content, as content as any man could ever be. He had Awena in his life and she looked set to stay there, always at his side, at least in spirit—a perfect way to describe Awena at any time. What more could he ask?

There was a stirring behind him, the whisper of small feet brushing against the carpet. A mouse might make such a noise. But this particular mouse was a child named Tom. His mother, Mrs. Hooser, had earlier brought a huge breakfast tray into the vicarage study. The boy must have followed her in and remained behind.

"That's so kind," Max had said to her, "but really, you don't have to do this." He'd started to say he'd eaten already but then realized she might catch him in the lie, as there were no traces of such activity left in the kitchen as normally there would be. Mrs. Hooser cooked with a heavy hand in the carbohydrate and bacon-grease departments.

"Nonsense!" she'd said, in her musical accent, as if she might burst into song. "I'll not be leaving you to starve on my watch."

I am *so* very far from starving, he'd thought. Apart from the wonderful meals he shared at Awena's house, there were any number of other tempting dining options, for Nether Monkslip was fast becoming a gourmet's destination, as witnessed by the recent opening of the White Bean restaurant.

When Max had learned his housekeeper's children were being left alone in the late afternoons with only periodic look-ins by a neighbor, Max had told Mrs. Hooser to have them come to the vicarage instead. The girl, Tildy Ann, now did her homework at the vicarage kitchen table. It was hard to say what her younger brother, Tom, did exactly. Max would often turn from working at his desk to find the child sitting with rapt fascination and endless patience, waiting for Max's attention. The boy was preternaturally quiet—so much so that Max suspected he was under threat of some dire punishment from his sister if he disturbed the vicar at his work. Max had overheard her once promise to shellac him if he didn't behave. Tildy Ann stood in loco parentis to Tom, since Mrs. Hooser, a single mother, was too overwhelmed most days to take on the job.

Often Max would find Tom pretending to read one of the massive tomes from the study's bookshelf, his dark head bent with intense interest over a book that weighed nearly more than he did, as he petted Thea, Max's Gordon setter and a silent (usually sleeping) partner in this vicar vigil. Sometimes, the pair of them would have fallen asleep, waiting for Max to do something. In Thea's case, the something was always to take her for a walk. What Tom wanted, apart from Max's presence, it was more difficult to say.

Max, as he headed toward the kitchen to make some hawthorn tea, noticed Tom's shoelace had come untied. Also that the boy seemed to have cut his hair himself. More likely, from the tattered look of things, his sister had cut his hair for him, using the rounded plastic scissors he'd seen her using for her paper dolls.

Max first tried teaching Tom how to tie the lace himself; the child willingly gathered one side of the bow in one fist, holding it for dear life. But his fingers were still too small and his movements too clumsy to loop the matching lace around the stem, and he kept wrapping the lace around his fist instead.

As Max was tying a double bow on the boy's shoe, the sound of breaking ornaments confirmed that Mrs. Hooser was dusting in the next room. Max gathered his newfound contentment around him like a cloak before going to investigate, more out of curiosity than annoyance. Tom and Thea padded in his wake.

Subject: Hello! And an Update

From: Gabrielle Crew (gabby@TresRapidePoste.fr)

To: Claude Chaux (Claude43@TresRapidePoste.fr)

Date: Thursday, March 22, 2012 6:48 P.M.

Claude—How lovely to receive your warm e-mail on a cold
and blustery English day.

Aside from the weather, Nether Monkslip is a lovely
village, quite cut off from the world—a drowsy sort of place.
It is just what I needed—right now, at this point in my life.
The loss of Harold was a rude jolt, a reminder, as if I needed
reminding, that life goes by too quickly. We must all seize our
own happiness as we can.

You asked if I had made new friends here. Indeed I have!
The villagers are wonderful about keeping me included. And
living over Frank and Lucie's shop, with its little white ceramic
pig propped beside the front door, I feel very much at the
center of village doings. Tomorrow I'm having dinner at their
new home. As I have said before, they have treated me from
the first like a long-lost relative. I nearly am a relative, as you
know. These distant relationships mean more as time passes
and fewer of us are left behind.

What a coincidence it was to open a magazine and see
Lucie's village pictured in its pages. Well, the article actually
was about a restaurant in the village, the White Bean, but the
village itself is fast becoming what the young people would
call a "foodie destination." Fortunately, I think, the village
really cannot sustain a huge influx of people. To a man and to
a woman, they keep themselves to themselves and they like
it that way.

I'm sorry I have to rush, but tonight is the crochet circle

I told you about and I'm running late now. It is true that the older one gets, the busier one gets. I've been asked to join the local writers' group, as well—I don't know about that! My scribblings I've always held private. But I did want you to know that, as always, I think of you.

Rushing now,

Your loving Gabby xox

CHAPTER 2
Writers' Square

Thursday, March 22, 7:15 P.M.

Later that same evening, Adam Birch was telling his fellow members of the Writers' Square the story of Nunswood, the thicket near the ancient menhirs up on Hawk Crest, and how it came by its name. He held the legal pad on which he had been writing all that afternoon, clutching his pen tightly in his fist like a child learning to write, a picture of concentration as the words had spilled from the pen.

"They say the nun was a 'real' sister of one of the monks at the abbey—his blood relative, you see—and she passed through Nether Monkslip with a group of nuns on their way to found a nunnery near Temple Monkslip. The legend is she's buried on Hawk Crest, with its steep, winding path leading to the top—buried at a secret location within Nunswood. Her grave is rumored to be not far from the menhirs, near the healing spring."

"Not quite healing enough, then, was it?" said Suzanna. "If she died, I mean."

"They say she was murdered," said Adam. "There's no cure for being murdered."

The members of the Writers' Square sat in one of the many homey nooks of Adam's bookshop, The Onlie Begetter, where stacks of old books were used as table legs, and coffee-table books were used as tables, lending a new meaning to the term. They gathered around a real table, a square wooden one—a coffee table scattered with pens and notebooks and novels and magazines, and illuminated by two Tiffany-style lamps and by the golden, cozy glow of the fireplace. The shop, offering both new and "antiquarian" books, featured a stained-glass window of Saint Francis de Sales, the patron saint of writing. Local antiquarian Noah had rescued the ancient find from a church scheduled for demolition.

The Writers' Square group had been named after *much* heated discussion, and in the end took its name from the square table they used for their meetings. Besides, it sounded so much more avant-garde than "Writers' Circle." They were determined, Frank in particular, to be avant-garde if at all possible.

Adam had been unusually busy that day, as the deadline loomed for the monthly magazine he used to promote his shop; he wrote it all himself, and set the pages using the desktop publishing software that had come bundled with his computer. Suzanna often was heard to remark that it looked as if the layout had been done by a man wearing sunglasses in a darkened, windowless room, with crooked columns of text unevenly spaced, sentences that mysteriously disappeared in mid-flow, and uncaptioned photos having no evident bearing on the topic at hand. A review of the latest legal thriller, for example, might be illustrated by a photo of a wild boar. It was called the *Village Voice* and it was hugely popular amongst the habitués of the Hidden Fox, the Cavalier, and the Horseshoe.

Waiting for Adam to put out the CLOSED sign on the shop door, Suzanna Winship and Elka Garth had poured themselves coffee in the shop's little kitchen alcove.

"Have you been to Cut and Dried since Gabby started working there?" Suzanna shook her head.

"You should give her a try," said Elka. "She's very trendy."

"Since when is blue hair trendy?"

"Well, her own hair *is* bluish, but that's just her style. It's that white so white, it looks blue in certain lights—very flattering. She's really good at sizing you up."

Suzanna leveled a gaze out of her chocolate brown eyes. "No one is good at sizing me up." She examined one manicured hand. "Many are called; few are chosen. That place is like something out of Miss Pitchford's day—she who, by the way, would call it 'the hairdresser's.' These days, except for an emergency updo, I go to Alfonse at the Do or Dye in Monkslip-super-Mare."

"You should try Gabby," Elka repeated. "Remember when I tried to cut my own fringe a few weeks ago? I looked like I'd had my head half chewed off by a wild animal. Gabby's the one who fixed it. Free of charge." She fluffed out the hair now lightly feathered across her forehead. "She's ever so good."

Suzanna eyed her critically. Apart from the half-inch outgrowth of white root showing skunklike at the part, Elka's hair was showing vast improvement lately. Elka worked long hours, seldom taking time out for herself. She even looked as though she might have dropped half a stone from around her middle. She was wearing her jumper turned inside out, and one of her hoop earrings was on backward, but even so . . .

"We'll see." Suzanna, in jeggings, heels, and an oversized cashmere jumper, settled against the cushions on one of the sofas. "But Alfonse is just getting used to me. It's hard to make a change. One feels one is being unfaithful somehow."

"Oh, I do know what you mean. It's like a divorce, isn't it? You simply—"

Frank Cuthbert had sat quietly throughout this discussion in an overstuffed chair by the fireplace, scanning his notes and sipping his glass of red wine. He wore rose-tinted glasses and a turtleneck under his tweed sports jacket, and his bristly white beard and hair had gone uncombed in his haste not to be late for the meeting. He looked like a bereted woodland creature emerging from the brambles after some sort of massive literary struggle for survival. Sadie, his bichon frise, lay somnolently at his feet, nose buried in her paws.

"Ladies, if you wouldn't mind . . ." he interrupted importantly, as Adam joined them. "Your pages?"

Pages was a professional term Frank had heard used somewhere. He liked tossing it into the conversation, along with the word *script,* which he condescendingly had explained to the group was short for *manuscript.*

Suzanna took a seat and began leafing through a copy of *Write What You Know* magazine. "There's an ad in here for a 'Certified Poetry Therapist,'" she said, briefly turning the open magazine so they all could see. "I never heard of such a thing, have you? What next, a comic book therapist?" She held the periodical at arm's length, reading aloud. "'Poetry can be a powerful tool for unleashing secret healing and creative forces in the psyche.'"

"You can be certified to do that?" asked Elka.

"I think one had probably better be, don't you? I wouldn't want amateurs probing around *my* psyche."

"I'm sure that's all well and good for some," said Frank brusquely. "But poetry is beyond the realm of our expertise in this group. Now, ladies, if I could just—"

"I don't think you need expertise. I think you only need a heart," said Elka earnestly.

"If having a heart were the only qualification, we'd all be famous," said Frank.

Elka hesitated. "I was encouraging Gabby to join us, you see. She told me she writes poetry sometimes."

Frank was hugely reluctant. "We'd have to put it to a vote."

"There are only four of us, with Awena gone." Awena, always a leavening influence, was absent because of her class at Denman College. With the group's encouragement, she was writing a book that encompassed her philosophy, her seasonal tips, her recipes, and her herbal remedies. Suzanna was predicting an Oprah endorsement. "We'd need a tiebreaker," said Elka. "As you know, we've had some attrition lately . . . the Major."

The Major lived alone now, surrounded by Benares brass, his retirement activities supervised with languid contempt by a Persian cat. He had dropped out of the group some time ago, as he found writing interfered with his golf game. He had been working on a military history of the world and had found this to be a mushrooming project. But the chapters he had shared with the group, characterized as they were by sweeping yet achingly dull summaries of historic events, would remain with them forever, as Suzanna had observed.

Similarly, Melinda Bottle, not long ago arrived in Nether Monkslip, had participated in the group when it had met on Saturdays, although *participated* might be too strong a term, since she seemed to have only a nodding acquaintance with the written word. She once submitted for the group's consideration an index card containing a home recipe for an avocado face mask. Elka had correctly surmised that the group meetings were an excuse for Melinda to get out of the house and away from her husband, who was reputed to be somewhat of a tyrant.

"Oh, for heaven's sake," said Suzanna, after some further discussion. "If Elka vouches for Gabby, that's good enough for me. A poet would provide a nice sort of balance."

Adam now picked up his legal pad to continue his read-aloud. The Writers' Square did not exist, as it might first appear, as an arena for its members to get on one another's nerves. These budding authors were, for the most part, extremely gentle with one another's creations. Anything that seemed to imply criticism generally came from one source, and that source was similarly accepted (for the most part) as just being true to itself.

"You don't feel," said Suzanna, when Adam had stopped to draw breath, "that the phrase 'blue as the sky' has been just a tad overused in describing the color of someone's eyes?"

"Yes, yes," said Adam. "I rather thought so, too. But it's deucedly hard to describe eyes, when you think about it. How would you have handled it?"

"I would have said her eyes were blue," answered Suzanna.

"And you call yourself a romance writer?" asked Frank.

"I take your point," said Suzanna. "Steamy blue eyes, then. My hero has steamy blue eyes, but go ahead and borrow that if you like."

"But you can't—" began Elka.

"What can't I?"

"Your hero is already steaming quite a lot, from what I've read of your book. He steams and smolders throughout. I would use another word for his eyes."

Suzanna gave this some thought.

"Moldering, then."

"Is that a word?"

"Yes. It means disintegrating," Adam said. "I don't quite think that's the word you want in this instance."

And so it went, throughout the long evening, a perfect illustration of why so little actual writing got done in the Writers' Square.

"'And on winter nights,'" Adam read, "'when the wind is heard in the trees, it is her voice calling for her lover, whom in life she darest not name.'"

They were all nicely settled into the session now, coffee cups or wineglasses full, and eyes bright, in the case of Suzanna and Frank, like owls on the alert for stray field mice or, in Frank's case, the stray comma.

Adam flipped over another page of his pad and cleared his throat. The brown cardigan he wore in the shop as a sort of dust jacket had been replaced, in deference to the cool weather and the bookish occasion, with a fisherman's knit jumper and a wool scarf looped artfully around his neck. In summer, it would be a Hawaiian shirt, his trousers held up with striped braces. Befitting his profession, Adam had a domed Shakespearean forehead, basset-hound eyes, and a quiet, scholarly manner. He had been amicably divorced for many years and seemed untouched by the general downturn in the book trade. He went to book sales and had uncovered a few gems, relying on instinct as much as knowledge. He sold mostly through an online presence these days, but he was a book lover to his fingertips and too often couldn't bear to part with his signed treasures.

Adam had set aside the other novel he'd been writing for years, having given up on a creation in which the literary world had shown either no interest or an active dislike. It had been a modern novel, experimental— so much so as to be incomprehensible. Suzanna described it as the written equivalent of a whistle only dogs could hear. Now he was writing something "popular," and was thinking of calling it *A Death in Nunswood*.

"'And now she lives the life beyond the veil, the veil we darest not pierce.'" Adjusting his rimless spectacles, Adam peered about the group, to see how they were taking this. "Future generations have called the spot haunted, and on All Hallows' Eve, few darest approach Nunswood at night."

It was all too much for Suzanna. From where she sat on the overstuffed chintz-covered sofa, feet tucked beneath her, she drawled, "Adam, darest I interrupt you to ask whether *darest* is a word?" She turned inquiringly toward Frank, their resident pedant. "I don't think *darest* is a word, do you?"

Frank pulled thoughtfully at his beard. "It *was* a word at one time."

"So was *codpiece*," said Suzanna. "Unless we're writing a historical novel about the Cultural Revolution of Henry the Eighth, I don't think we need to revive the worst of the old language."

"It is Poetry," said Adam. The uppercase *P* was clearly implied. "I am using Poetic License." Ditto the *L*.

"It's a word if it has letters," said Frank. Suzanna looked at him, for once not quite knowing what to say.

"DKNY has letters," said Elka Garth doubtfully. Elka was writing a cookbook, a collection of baking recipes. She was hamstrung by the fact that her methods and measurements were intuitive, honed over years of operating the Cavalier Tea Room. She could eyeball with scientific precision how much flour to pour into the "big chipped yellow bowl," for example, but she had had trouble translating this into grams.

"Hmm," said Frank and Suzanna together.

"Let Adam go on," suggested Elka. "I like this story."

Adam, a gentle soul, his petals easily crushed, looked gratefully at Elka, his brown eyes magnified by the thick lenses of his glasses.

"Go on," said Suzanna, but in a low voice. "It might cure my insomnia."

"Is there really a magical spring where a murder was committed?" asked Elka. "Formed at the spot where the nun's blood was shed?"

"That depends on who you darest ask," replied Suzanna.

"Whom," corrected Frank automatically.

"What?" said Suzanna.

"That depends on *whom* you ask," said Frank.

"*Real*ly?" Suzanna managed to pack quite a bit of feeling into the two syllables. "Then I'll ask the right person next time," she said. "And the spring," she continued, turning away from Frank, the Grammar Czar, "has been around since anyone can remember. It used to be called 'Blood Spring.' Still is, by some of the village wrinklies. Its healing properties have been well known for centuries."

"Absolutely," said Elka.

Suzanna nodded. "It's not talked about much—they want to keep the tourists away." "They" were understood to be the members of the Nether Monkslip Parish Council. "When I first came to Nether Monkslip, I took out a book on the subject from the perambulating library. And, of course, Awena knows all about it."

"Thank you, Elka and Suzanna," said Adam. "If I may I'll insert a bit of background here, since *some of us* at least seem to be interested. Monks from the old abbey at some point took over the pagan spring, which had been there, as Suzanna says, forever—adopting and caring for it. Interestingly, they didn't choose to obliterate the pagan symbols they found scattered about, often carved into the stone menhirs. They incorporated them with their Christian symbols."

"That was broad-minded of them," said Elka.

Adam nodded. "This live-and-let-live attitude persisted until the Reformation and the dissolution of the monasteries. The spring was forgotten. It was rumored that when Henry's men came to destroy the "popish" symbols, a monk from the nearby abbey, on the orders of the abbot, buried some of the monastery's treasure at the spring."

"Very good idea, that," said Elka.

"I'm thinking of turning the story into a screenplay," Adam said.

"Oh!" said Elka, to whom screenplay writing was a dark art, like necromancy. "Do you know how to write a screenplay? Don't you have to format it and things?"

"Well, it's just dialogue, really. Beckettian. Brief, punchy sentences. You know."

"What's the title?"

"*Wait for Spring.*"

"I'm waiting."

"I mean that's the title."

Frank said, "I thought of turning *Wherefore Nether Monkslip* into a screenplay." *Wherefore Nether Monkslip*, or *WNM* as it was called by those who felt they'd read or heard about it *at least* a thousand times, was Frank's contribution to the folklore of the region. Originally, it had debuted in pamphlet form. Frank had typed every word in a slow hunt and peck at his old typewriter and then had had photocopies made at the stationers in Monkslip-super-Mare, complete with his later insertions and crossings-out. Later, he'd splurged, dipping into his savings to have the pamphlet published by a vanity press. (That he had not consulted his wife, Lucie, over this decision was still a hot topic in the Cuthbert household.) Copies were available for purchase, as he liked to say, everywhere—that is, at the Hidden Fox pub and, more recently, at the little shop attached to the post office. He had in the meantime secured another blurb for the back cover (to add to the one from Jack Ralston-Fifle, Historian and Author), this time from "Literature Authority Ivor Blattfallen." It read, in total, "Frank Cuthbert's finest effort to date," which neatly managed to sidestep several issues, including the fact that it was Frank's only effort to date.

"I thought *Wherefore Nether Monkslip* was more a rambler's guide to the area," said Suzanna.

"Oh, I've much expanded it beyond the early drafts. I've added characters, you see, to flesh the whole thing out."

"Ah," said Suzanna.

"I've just been reworking chapter sixty-seven," said Frank. "I'll read a few paragraphs aloud, shall I?"

Suzanna listened patiently—as patiently as Suzanna could, like someone waiting for the results of urgently commissioned chest X-rays or an autopsy report—and finally broke in to say, "Frank, the *clichés*! Why don't you just have him twirl his mustache while you're at it?"

"You feel the character is a cliché, Suzanna?" Frank fairly bristled with tetchy annoyance: It was as though the hairs in his beard stood on end. Frank, for all his writerly optimism, occasionally succumbed to moments of self-doubt. Sadie awoke and stood beside him, a look of anxiety on her face.

"Is that what you're implying?" Frank demanded.

"I *imply* nothing. I clearly state that you're hamming it up too much. Do you want my help getting published or don't you?" Suzanna, with her tenuous and fading connections to the world of London publishing, frequently adopted this sort of attitude, best described as "take it or leave it." Only Suzanna emerged unscathed from the resulting spats, her wanton disregard for opposing opinions intact. She was one of those lucky people born without filters; for the most part, she simply didn't care what others thought.

"I'm thinking I might put an excerpt on the Internet," Frank told the others, gazing darkly ahead and avoiding Suzanna's eyes.

"Oh!" Elka was enthusiastic. She sold her marzipan creations over the Web—tiny, exquisitely crafted animals and flowers—but had hired a firm to build her Web site and process orders. How they did this was, to her, an even darker art than scriptwriting. "Do you know how to Webmaster?"

"It's child's play. In fact, my grandchild has offered to help me."

Elka turned to Suzanna. "How's your book coming along, then?" Suzanna, when last heard from, had been writing what might politely be called a romance with erogenous interludes.

"Swimmingly. Have a look." Suzanna handed her a notebook with a cardboard cover of a vivid paisley design of pinks and greens.

Elka read a few pages in silence, then put down the notebook, as if its pages might ignite in her hands.

"I've never seen our vicar surge or pulse, now that I come to think of it," she said at last. "Max just . . . well, he's just *there*. He is what he is."

"Who said I'm writing about Max?"

"Puh-leeze. 'Black hair falling rakishly over one gray eye, and a devilish grin'?"

"Yes, so? That describes hundreds of men."

"'A devilish grin that belied a . . .'"—she reached for the line again—"'a compassionate and tender nature'? And what happened to his other eye, by the way?"

"Dozens of men," insisted Suzanna. "I can fix that bit about the eye."

Adam, who had left momentarily to replenish his coffee cup, rejoined them. Elka told him, "I think Suzanna may have discovered a new romance novel subgenre. Vicar porn."

"Really," said Adam. "I'm not sure if it's all that new. Anyway, I thought you were writing your memoirs?"

"I can do both. It's all the same thing, when you really think about it, isn't it? I've already had my author photo taken. So I'm ready, whenever the iron's hot."

"You just have to finish writing the book."

"Goes without saying." She waved a manicured hand, as if casting a spell over the pages in her notebook, making them write themselves. "Won't take long."

"I worked on my book for years, as you know," said Adam. "*Years.*"

She might not have heard, for Suzanna was not open to suggestions that anything about this book-writing process might be time-consuming or labor-intensive. "Now all that's needed is a prominent socialite to host my book launch," she said.

"Apart from having an actual book to launch, you mean?" said Frank.

"Nether Monkslip doesn't have a socialite," said Elka, having mentally surveyed the field of potential candidates. "Prominent or otherwise."

"That is true," said Suzanna. "There is a gaping void in our socialite department. Excepting the folk at Totleigh Hall when they're about, which they hardly ever seem to be."

"*I'm* thinking of writing a memoir next," said Frank. "If the book doesn't take off. It's funny, but I'm still not hearing back from any of the agents I mailed it to." They were all thinking that the market for Frank's memoirs would be approximately five people. Frank came from quite a small family.

"Did you hear anything back from Thaddeus Bottle?" Elka asked Frank.

"No," said Frank shortly. Frank had sent a copy of his book to the playwright and actor on his arrival in Nether Monkslip, along with a polite request that he do a guest appearance at the Writers' Square. The reply, when it came, had been scathing.

"You might try approaching him again," said Elka tentatively.

"Let me think about it."

"It's just that I—"

"Okay, I've thought about it. And the answer is no."

"I think you're wise," said Adam, who may have been reminded of a recent visit by the author (the *semi*famous author, Adam corrected himself) and how he'd tried to browbeat Adam into stocking copies of his plays. No use telling the man scripts didn't sell. What a pompous know-it-all.

"I gave Thaddeus a summary of my book to read," Adam told them. "He glanced at it and said, 'I have not read anything so not worth reading than this in a long time.'"

They all made shocked, gasping sounds. "Oh, Adam. How horrible for you. And how horrible of *him*," said Elka.

Adam shrugged. "S'okay. Maybe he's right."

"I don't see," said Elka, "how anyone so lacking in taste about everything else could be right about this. I mean, just look at that house of his."

They all loyally nodded their heads.

A small grin lifted the corners of Adam's mouth. Could Elka be right?

"She's absolutely right," Suzanna assured him. "He always struck me as an idiot with a first-class mind, if you follow. Not precisely dim, but that ego gets in the way. And that emaciated stick of a wife, Melinda. What is *up* with those two?"

Elka agreed. "Pay absolutely no attention. If I were you, I'd be more worried he's over there trying to remember what he read so he can steal it from you."

"Do you really think . . ." Adam began, alarmed. Clearly this possibility had not occurred to him.

Frank nodded. "Look, no one is crazy about that guy. He seems to have moved here just to lord it over all of us peons. And this just proves it. I doubt he even read your summary. He just pretended to."

Now Adam was beaming. What good friends he had. Oh, they might demolish one another's work at times, but they never would allow anyone else to do the same. Thaddeus had unknowingly just solidified his position as an outsider doomed to remain outside. It took long enough for a newcomer to be accepted into the fold in Nether Monkslip. With Thaddeus, a long time might mean forever.

"How do you spell *playwright*?" asked Elka, who had volunteered to take minutes of these meetings. "P-l-a-y-w-r-i-t-e?" It was felt that what they were doing in the Writers' Square was of such importance to future generations, it needed to be documented.

"You would think so, wouldn't you?" said Suzanna. "But I'm not certain we need to memorialize Mr. Thaddeus Bottle."

"So, our next meeting . . . let me see . . ." And here Frank pulled a calendar from the stack of papers before him. "Yes, we're on the calendar for April nineteenth." Frank had assumed a leadership role although, in theory, and in keeping with the stated avant gardeness of the group, its manifesto was that "all were equal, all voices to be heard" (Frank Cuthbert, *Minutes of the Writers' Square—Founding Meeting*).

Suzanna held up her hand. She had assumed a recently vacated position in the role of Village Bossypants, and now reigned unchallenged, the *capo di tutti capi* of the Women's Institute. She had taken on this mantle with a great deal of style and verve, and reveled in a role that provided an outlet for her otherwise-thwarted ambitions. Still, things were not as bad as what the villagers had experienced with her predecessor, and no one could question that Suzanna had brought new life to the sessions. Most recently, the Women's Institute had provided a "Know Your Bits" evening, a feminist offering boycotted by Miss Pitchford and several others. The topic had, of course, been Suzanna's idea.

"Let me stop you right there," she said now. "We've got a conflict. The Women's Institute meets that night instead of the usual. We have a guest speaker—the chef from the new restaurant." She picked up a copy of *Glossamer Living* magazine and began thumbing through its thick, shiny pages. "All of you did see the article about the White Bean?"

The talk of the village for weeks had been the opening of the new restaurant—an establishment featuring organic, local-sourced, and sustainable food. The place had received significant attention in the local-and-beyond press. It was, they said, "ecofriendly," having been renovated with reclaimed and recycled materials by an uber-trendy outfit called ARchiTecture (+Y+) DEsign.

"We're lucky to get Fabio as a speaker," said Suzanna. "Fortunately, I grabbed him and his brother before the restaurant took off and they got so busy."

"You are speaking metaphorically, of course," said Frank with feigned innocence. "What *is* the brother's name? I keep forgetting."

"I think it's Umberto," Suzanna replied vaguely. She sighed as deeply as her undergarments would allow. Suzanna had sworn off tummy tamers, which she likened to the whalebone corset, when Awena had "swooped in and stolen Max," although the ban hadn't lasted once she'd set eyes on Umberto, also known as Grimaldi the Elder. She had last night asked her brother Bruce if she could borrow a scalpel.

"I don't see how else I'm going to get out of this thing. I might need the Jaws of Life."

"That is really bad for your circulation, you know," Bruce Winship had said.

"So is spinsterhood."

Leaning over with difficulty to pat Sadie, Suzanna said, "Fabio is married," hoping to deflect attention from the fact it was the elder of the Grimaldis she had set her sights on. "Completely off-limits as far as I'm concerned. Anyway, we'll have to move the Writers' Square meeting by a few days. Thursday's the only day he was available." She flipped through her mobile phone's calendar with brisk efficiency, as if masterminding an invasion. "Let's see . . ."

"Last year, we had the Royal Wedding Bank Holiday buggering things up," mused Frank. "So there's that to be grateful for this year—no wedding. I don't see Prince Harry getting married anytime soon, do you? Of course, the Olympics and the Diamond Jubilee this summer will pose a challenge."

Thus, thought Adam, are major historic events reduced to their elements in Nether Monkslip.

Suzanna said, "Let's say next time we'll meet on the Tuesday prior to the WI meeting unless you hear differently from me. I'll send out an e-mail."

"So we've tabled the idea of a guest speaker for now, have we?" asked Elka.

"Until we can do better than Thaddeus Bottle," said Frank. "I'm thinking now it's too bad Lucie's invited him over to the house for dinner."

"I keep hearing he needs no introduction," said Adam, smiling, still warmed by his friends' defense against Thaddeus Bottle's ugly attack.

"Good," said Frank. "Because he won't get one from me."

Subject: Nether Monkslip

From: Gabrielle Crew (gabby@TresRapidePoste.fr)

To: Claude Chaux (Claude43@TresRapidePoste.fr)

Date: Friday, March 23, 2012 12:48 P.M.

Dear Claude—It was so good, as always, to hear from you.

Nether Monkslip is starting to feel more like home to me than anywhere I've ever lived. I hope Bernadina—the estate agent I told you about—I hope she can find something reasonable for me to lease. Prices here are "defeating the current negative trend," she says. Everyone is hearing the call of the charming old-world village, the slower pace of life, and the return to a simpler time—especially those of retirement age. But, in fact, many of the people who have relocated here have not retired, but simply have moved their businesses online.

Not all of the newcomers are my age. Popularity is giving the village the life it needs, attracting both young and old. More babies are appearing, and our handsome vicar is kept busy with baptisms. A village needs children, or it will die out.

Of course, everything is illusion, isn't it? You might be living peaceably in a village like Nether Monkslip, a place where they plant vegetables according to the lunar calendar. And then one day your world might end.

I do so miss Harold at times.

But like you, I love this time of year, with its spring flowers. There is the "gentle rain" of Shakespeare's day, perhaps a bit less of it now, with global warming. There have been drought conditions in much of England, but Nether Monkslip has been spared. Right now it's raining, and that's bad for people like me in the hair business. It's like working in a car wash in that regard. I thought I'd use the free time wisely and write to you, and maybe work a bit on my poetry.

For the most part, I am content, anxious only to try out a recipe for carrots with dill—a recipe given me by Awena Owen, the one I told you about. The woman who runs the New Agey shop. It's funny how everything old is new again, with everyone going back to the basics. Bless her, but my generation, and yours, "invented" organic food.

Love, your Gabby

CHAPTER 3
Captive Audience

Friday, March 23, 6:00 P.M.

The man who needed no introduction was at home preparing for what he thought of as the evening's performance. Every public appearance was to Thaddeus Bottle a presentation—a chance to display his good looks and exercise his actor's voice; a chance to shine, and to impress his (usually captive) audience. After a lifetime of getting if not the best seat in a restaurant, at least the sort of seat saved for a life peer, Thaddeus knew his worth—even if he usually overestimated it. The fact that his name had not yet appeared on an Honours List was, he felt certain, an oversight that would be remedied in time. His career had been so long and, well, long. And besides, "Lord Thaddeus Bottle" had such a ring to it. Wouldn't his parents have been proud?

Proud? They'd have been struck dumb.

He was a man of short but imposing stature, with a physique that owed much to the men's slimming corset he wore around his midsection, for Thaddeus was as vain, if not vainer, than any actress when it came to maintaining a youthful appearance. In the same way, his stature was elevated by the shoe lifts he wore any time he was likely to run into his "legions of fans," as he thought of them. In London, he had clung fondly to the belief that his fans included the butcher, the baker, and the bookie around the corner; around no one except his wife did Thaddeus let down his show-must-go-on facade. In the same way, he allowed no one to use the familiar or shortened form of his name; it was never Thad or Thaddee, but Thaddeus.

He was dark of eye and hawklike of nose, and made a striking impression he liked to highlight by keeping his head thrown back, chin and nose in the air, so people could enjoy his Roman-coin profile. His crowning glory was his thick mane of brown hair, always described in his performance reviews as "leonine," as though the hair had taken on a life of its own and would soon deliver its own lines onstage. Thaddeus Never Thad used a special shampoo to bring out the highlights in that mass of hair, which was, in fact, quite beautiful. The shampoo cost fifteen pounds for a small bottle, and he reported it to Her Majesty's Revenue and Customs as a business expense, lumped under the "business equipment" category, along with his blow-dryer and curling iron, the corset and the lifts, so as not to invite indelicate probing by Her Majesty's tax compliance professionals.

His wife of seven years, Melinda, was primping in the next room. She was not a stage professional, or Thaddeus would have tried to pass his expenses off as hers. Although she was or had been a professional society beauty, this was not an occupation widely recognized among the cube dwellers of HMRC. Melinda would have argued that it should have been, given the amount of work that was involved, particularly lately, as she was far from being in the first flush of youth. Also, playing handmaiden to the great writer/actor should probably have counted as full-time employment in the case of Melinda Bottle.

Her brunette good looks had brought her to Thaddeus's attention when she was still married to her former spouse, which union was to prove a minor inconvenience. One glance, as she would later recall, from

Thaddeus's piercing dark eyes beneath thatchy white eyebrows and she had been his. Thaddeus had been a widower, whose wife had been found (alive, of course) in flagrante with her lover, which exposure dovetailed beautifully with Melinda's own infatuation with Thaddeus Bottle.

In short, having seen him, Melinda had been determined to conquer him. She had been so besotted, she hadn't noticed the difference in their ages. She had been captivated, ignoring the years that separated them and seeing only the dashing figure of his early publicity stills. She supposed a shrink would say she was looking for a father figure. Too right, as she now understood. Her own father had been a right bastard, and Thaddeus was living up to his legacy. Funny how you don't realize the fatal, familiar choices you're making before it's too late to go back. Life doesn't come with a rewind button. Or even, in Melinda's case, a pause button.

Thaddeus had all the glamour of the West End stage at his back; her first husband, Jack, wealthy even after the worldwide stock market meltdown, could not compete, for Melinda had secret dreams of one day appearing before the footlights with her new husband, an ambition as yet unrealized. It was dawning on her that it might never be realized, now that they'd come to live miles from the London stage. Too late she would comprehend she should probably have asked Thaddeus for an impartial assessment of her acting abilities *before* she married him. He was blunt in his judgment now: She had zero talent as an actress. If she'd ever had talent, he'd said, in a contemptuous tone that still stung to recall, the talent would have made an appearance long before.

Whatever reasons she'd had for marrying him, he'd certainly not married her to advance her nonexistent career. He'd married her for her looks and for her relative youth. For he, at seventy-eight, was a man of consequence, and he needed someone of an appropriate age to play the part of wife to a man of such masterful consequence as he.

It was all too late, in any event, thought Melinda now. By the time she began to suspect she should have looked before she leaped, her now-ex, Jack, had already moved on to greener pastures. He'd been having an affair during the last years of his marriage to Melinda, a fact he kept well hidden during the divorce proceedings—and the green pastures were owned by a wealthy and titled widow ten years his senior. That certainly, thought Melinda, explained a lot.

Current spouse Thaddeus having taken over the large mirror in the master bathroom, Melinda was making do with the vanity table by the bedroom window. They had purchased the house a year ago. The previous owner had added a bulbous modern appendage at the back, and Melinda, trying to make the old blend with the new, had had to call on every small talent in her interior decoration arsenal since they had moved in. Not to mention home repair: Like many such modern constructions, the house was all style and little substance, "restored" by what turned out to be a fly-by-night contractor. Out of place in the village proper, the house, mercifully, was situated some distance past the train station and at the end of a country lane hidden by trees. Although it was the second-largest house in or near the village of Nether Monkslip, they had bought it for a song. The reasons why were not apparent until they'd moved in. Thaddeus had insisted the house needed no inspection—an interesting choice, since Thaddeus's own skills in home repair were nonexistent. The estate agent, Bernadina Steed, had warned them that she saw potential problems, which was why Bernadina had become a rather trusted friend since the move into the house. Melinda had come to rely on her, first of all, for recommendations as to trustworthy local repairmen and other experts, and, second, for her no-nonsense and forthright approach to life. Despite outward differences, the two women had found they had much in common—things that others might have seen as a hindrance to friendship.

Melinda, if anything, was looking for a way out, a release valve. Common cause against Thaddeus was one such release.

The enemy of my enemy is my friend, thought Melinda.

She now critically surveyed her appearance as she twirled a lock of coffee-colored hair around her curling iron, a match for her husband's. She'd been styled and highlighted just that morning at the Cut and Dried. But the nearness of the village to the English Channel and the time of year meant humidity, and that meant constant vigilance on Melinda's part to ensure the curl did not expand, spongelike, by the end of the day.

As she preened and primped, adding a little wing of black eyeliner to the corner of each eye, she thought about the choice she'd made. Choices, rather. The glamorous life she'd pictured when she'd married Thaddeus had lasted exactly five years, which time Melinda had largely spent, like Lucy Ricardo, trying to talk her husband into putting her into a show or even writing a play just for her. In the sixth year, Thaddeus had started talking about retirement. In the seventh, it had become clear that he pictured retirement as meaning a return to the village of his youth. It seemed he had fond memories of his time here, the son of the local saddler.

"Big fish in a small pond" was the phrase that kept going through Melinda's mind.

A nearly empty martini glass rested on the dressing table, at her left hand. Thaddeus never seriously objected to her copious drinking, since alcohol helped keep her thin. So did smoking, but he'd made her give that up, due to the secondhand dangers.

Now she took a final sip as she opened her jewelry box and pulled out the antique earrings Thaddeus had given her as a wedding present. They were still her favorites, second only to the antique pair she'd lost a few weeks before, which had been an engagement present.

She'd be willing to bet these earrings and everything else in the jewelry box that what Thaddeus really liked about this place, Nether Monkslip, was the chance it gave him to lord it over the peasants. But he'd been shocked to realize the peasants had mostly moved on, and more sophisticated urban escapees had taken their place. Thaddeus was a celebrity, to be sure, but—much to his disappointment—he was not being hailed as a god.

She held the earrings up to catch the last of the light. They were a Victorian design of gold and enamel in the shape of two butterflies. They dangled fetchingly from her earlobes, catching the light as it bounced off the tiny embedded diamonds.

She switched off the curling iron. She didn't see how, at the age of forty-five, she was expected to survive if she left him. Her foreshortened view of her future clouded every judgment, every decision. It was like reading a map using a magnifying glass—she could not see anything to the north or south, anything beyond the area of focus. She knew that if she pulled back, if she lifted her gaze, she might be able to see the whole path ahead, but somehow the will to do that had deserted her. Thaddeus controlled everything—her, her looks, her friends (he did not approve of Bernadina, of course), her makeup, the very food she ate.

And the purse strings. Always, and at the bottom of her indecision, lay that simple fact.

Thaddeus held the purse strings very tightly indeed.

Subject: The Villagers

From: Gabrielle Crew (gabby@TresRapidePoste.fr)

To: Claude Chaux (Claude43@TresRapidePoste.fr)

Date: Friday, March 23, 2012 6:30 P.M.

Claude—You asked about the people in my new village.
I suppose I'll start with the Reverend Max Tudor, one of the
most appealing men I've ever come across. He's an Anglican
vicar, but he's not one of the preachy sorts of vicars, if you
follow. He is in love with the woman who runs the local New
Age shop, and she with him—they fondly believe no one
notices this, which is rather sweet of them, we all think. They
are a charming couple, and made for each other, so no one
can help but wish them well. Watch this space for an
announcement of a wedding, or so we all hope. What a
celebration that will be! We—the villagers, and I have quickly
come to count myself as one of them, you see—we have
rather banded together to try to ensure Max's bishop doesn't
get wind of this news before Max and Awena are ready to
announce the banns. Awena is . . . well, she's rather a
spiritual person and goes her own way in the religion
department. There may be trouble if the purple-robed
brigade learns of this too soon. They'd be worried about what
the press may make of it, of course. Otherwise, I am not sure
they'd care, although some people will, of course. Some
people always care too much about others' business, as we
well know.

I did tell you I've been invited to join the local writers'
group? I gather the standards for membership are minimal,
simply a pen and a notebook and a desire to write. "We let
Frank join" is how Suzanna Winship, the doctor's sister, puts

it. The desire to write is there inside me; I suppose it always has been. They say it's never too late. But what could I write about? I've lived a life of little incident. I'm too shy to read aloud my little scraps of poetry (I suppose people would call it poetry, for lack of a better term), and I gather reading aloud is another requirement of joining the group. Maybe it's time to outgrow that reluctance.

I have to run now—tonight is Lucie's dinner party. I am happy, keeping busy. I hope you are happy, too.

Your ever-loving, Gabby

CHAPTER 4
Dinner Party

Friday, March 23, 7:00 P.M.

Lucie and Frank Cuthbert lived embraced by peaceful woods in an old Georgian house at the west end of the village, on the road to Chipping Monkslip. They recently had moved there from the cramped quarters over their shop.

Rather than take the Land Rover, Max had slogged his way over on foot, passing St. Edwold's graveyard with its enormous Plague Tree, dodging puddles, and using his umbrella as a windshield. The weather, which had threatened rain for most of March, had seldom delivered, and parts of the South West were officially facing a serious drought. But when it did rain, it tended to pour, as now, chucking it down, with high winds added to stir the River Puddmill's waters into a froth, and to rattle shutters and windows. Oddly, there was never quite enough water to alleviate drought, but enough to disrupt the various trade routes to and from Nether Monkslip, and, on occasion, to swell the normally placid river into a surging torrent.

Max arrived at the house to effusive greetings and cluckings from Lucie Cuthbert, who helped him peel off his wet raincoat and hat and divested him of his umbrella in the entry hall. The other dinner party guests were already gathered in the Cuthberts' living room, for Max was last to arrive: He'd been held up by a last-minute phone call from a parishioner asking about available wedding dates at St. Edwold's. As he rang off, Max thought placidly how nice it was that when the time came, he would be able to pick and choose practically whatever date he and Awena liked.

Max, joining the others, counted off the eight for dinner. Representing the men's team were himself, Thaddeus Bottle, Dr. Bruce Winship, and Frank Cuthbert; for the women, Melinda Bottle, estate agent Bernadina Steed, and Gabby Crew, in addition to their hostess, Mme. Lucie Cuthbert. Max recognized Gabby as the eldest of the three hairstylists who had passed by his window yesterday morning.

Lucie settled everyone with their drinks before going to check on the meal. They all politely eyed one another as they sipped their aperitifs and breathed in the beguiling aromas coming from the kitchen.

As with Gabby, Max had only a nodding acquaintance with Bernadina Steed. She sold properties in the area, and her photo, with its slightly manic expression, often appeared in ads in the *Monkslip-super-Mare Globe and Bugle*. From what little he knew of her, she was a clever and attractive middle-aged divorcée with time and money to devote to her springy, youthful appearance. She had dark corkscrew hair that curled softly at the chin, and she wore a smart navy suit over a striped silk shirt. At her neck was a string of oversized red beads, and strapped to her feet were matching red shoes with heels that must have played havoc with her ability to walk on the cobblestone streets of Nether Monkslip. Her tan (an artifact, he heard her saying, of a recent trip to the south of France) was fading to a somewhat orangey glow.

Dr. Bruce Winship, Max noticed, seemed to be paying her special attention. Bruce appeared to be sucking in his stomach and puffing out his chest, in perfect imitation of the courting pigeon; Bernadina appeared to be reciprocating with sidelong glances of appreciation for this astonishingly macho display. Bruce's sister, Suzanna, who privately worried he might be in danger of becoming one of those quaint bachelor doctors so beloved of novelists of the thirties and forties, would approve of this mild flirtation, thought Max. Max knew too well the penchant of the women of Nether Monkslip for playing matchmaker.

Bernadina stole a moment from gazing into Bruce's eyes to introduce Gabrielle Crew.

"Please call me Gabby," she said. "Everyone does."

Max politely shook Gabby's hand, noting its surprisingly firm grip. He supposed her line of work explained the grip, but overall she was a vigorous-looking woman, if older than he'd first thought. Closer inspection revealed the crosshatching of fine lines on the plump skin around her eyes and mouth.

Lucie, an energetic woman in her late forties or early fifties, briefly emerged from the kitchen, a white dish towel looped over the leather belt at her waist. Max often thought of her as the backbone of the Cuthberts' marriage, the frame that gave her husband's blue-sky ambitions something to cling to. Both were of the artistic temperament, but in very different ways. La Maison Bleue, the village wine and cheese shop, ran on the engine of Lucie's steely determination. She was what the French would call *jolie laide,* or pretty-ugly, with distinctive large features that taken as a whole were unforgettably attractive. At the same time, one look at Lucie and one's thoughts inevitably drifted toward Madame Defarge in *A Tale of Two Cities.* That strong and unstoppable will shone through.

Max complemented her on one of the appetizers, a soft white cheese spread on toasted slices of French bread. It was, she told him, a Lyonnais specialty called *cervelle de canut* and made from *fromage blanc,* herbs, shallots, olive oil, vinegar, and salt and pepper. "The name means 'silk worker's brains,'" she told him. "Try not to think about it."

Max would not let it put him off. He had never eaten so well as since coming to Nether Monkslip. Awena was an excellent cook, for a start, her specialty being the ability to prepare any dish so no one suspected they were eating a vegetarian meal. Max had lost what little spare body fat he'd possessed under her gentle ministrations and had never felt as sound and whole as he did now. Lucie Cuthbert was likewise an excellent cook, but of the butter, cream, and goose-liver pâté variety.

Lucie, taking Gabby's arm in hers, told Max, "We call her 'Auntie'; she and my mother were like sisters. You may be interested to know Gabby and her husband were missionaries for a while."

"Oh, but that was a long time ago, Father," said Gabby. "I'm sure everything has changed. We came back to live in England some time ago."

Max mentioned an Anglican group often involved in missionary work.

"No, Father, this was a Catholic organization. My husband was a very devout Catholic."

"He is no longer with you?" Max asked her. She cocked her head, straining to hear, and he repeated what he'd said.

"He died last year."

"I'm very sorry to hear that," said Max.

She nodded. "It's more difficult than you realize it's going to be. But Lucie and Frank have been very kind, very welcoming, in giving me a new place for a new start. I don't know if you're aware I am living in the shop over their store. I work at the Cut and Dried."

"Gabby comes from a long line of hairdressers," said Lucie.

Gabby nodded. "My mother and grandmother owned a hair salon."

Max became aware of a man hovering in his peripheral vision, waiting to cut in. He had been standing very near Bernadina, but having failed to entice her away from Dr. Winship, he seemed momentarily at a loss. Less by process of elimination than from the look-at-me signals the man gave off, Max knew this had to be Thaddeus Bottle. He had a frame designed for leading-man parts and, Max was to learn, a wonderful bell-like speaking voice. Brown hair sprang back from a widow's peak—a luxuriant mane that was thinning ever so slightly, to judge by the gleaming scalp visible at the part.

It was somehow made clear to the observer that Thaddeus was well aware of his many wonderful attributes. Max half-expected him to position himself by the window so as to—*Oh, wait for it. There he goes.* Thaddeus walked over to one swagged window, ostensibly to admire the darkening garden. The setting sun cooperated by silhouetting his features against a sudden burst of golden backlighting. It was all nicely staged, and Max could not help but think it *was* staged. The others were too taken up by their conversations to notice, and after a while Thaddeus dropped the pretense of a sudden rapt interest in horticulture and rather sulkily rejoined the group tugging at his collar, which seemed to irritate him suddenly. Max hid his amusement by taking a small sip from his glass.

A new figure appeared beside Max and said, "Hullo." The woman held out a hand in greeting. "I'm Melinda Bottle. I think we've met before."

"Yes, of course," said Max.

They had chatted briefly during one of the interminable queues in the village post office, a queue resulting from the postmistress's need to pass along all the news of the day to whoever stood before her counter. This could be a matter of some minutes while the news was assessed, verified, and passed up and down the queue for additional input and analysis. Max recalled that Miss Pitchford had been in the middle of the queue, which seemed to be adding to the rebuttal time needed for this intricate, time-honored method of news dissemination, for Miss Pitchford was bound to uphold her reputation as the purveyor of only *accurate* village gossip. As she was generally the Q source for every rumor, villagers often felt it was best to consult her for clarification should any questions arise.

On this occasion, Max recalled, the postmistress had been even slower than usual, as tidbits about the Royal Couple had to be communicated to each and every customer, with time allotted for each and every customer to comment and speculate at length.

Max, who had been in rather a hurry, and much good had it done him, had greeted Melinda Bottle politely but with only half his attention, for the queue was making him late for an appointment and he was preoccupied with what he could do, short of faking some sort of fatal seizure, to move things along.

Thus in meeting Melinda Bottle, he had formed a hazy impression of a thin but attractive woman, the impression of attractiveness reinforced now that Melinda was done up in her finery, with glistening hair and stagy makeup, the impression of thinness emphasized by the prominent collarbones on display at the top of her dress. She wore sky-high platform shoes, and it seemed to take all her effort to stand in them without swaying as she sipped her aperitif.

On the day of the Great Post Office Wait Your Turn, she had been in mufti, wearing some sort of yoga costume of stretchy black fabric and clutching a purple mat under one arm. He had been standing ahead of her in the fumes of the flowery perfume she seemed to favor, since she was wearing it again now. Back then she'd been dressed for the winter in a short but bulky winter coat over the yoga togs, with a woolen scarf wrapped high around her hair and neck.

She'd had a package destined for mailing to London, and she could be heard to mutter that she could have delivered it herself in less time than this was taking. The postmistress might have heard this, for Melinda received a rather deliberate and piercing appraisal as Mrs. Watling abruptly stopped her monologue to peer at Melinda over the top of her pince-nez.

"Lovely to see you again," said Max now. "Did you ever get that package mailed?"

She laughed. "Yes, but the price was a relentless grilling by Mrs. Watling. How long do you have to live here before you're no longer considered an outsider?"

"Oh, I don't know. I'd give it twenty more years. Until then, you're still considered a Townie."

"Gawd," she said.

After half an hour or so, Lucie, who had been dashing in and out from the kitchen, announced that dinner was served. They willingly trooped into the dining room, where they found a beautifully set table complete with scented candlelight and a low floral centerpiece of velvety tulips and pansies.

There was a bit of a kerfuffle as they went to find their places.

"Here you are, Gabby," said Lucie, indicating a place next to her. Despite the small size of the party, Lucie had provided little place cards with names written in beautiful calligraphy. It was an old-fashioned touch he hadn't seen done for years.

But Gabby, her attention seemingly caught by one of Lucie's paintings, ignored Lucie's instructions. Max already thought that perhaps her hearing wasn't good—he had had to repeat that question he had put to her during the predinner drinks, but then there had been a great deal of chatter in the small room.

Then Gabby dropped something from her purse, and there was a scramble to retrieve it.

And she ended up sitting by Max, who was flattered to realize she had maneuvered to arrange this proximity by switching her card with Bernadina's. Max assumed she had some personal matter she wanted to discuss with him, or perhaps she found some comfort in sitting next to a man of the cloth. In his role as vicar, this sort of thing often happened, particularly with the recently bereaved, like Gabby.

While pulling out her chair for her, Max noticed she wore an enameled medallion that depicted the Madonna standing on a globe with hands outstretched against a pale blue sky. It was beautiful both as a piece of jewelry and as religious art, and Max complimented her on it.

"The nuns gave it to me as a school prize in a spelling competition. I was good at languages; in fact, they finally convinced me to go to university in France. I always wear it, the medallion, although I follow no particular religion. As I told you, Father, it was my husband who was the devout one. I do go to church, but the necklace is more like a talisman for me. I suppose you'd say I wear it in a superstitious way—isn't that odd, that we 'rational' people do these things? I'm afraid to be without it, as if something might drop from the sky if I didn't—some horrid fate befalling me."

Max, settling his napkin in his lap, stole a glance her. He was strongly reminded of the prototypical Miss Marple, who, according to Agatha Christie, shared some traits with the creator's own grandmother. Gabby was tall and thin and looked to be in her mid-sixties. Her thick hair, glossy white tinged with blue, had been twirled into an elaborate bun that rested heavily at the nape of her neck; in her strong features she bore a slight resemblance to Lucie. With that bright gleam in her eye, she also looked like the type of person who never missed spotting a trick. Max wondered if, like Christie's grandmother, she had the worst opinions of people and was often right.

Dr. Winship, overhearing their conversation about the medallion, said, "That's a form of religion right there, I'd say. Going back to its earliest history, mankind has fought fear with totems and amulets against evil."

Gabby smiled. She had a lovely smile, serene yet wistful. "I would agree with you. But I don't seem able to help myself. I couldn't bear to lose this necklace. It connects me to the past. And to the present."

"I recently read," said Max, "that early Christian icons represent the animal, vegetable, and mineral worlds because the artists used an egg tempera paint made with elements of all three."

"I wonder what the world would be like without religious art," said

Bruce Winship, at Gabby's right. Her maneuvering with the place cards had disturbed Lucie's matchmaking efforts, Max realized, for Bernadina, now sitting across the table from him, should have been seated between himself and the doctor.

"I suspect it would be a much bleaker place," Max replied. "One doesn't have to believe in a divinity to see that." Turning to Lucie, who sat to his left at the head of the table, he said, "This salad is superb."

Everyone nodded their agreement. The spring salad was a mix of romaine lettuce, spinach, tomatoes, mushrooms, and sprouts, all lightly dressed with a raspberry vinaigrette.

"The mushrooms came fresh from Raven's Wood this morning," Lucie told him.

"There are wonderful specimens in Raven's Wood," said Gabby. "Orchids, too, so I've heard."

"I picked them myself," said Frank with pride.

"And I sorted through them to make sure they were safe," said Lucie. "My husband is not a countryman by birth, you know."

"Or a chef by training," Frank admitted.

"I never took a cooking class in my life," said Lucie. "One just knows."

Max smiled. "The French seem to be born knowing how to cook."

"As do the Welsh," said Frank, with what looked alarmingly to Max like a wink. Since that was so obviously a reference to Awena and her peerless vegetarian cooking, Max hurriedly changed the subject. He said to Lucie, "But I was forgetting: You're not actually from France, are you?" Lucie's English, while perfect, was accented with something that sounded French to the ear.

Lucie shook her head. "Not the mainland of France, no. I'm from the Channel Islands; my mother was French. And for a while, I lived on the Isle of Wight." Max knew it was a matter of some particular pride in the Channel Islands that while they were possessions of the British Crown, they were volubly and idiosyncratically independent from it.

Lucie illustrated this with her next words. "Most people don't realize we were occupied by the Germans during the war."

No need to ask who "we" were, or which war. For Lucie and many of her generation from that region, there was only one war.

"I was, of course, not yet born," she said, "but the stories around the dinner table were all of the German occupation of the islands. My father was evacuated with his school to England. He was separated from his parents—my grandparents—for five years. The breaking of that bond took a long time to repair. My mother was orphaned at five—even worse. And that was just the emotional damage, terrible as it was: My grandparents often said they would have starved if not for the late arrival of the Red Cross supply ship."

Gabby nodded in sympathy as Lucie spoke.

"So horrible," murmured Bernadina.

"I was too young to remember," said Thaddeus.

"As was I," said Gabby.

"They built Nazi concentration camps," Lucie went on, eyes alight with outrage. "On British soil. For forced laborers, to build the fortifications. Can you imagine?"

They could not.

"We weren't liberated until 1945." She had again unconsciously adopted the "we" of handed-down suffering. "The shortages were dreadful. Food, of course, was all that mattered, and warmth, but for a while it was the everyday things that you don't miss until they're gone."

"In my mother's day," said Gabby, "they had already learned to make do. I wonder if we in this age of convenience would be as resourceful now. If we could even survive. Even the least important things could become important—human dignity demands a keeping up of appearances, doesn't it? Little things: Berries for lipstick and rouge—and when berries weren't available, they'd grind up the lead in a red pencil and smear it on their cheeks. There weren't the shelves of cosmetics we women have today."

They had reached the main course, and Bernadina, sipping at the excellent wine, was commenting on one of the paintings that hung on the Cuthberts' wall. The wallpaper looked like prison stripes to Max, but he assumed the pattern was the height of chic. Lucie was renowned for her good taste.

"How exquisite," Bernadina was saying. "He is a master, is Coombebridge. One day, he'll be worth a fortune. One day *soon*—he must be quite old by now. He never does portraits, though. I find that interesting, don't you?"

Dr. Winship turned his head to glance at the painting. "I read somewhere that he does do portraits. He just won't sell them."

"I happen to own several of his works—purchased, I can assure you, before he was discovered and rocketed out of my price range," said Max.

"I suppose he can do as he likes now." This was Thaddeus, and it was spoken with what sounded like wistful envy.

Gabby said, "My husband painted a similar scene. He must have visited this area at one time, before I met him."

"He was a painter?" asked Max.

She nodded. "Quite a good one. The paintings aren't worth much to anyone but me. I've been meaning to get them professionally appraised."

This was a topic Max knew something about. He recommended a gallery hidden among the gelato-colored houses of Monkslip-super-Mare, and invited her to drop by the vicarage, where he could provide her with the owner's contact information.

Thaddeus now began to show off in a foreign language, having presumably exhausted the possibilities of English. "*A l'œuvre on connaît l'artisan.*' 'The craftsman by his work is known,'" said Thaddeus to Lucie with a false modesty and flawless accent, turning on what Max felt sure Thaddeus regarded as a bewitching smile. He did have a charming manner, provided one was easily charmed. Overall, Max did not think that Lucie was effortlessly captivated by the actor and playwright, his gifts now on full display in the small confines of her dining room. Still, a few minutes later they were both smiling, as if they were in on a secret joke. Thaddeus seemed to miss the limelight he so recently had relinquished, and was working hard to regain it.

He had, Max noticed, an unfortunate tendency to punctuate the end of his sentences with a Putin-like self-satisfied smirk. He had slightly protuberant front teeth, like a sleeping dormouse, an impression enhanced by a tendency to breathe through his nose. Perhaps overcompensating to hide this minor affliction, he had a habit of pressing his lips tightly together when he'd finished speaking. It must have amounted to quite a handicap for a man expected to orate from a stage.

Thaddeus Bottle might well turn out to be that most irksome of human specimens: the underpraised genius. Max had found that sort of pit bottomless and unfillable unless disaster brought it low. And even then, especially then, the pit often found someone else to blame for its troubles.

But Max was genuinely fascinated by people and had a natural ability to respect differences. In his MI5 days, this was a much-needed quality, when he was forced into forming friendships with some of the world's worst thieves and tyrants. Nowadays, it merely helped him cope with nuisances like Thaddeus Bottle.

Now Thaddeus was trying to fold them all into the conversation so they could benefit from his views: "The problem with being a character actor is that after a while the audience comes to know and recognize you too well."

"Surely the mark of a good actor is to slip into a role so that the audience doesn't recognize you?" asked his wife, innocently enough.

"Everyone's a critic," he snapped. As if suddenly realizing they were not alone, this loud remark, which had silenced the other conversations, was followed by a look around the table of pained forbearance.

"I didn't mean to criticize," Melinda said meekly.

And she had not, in Max's opinion. It was Thaddeus who seemed to be too quick on the draw.

It was then Max began to notice Thaddeus was monitoring every bite of Melinda's food intake, as well as her behavior. In contrast with Gabby, who ate heartily, if somewhat mechanically, and Bernadina, who ate voraciously, as if the world were coming to an end, Melinda toyed with her food, pushing it into little piles on her plate. Max saw her actually put down her fork in response to a critical glare from her husband. It was disturbing, if only because Melinda was too thin to begin with, *too* fashionably thin.

Now Thaddeus was telling Lucie, "We were here on holiday when we saw the house was up for sale. In fact, it was the *only* home we saw for sale."

"Properties don't often appear on the market around here," said Max.

"So we gathered!" said Thaddeus. "Well, we obtained an order to view from Bernadina here, and when we saw the inside of the place, we just fell in love with it. I grew up here in Nether Monkslip, you know. Of course, it needs a lot of work. . . ."

"A lot," put in Melinda. "A lot of work."

"That is the charm of these old cottages," said Bernadina smoothly, with the practiced calm of the estate agent assessing termite damage and crumbling foundations. "You can make them your own in any number of innovative ways."

"I'd be happy if the water heater would innovatively heat the water." At a fiery glance from her husband, Melinda added meekly, "Of course, we do love it. *So* charming. I do so love the country."

Max wrestled with a smile. He'd met few people less well adapted to country life, but then he remembered he himself had taken some time to acclimatize. That he now could recognize a few wildflowers like bluebells and primroses was a source of immense personal pride.

But watching Melinda, he had the distinct feeling it would be a long time before she came to grips with the flora and fauna of Nether Monkslip.

CHAPTER 5
Hardwired

Stimulated by Lucie and Frank's excellent wine, Thaddeus began to relive his successful roles on the stage, where he had commanded top money for his appearances. Max listened, wearing a look of polite forbearance. Looking around the table, he saw several faces that looked enthralled by these tales. Melinda's was not one of them.

Now Thaddeus started name-dropping. He needs to polish his technique, thought Max, as he had a tendency to pause after the drop to make sure the listener had caught the name and was suitably awed. A more adept name-dropper would have mastered the art of the careless, incidental, breezy drop.

"A friend of mine," Thaddeus was saying, "at the New College in *Oxford* is a professor of the history of the theater. One night while we were having dinner with the *French* ambassador, he told me there is no doubt whatever that the Earl of Oxford wrote the plays. One has only to read them to see the fine hand of an aristocrat at work."

Max turned to Lucie, hoping to steer the conversation away from Thaddeus's triumphs. "What a wonderful meal," he began.

"Actually," said Bruce Winship, "I have always understood there to be the most tremendous doubt on that subject, if only because the earl was dead at the time he was said to have been writing many of the plays."

Thaddeus waved away this minor discrepancy, giving Bruce the benefit of a pitying glance for his ignorance. It was the merest twitch of the skin near the eyes and lips, but it spoke volumes. It's no doubt the result of years of theatrical training, thought Max, but difficult to take when one is on the receiving end.

"All the experts agree with me on this," said Thaddeus.

"It gives new meaning to the term *ghostwriter,* in any case," said Bruce. Recognizing that they would never resolve in one evening a dispute that had obsessed academics for decades, he decided on a change of subject. "Have you heard the rumor that Royalty is in the area?" he said.

Wonderful if true, thought Max, immediately wondering if he could work them into a sermon.

Bernadina looked thrilled. "I wonder if they're house hunting," she said.

"I think," said Gabby drily, "they already own several houses."

Lucie's glance rested affectionately on her Gabby, who shared her Gallic suspicion of all things monarchal.

"*Liberté, égalité, fraternité,*" she said, raising her glass of wine. She seemed to notice for the first time Gabby's jumper of fluffy green wool, its long sleeves embroidered with beaded flowers of white and yellow.

"I would bet that jumper is one of Lily Iverson's designs," said Lucie.

"Yes, isn't it gorgeous?" said Gabby. "That woman is so talented."

"But it's not too warm in here for you, is it, dear?" Lucie asked. "I can adjust the thermostat. In fact, it's so high-tech, I think I could roast potatoes with it."

"I'm fine, thank you," said Gabby. "The weather, though—it's been so changeable. A heat wave one minute, cold rain the next. I don't know what to wear."

"I've started keeping an umbrella with me at all times," said Lucie. "And a shawl."

"I feel the cold the more I age," Gabby said. "Don't you?"

Lucie knew Gabby was in her late sixties, but she looked far younger. She had clear eyes, few wrinkles, and perfect teeth, which may have added to the illusion—her teeth were so perfect, they might have been implants. She wore perhaps a little too much makeup; her cheeks were painted a hectic red—little dots of red, like a marionette's. She had outlined her lips in a matching shade. Her posture was strong and her back straight within the long-sleeved jumper, and her white hair, which gave off a light scent of orange blossoms, gleamed in its impeccable twist.

Outside, the rain rattled against the terrace beyond the French doors like a shower of pebbles, splashing hard and hail-like against the little panes. Lucie's eyes were caught by Father Max's, and she returned his smile. So nice, she thought, that he and Awena have found each other at last. It took them long enough.

Her husband was saying, apropos of what she didn't know, "This is why England is going to the dogs." Frank had been strangely silent throughout the meal, but before their guests had arrived, he'd made his displeasure with Thaddeus clear. There would be no return engagement chez les Cuthberts for Thaddeus Bottle.

"I wouldn't be so sure," said Max. "There are some things we do uncommonly well, or used to do. Architecture, for one."

Bernadina and Melinda nodded in agreement.

"Furniture, for another," put in Dr. Winship, flinging a quick glance at Bernadina, seeking that same approval. "And paintings, like that Coombebridge on the wall there. And writing: plays and books and poetry. And—"

"I take your point," said Thaddeus disagreeably, with a grating sneer. "However, you are talking about the England that used to be. Now, where we had architecture, we have seedy-looking council flats that won't last another decade, but only if we're lucky. And the Millennium Wheel—whose idea was that?"

Max couldn't say he opposed Thaddeus's views on architecture, but what was it about the man that made him want to disagree, if only on principle? And what made Thaddeus an expert anyway? The Bottles' new house was a known eyesore.

"At least we're finally getting a good reputation for cooking," he said.

And Max said a few more words in this vein, adding an endorsement for sustainable resources. Thaddeus began feigning a deep interest in Max's remarks, a pastime that soon paled as the conversation stayed resolutely on the topic of the world's food supply in general and away from himself.

"It is certainly better than what the English served for so long," sniffed Mme. Cuthbert. "I wouldn't feed that to Frank's dog."

"I'm not sure Sadie would eat it if you tried," said her husband.

"That," said Lucie Cuthbert, "is only because you treat that dog like it is human."

Frank's mouth fell open in mild surprise. He did regard Sadie as human.

Gabby said, "What do you all think of the new restaurant in the village?"

Max recently had come to realize that as a topic, the new restaurant had nearly displaced complaints about the planning committee for the Easter egg hunt.

"Excellent—the Grimaldis are doing very well," said Bruce. "Suzanna used to call them 'Primo' and 'Secondo,' although this pair doesn't seem to be struggling anymore like the brothers in *Big Night*. They've probably been set up for life with all the free publicity they've been getting. Of course, it's not certain we want to attract all these foodie sorts from London."

"Why not?" wondered Gabby. "The salon could use new customers. Hair only grows so fast, you know."

"They want to move here, and that raises the price of housing; that's why not." As soon as Bruce said the words, he saw his mistake. Bernadina Steed made her living selling homes at inflated prices. And her clients Thaddeus and Melinda could be said to be Exhibit A in the foodie category, genus Yuppie, usual habitat: London. "I meant, well—I didn't mean anyone here, of course."

Max's glance strayed across the table to Melinda Bottle. She was drinking quite heavily by this point. Her husband, Thaddeus, took an abstemious sip from this own glass, peering critically over the rim at his wife and looking much like a hanging judge getting ready to pass sentence. She was drinking the way a woman might drink after having at last stumbled across an oasis in the desert—that is to say, thirstily and without inhibition. That she did not appear to be drunk might be taken as a sign that her capacity, after long and arduous training, was larger than that of the average person. Her dinner sat before her, virtually untouched. If someone would invent an alcoholic beverage infused with vitamins and protein, thought Max, she might just manage to pack a few pounds onto her small-boned frame. Max had seen whippets with more body mass. He asked her a question about her new home, and he saw he had underestimated her condition, for she dragged her head around to listen with the intense concentration of the very, very drunk. Even so, having gathered her full attention, Max had to repeat himself.

"Oh, very nice," she said. "It's nice." This seemed to deplete her supply of adjectives, so he asked her how she was settling in. This provoked much the same sort of response. "We like it here. S'nice."

Max could overhear Bernadina telling Lucie she had known actor/playwright Thaddeus from before, in London.

"But only slightly," she said. "In that way you feel you know an actor once you've seen him on the stage." Bernadina's voice rose above the pleasant hum of other conversations. "I'll never forget him," she went on, with a nod in Thaddeus's direction, "as Bertrand in *Eggplant.*"

Melinda lifted her head at this, but groggily. There it was again, thought Max. That sense of tension, moving not through but somehow beneath the civilized surface of the lovely room, like lava bubbling at the lip of a volcano. Thaddeus seemed always to be at its source.

"I just ah-*dore* the theater, don't you?" Bernadina was saying. "Nether Monkslip needs a local theater, I've always thought."

"There is an amateur drama group that puts on the occasional play in the Village Hall," said Lucie. "We all find it, well . . . I can guarantee it's like nothing you've seen before."

"Experimental, is it?" asked Bernadina.

"It somehow always ends up being so," answered Lucie. "More haricots verts?" Ladling a large portion on Bernadina's plate, Lucie said, "Wouldn't it be wonderful to have a real actor appear in one of our little village plays? What do you think, Thaddeus?"

Thaddeus greeted this idea much as the early Christians might have viewed an invitation to one of the gladiator shows at the Colosseum. That is to say, he pulled back his lips in a horrified grimace, perhaps meant to be a condescending smile, and said, "I have come here to escape the hurly-burly of the stage, the crowds, the fans, the constant currying of favor, the requests for autographs and endorsements. Besides, 'the laborer is worthy of his hire.' Isn't that what the Bible says, Rev?"

"Hmm?" said Max.

"I do not," explained Thaddeus, "engage in *amateur* theatricals."

"Actually," said Max, "I'd much prefer it if you didn't call me that." "Rev," a nickname made popular by a recent television show, bothered him not at all coming from other people. He found it did bother him coming from Thaddeus.

Lucie had anticipated that Thaddeus wasn't the type to do anything without financial compensation.

"I'm afraid," she said, a tad icily, "that these are charity dos. People donate their time. The proceeds always go to a worthy cause. Because," she added with pointed emphasis, "'it is more blessed to give than to receive.' Isn't that right, Father Max?"

Max, who had no desire to be caught in the middle of a game of dueling Bible quotes, a game with limitless variations, said to Thaddeus, "Perhaps when you're more settled into the village, you'll feel differently," guessing that the man would not long be able to resist the lure of being a big fish in a small pond, and not realizing how closely his thoughts tracked Melinda's own.

As much as Max felt he himself could resist for a very long time the temptation to see Thaddeus in a live performance, still he recognized that the actor might be a draw for people in the neighboring villages. A little flattery—in fact, bucketfuls of flattery, lavishly applied—would probably be all that was needed.

Still, Thaddeus's tone held endless reserves of scorn for those who could not appreciate the finer points of the dramatist's art—a group that, judging by her expression, included his wife.

"Somehow I doubt very much that I'll change my mind," said the actor.

At Max's side, Gabby continued to work her way through her meal in her precise and meticulous way, every small mouthful savored. She also ate every scrap on her plate, using a piece of bread for a dainty mopping up. Lucie offered seconds, which she accepted, and the whole careful procedure began again. Max wondered that the woman didn't weigh twenty stone, but she was fit and trim, even muscular, quite tall, and weighed perhaps less than ten stone. "Well preserved" was the only possible phrase.

A runner himself, Max asked, as diplomatically as he could phrase it, how she stayed so fit for her age. "Do you walk or run?"

She smiled. "Run? Good heavens, but I'm flattered. Not at my age. Hardly." She finished the next morsel and carefully set down her knife and fork before she went on. "My mother taught me how important it is to exercise and stay fit. That you have to be ready for whatever life throws at you, and for that you have to keep up your strength. It was good advice. So I walk as far and as often as I can. The area around Nether Monkslip is perfect for that, is it not? One day I walked nearly to Monkslip-super-Mare. And I recently signed up with Tara for yoga classes, over at Goddessspell. It's a shop run by a really interesting woman named Awena Owen. I think you know her?"

There was a mischievous note to this last, and a strange silence as she waited for his reply. During Gabby's conversation Max felt, rather than saw, Lucie looking up from taking another piece of bread from the basket, and the questioning glance she exchanged with Frank. Max's reaction was guarded: He and Awena had taken such care to keep their relationship away from the prying eyes of the village.

"Yes," he said, staring down with studied neutrality at the haricots verts on his plate, as if they might escape without careful monitoring. "Awena is remarkable. This parsley—is it that flat kind?"

But Lucie had fallen noticeably silent. Now with an effort she turned and looked at Max as if he had taken leave of his senses. "Yes-s-s," she said carefully. "It is what they call flat-leaf parsley."

"Oh! Just that . . . it's delicious. I'll have to ask A—I mean, Mrs. Hooser to prepare some for me this way. Perhaps you'd be kind enough to share the recipe with her? With Mrs. Hooser, that is?"

As Mrs. Hooser was incapable of boiling water without setting the kitchen curtains aflame, Lucie's look of staggered skepticism remained fixed in place: eyebrows raised, a moue of surprise on her lips. The French have perfected that look, thought Max, wriggling under the scrutiny. They should patent it. He smiled weakly. "Mrs. Hooser needs all the help she can get."

"That is obvious," replied Lucie judiciously, after a pause while she considered this truism. "Of course. I'll be certain she gets a copy. More beets?" she added brightly. "They had fresh ones at the market today. It's a sure sign spring is coming."

Everyone declined the offer except the apparently bottomless Gabby. For pudding, Lucie served a lemon tart topped by a mound of frothy meringue. This also vanished. Every crumb, this time, on every plate but Melinda's.

Gabby remained focused so completely on her food that at one point she didn't hear Bernadina asking if she would consider buying a three-bedroom home. Bernadina repeated the question.

"Too much room for me," Gabby answered briefly, shaking her head. She seemed to take little pleasure from the food; she ate with the focused concentration of a woman eating only because she understood food to be good for her.

Gabby's intensity was in complete contrast to Melinda Bottle's. Melinda continued to pick nervously at her food, even the hard-to-resist lemon tart.

"There is much to be said for the old remedies used by our ancestors," Gabby was saying, voluble now that dinner was finished. Lucie had given them small tulip-shaped glasses of a rare port to finish the meal. "The homeopathic cure. I was reading the other day that olives are good for preventing seasickness . . . something about the tannic acid."

Doc Winship said, "Yes. I suppose that would explain why the average life expectancy in the Middle Ages was about thirty-nine."

"Bruce is our resident voice of scientific reason," Max explained to Gabby.

"Someone has to be, around here," said Bruce Winship. "How's that sprained ankle of yours doing, Max?"

"Much better," said Max, smiling. With a nod in Gabby's direction, he said, "Awena applied a homeopathic remedy—some sort of salve made with sage and other things. It really seems to be working wonders." Max had walked and even danced on his ankle too soon after he'd injured it on the ice at Chedrow Castle. He had wondered himself, Is it the salve or is it her?

"What's in this stuff?" Max had asked her.

"Snakes and snails. You know—the usual New Age, Wiccan hocus-pocus."

"Seriously."

"Wildcrafted sage. Jojoba oil. Coconut oil. Beeswax. Nothing too exotic."

Now Bruce was saying, "Nonsense. It's the painkillers I gave you."

Max debated whether to tell Bruce he'd stopped taking the painkillers because they made him drowsy. Mrs. Hooser had more than once discovered him, Tom, and the dog, Thea, fast asleep, like creatures fallen under a spell in a Grimms' fairy tale. Awena's massaging whatever it was into his ankle had brought the swelling down in a nearly miraculous and drug-free way.

Max said diplomatically, "I'm sure it's a combination of all the attention my ankle's been getting."

This seemed to mollify Bruce, who confidently pronounced, "The placebo effect is undeniably real."

"Undeniably," said Max, thinking, No. It was Awena and her salve.

"Speaking of your ankle," said Bruce, "I'd like to hear more about the trouble up there at the castle." Bruce, to his disappointment, hadn't seen Max to talk to about the case for several weeks. The criminal mind was a pet topic with him. "I was amazed to learn who the killer was," Bruce went on. "It just goes to prove my theory."

"Which theory is that?" asked Max, smiling, knowing perfectly well.

"That we are all hardwired to kill." Dr. Winship thoughtfully rubbed his chin between thumb and index finger, fully astride his hobbyhorse, showing off for Bernadina.

"I don't think we are," said Max. "Not in the sense you mean."

"It's the only thing that explains the phenomenon of the 'normal' guy next door who suddenly goes on a rampage," Bruce insisted. "It only *seems* sudden, although the signs have been there all along, if only the wife and family had thought to look for them. Extreme displeasure shown over the overcooked broccoli and so forth."

"You don't ever suspect loved ones, though, do you?" said Gabby. "If you do suspect, you quickly ignore the warnings."

"Precisely. Because it's not in your best interests, or so you may tell yourself, to ask too many questions. You know full well you may not like the answers. That is how these people manage to survive and reproduce, passing along their propensities to the next generation. Unless they kill their wives first, of course."

"That is such a dark view of mankind," said Max.

"Oh, you would think so!" said Bruce. "But ask any evolutionary psychologist. We didn't get where we are by being *nice* to one another."

"Perhaps that is true, in the darkest past of mankind. But the message for modern times surely is that if we don't tame our baser instincts and start pulling together, we won't survive as a species."

"I'm not sure you aren't both saying the same thing," put in Bernadina. "We may be hardwired to kill, but civilization has taught us to keep the urges in check."

Bruce's chest swelled a bit more.

"Precisely," he said. "The only question is, when does the hard wiring kick in? Under what circumstances? What is the trigger—if you will pardon the pun."

"You don't have to look far in the past to see where the hard wiring has taken over. Just read the daily headlines," said Gabby.

Lucie and Frank nodded. "Just look at all the wars," said Lucie.

Thaddeus seemed to have lost the thread of the conversation as he sat thoughtfully sipping his wine. In true connoisseur fashion, he made little slurping noises to introduce air into the drink.

"So you believe," said Max, "that there is something adaptive about murder? In the Darwinian sense?"

"I believe there was, and, in the mind of today's killer, still is. It is all about survival. If someone is in the killer's way—well then! Murder is the easy way out. For someone of that mind-set," Bruce added hastily, since this didn't seem to be going down too well with Bernadina.

"But you can't justify murder, claiming that it's something inherent in the nature of mankind," said Max. "That we can't help ourselves. And I don't think you can ever entirely rule out environment as an influence."

"No, indeed. And in fact, when what I will call the 'murderers amongst us' try to justify and explain away what they have done, that is when they get most creative. I am talking of that ordinary neighbor, that 'normal' guy, often to be seen cutting his lawn and trimming his privet hedge on the weekend. Their explanations would astonish you, and often boil down to either a sense of entitlement—those are the deeply disturbed ones—or a sense that they are protecting what they hold most dear. Those are the deluded ones."

Max felt he knew what Bruce was getting at. Most criminals not only cared about their families, thought Max, but used family values as an excuse for the most reprehensible of crimes, justifying atrocities by claiming they were doing it to protect their loved ones—who were more important than anyone else's loved ones, apparently.

"I'm not sure," he said, playing devil's advocate, "that murderers can be neatly stacked into categories like that."

"Oh, yes, they can!" said Bruce. "The paranoid killer lives in a world of his own, in a class by himself. Do you know, I have read that the paranoid is mesmerized by other people's eyes. He sees them as mirrors, you see, and is tremendously worried that they can 'see through him.'"

"All very scientific," said Max, "but—"

Bruce was not to be deterred. In the flickering candlelight, his own eyes glowed, shining and mysterious. At least he hoped they did: Berna-dina was a damnably attractive woman.

"The ecologist or scientist is the new 'trusted person,' have you no-ticed?" he said. "At one time, it would have been the vicar or the village policeman."

"Or the village doctor," said Max.

Bruce laughed. "Point taken. And in any mystery of the golden age of mysteries, this trusted person would turn out to be the killer," added Bruce, not remotely offended by the prospect. "Doctors have access to drugs, making murder easy. And some of them go once too often to the trough."

"What do you mean?'

"Become addicted to this or that. Poor judgment is the result."

"I've never," said Max ruminatively, "thought of murder in terms of poor judgment, but it's certainly one interpretation."

"Oh, to you, murder may be seen as a moral lapse. Which it is. But some people, I do insist, are born to kill."

Lucie, who seemed to be growing more and more alarmed by this dinner-table conversation, put in firmly, "Cheese and biscuits?" This was said in such a way it carried a world of condemnation, even though she didn't so much as raise her voice or an eyebrow. Bruce fell into immediate, contrite silence. It was not to last. Once the platter was passed around the table and everyone had marveled over the selection of Brie, blue, and cheddar, Bruce began opining on yet another uncomfortable topic. It was the only way Bruce knew how to impress, Max decided.

"The plague," Bruce was saying. "A perfect example of the folly of the medical profession. Sometimes one wonders if we've traveled very far since those days. The disease that wiped out much of mankind in the Middle Ages was caused by the *Yersinia pestis*—bacteria—but they blamed the cats. Of course, the cats were the main hope of stopping the spread of the disease by killing the rats."

This time, Lucie succeeded in derailing him.

"I think the weather is letting up," she said.

They turned as one toward the window, where they could see the rain had dwindled from a steady bombardment to a trickle. There was common agreement they should seize their chance now and leave before it started in earnest again. It was nearly ten-thirty.

In the hallway as they were sorting out their coats and umbrellas, Max heard Melinda say to Gabby, "See you Monday. I need a few more highlights around the temples, I think."

"Do you really think that's a good idea? In this weather? It's so drying. We don't want a lot of frizz." Gabby reached out one hand and touched the hair at the side of Melinda's head, gently pulling at one lock in an assessing way. She shook her head doubtfully. "Maybe with a conditioner. Anyway, you need a trim. See you Monday."

"Can you talk about this later?" fussed Thaddeus. "We have to rush. We left Jean inside, and he'll be wanting his last walk of the day." Melinda turned anxiously toward her husband, exuding unease.

Max watched the interaction, concern darkening his eyes. "And I should get back to Thea," Max told Lucie. "Thank you for a wonderful meal."

Max was walking away as he heard a voice call after him, "Evening, Rev." He didn't have to guess who it was, and he pretended he hadn't heard.

Subject: Social Whirl
From: Gabrielle Crew (gabby@TresRapidePoste.fr)
To: Claude Chaux (Claude43@TresRapidePoste.fr)
Date: Saturday, March 24, 2012 3:48 P.M.

Dear Claude—I've been rushed off my feet today! A visit to
the salon in a village like Nether Monkslip is an occasion, for
men and women. The exchange of gossip and ideas—well, I
perhaps wouldn't go so far as to call them ideas, but the
exchange of information is crucial to the transaction.
Everyone is offered a strong cup of tea, or wine in the
evenings, and we don't mind if they stay awhile. It is not
much different from a salon in a town or city, but in Nether
Monkslip, in this as in all things, making the most of little
occasions is their specialty. They have learned the secret to a
good life, these villagers.

Small things count for much, but sometimes in a not-good
way. There was great excitement in the salon when some hair
clips went missing the other day. I think Thaddeus Bottle took
them just to cause mischief—dreadful, odious man!—but it
hardly seems worth mentioning to anyone, since I didn't
actually see him take anything. This hardly qualifies as news,
but Annette was in a state. She is a good soul, but excitable.

I'm quickly gaining clients. In fact, I'm busier now than I
was when I was younger, when standing on my feet all day
wasn't such a strain. But being an expert colorist is a slowly
acquired skill, much like being a chemist. Get it wrong and
you never get a second chance with that customer.

The weather here in the South West has been a welcome
relief from what I've been used to—climates either too warm
or too cold. It's been wet, yes, but not that freezing wet that

creeps into the bone. Orchids will soon appear in Raven's Wood—quite rare, probably arrived on the wind from France.

Do I miss my dream of owning my own shop like you and grandmother? Not at all. Ownership is just one thing after another. I work only because I enjoy the artistry of it. Let someone else have the business headaches.

I was telling our vicar last night how the nuns encouraged me to go to university, and I've been thinking a lot about that conversation. I did try to stay the course, but I quickly knew it wasn't for me. I wanted to read, not be told how to read.

The nuns did their best, but they didn't have time for everyone, and besides, they thought it was bad to "coddle" their pupils. It was important that we be strong, that we offer up our suffering. I did absorb much of their philosophy. But oh! How I also longed for tenderness from someone—from anyone, really. Then along came Harold.

The only thing of importance that came out of my time at university was Harold.

That I married a missionary was a legacy of all those years with the nuns, I think now. I wanted to do good. I wanted to feed the hungry and shelter the poor. I like to think I did some good here and there. But after a while, I just wanted to enjoy what was left of my own life. One gets too old for that sort of hardship. And then Harold died. . . .

Sometimes, I do miss him so. He was always *there.*

But why do I tell you what you already know? You must forgive my rambling on. I am an old woman now, you see— it's official! More tomorrow. As always, writing to you brightens my day.

All my love, your Gabby

CHAPTER 6
Predawn Visitor

Sunday, March 25, 5:00 A.M.

Max learned of the death Sunday, when he was awakened by a rapping on the front door of the vicarage. His alarm clock told him it was 5:00 A.M.—for Max, a normal time of rising—but it felt like 4:00 A.M., for his body had still to adjust to the clocks having been moved forward one hour for spring. Besides, the sun hadn't read the British Summer Time bulletin and was still asleep.

He'd spent a few moments the night before changing the clocks that he could—the clock on the microwave oven had defeated him. But it was the combined cacophony of the alarm by his bed and the pounding of the door knocker that woke him. Thea began nudging him with her wet nose on the off chance the other two alarms weren't doing the trick.

"Good girl," said Max. "Go see who it is."

Obediently, the dog threw herself headlong down the stairs, barking madly. *This is the life! A chance to show what I'm made of!* Max had encouraged this behavior in case of the one-in-eight-million chance a crook might approach the vicarage with theft or mayhem in mind. Max's old habits from MI5 and living-in-London days died hard.

He shrugged his way into a wool Black Watch robe over his pajama bottoms and padded barefoot down the stairs. Calming Thea with a good-girl pat on the head, he opened the door.

To find, to his mystification, a distraught and disheveled-looking Melinda Bottle on the doorstep. The rain had started again during the night, and water had collected on the stoop—shallow puddles bulleted by droplets as water continued to spill over the lip of the roof. Melinda was wearing some sort of negligee and a matching white robe edged with ostrich feathers. Like the porch roof, she dripped with moisture. Devoid of makeup, her face glistening with night cream, she wore a scarf hastily tied around her head. She looked like Jemima Puddleduck in need of rescue from a fast-talking fox.

"Help!" she cried. She stopped for a deep breath, hand against her heart, as if the single word had cost her her last gasp. "Come and see. Please. There's something wrong with Thaddeus. I think . . . I'm sure he's *dead*."

The wet morning was unnaturally still, with a muffled sound track punctuated occasionally by the squawk of something attacking or something being pounced upon. Max was still learning to live with the alarming nonhuman squeaks and squawks of the village, its hidden dramas played out under a canopy of distant stars. Nether Monkslip, unlike the London of Max's recent memory, was so isolated that the universe on most nights was revealed in all its glory, a living, moving testament to its creator, a stubborn rebuke to the notion of a universe that "just happened." But on recent nights, the moon had snaked against a black sky like a sliver of fire.

On the short walk over to the Bottle house, Max—who had stopped only long enough to pull trainers on his own feet, grab a torch, and tuck a mobile phone in his pocket—had pulled what details he could out of a rattled Melinda. She said she had fallen asleep downstairs while watching an old movie, and when she woke up, it was early morning. She had gone upstairs and in the dark had gotten into bed, slipping under the covers on her side. Something, she told Max, wasn't right.

"For one thing, Thad snores. Really loud. Loud enough to wake the d—" She swallowed hard on the word that still trembled on her lips. In the paleness of the streetlamps on Church Street, her face had been ghostly, a pasty white under the slick of night cream, and devoid of color, her eyes sunken into cadaverous sockets.

He could see that beneath the cream and outside the benefit of Lucie Cuthbert's flattering candlelight, Melinda had a somewhat thick, roughened complexion. He realized then she was older than she appeared without makeup to mask the little commas at the sides of her mouth and the crinkle of lines at the corners of her eyes. Still, she looked more like a sleep-deprived toddler than a mature woman. The vampy, if undernourished, sex kitten of the evening before had been replaced by a frightened girl.

"I mean *loud*," she said. "A beached whale—if they snore."

She seemed hung up on the memory of Thaddeus's snoring, as if by repeating this single fact she could come to grips with the new reality of life without Thaddeus, a man who would never disturb her sleep again.

"You didn't realize . . ." Max began delicately.

"It's a California king-size bed," she said. Incredibly, there was a certain thrill of pride of ownership in her voice. "I always sleep on the side of the bed nearest the door. I had done this a hundred times, a thousand— just slipped in quietly so as not to disturb him."

She had followed Max as he made his way toward the house, scuttling along in fuzzy bedroom slippers with kitten heels, Max loping ahead. It was clear she was in no hurry to return to the house anyway. Max had at this point realized she could never keep up and had left her on the High Street to follow as quickly as she could, first asking if she'd left the door unlocked. Jogging past the train station, Max made a left into the dirt-turning-to-gravel lane leading up to the house. His shoes squelched as he sponged his way down the sodden path.

The Bottles' house had once been named, with blinding optimism, Happy Ending, but it had been renamed—absurdly and with the lack of humility that characterized its male owner—King's Rest. Its remodeling, under whichever name, had caused a commotion in the village, and Max, as he made his approach, was reminded of all the reasons why. The addition to its back side was too big, incorporating all that was ugly and inconvenient in the modern for the sake of making a showy statement. It now harkened back, absurdly, to what could best be described as a blend of Tudor and Mayan architecture, and Max thought it the perfect embodiment of all that Thaddeus stood for—all look-at-me flash concealing a flimsy foundation, shoddy workmanship, and cut-rate amenities. The man who originally had remodeled the place had become famous for business practices consisting of offshore accounts and ghost companies, and he had last been spotted on a private beach a few miles from Majorca, avoiding the attentions of the courts and the media, and in the company of others of his kind. For a while, he had tried to interest various of the villagers in his schemes but, unfortunately for him, cooler business heads had prevailed—he had made the mistake of forgetting most of them were canny, and honest, businesspeople, with long histories among the financial cognoscenti of London. He was soon sent packing with his beach umbrella.

The Bottles' dog, a beagle, greeted Max at the door with a frenzied, worried barking. Jean, he thought its name was. Max stood quietly, waiting for the dog to calm down. Finally, Max offered the open palm of his hand for inspection, as a sign he came in peace, and Jean allowed him to pass inside.

The home of King Thaddeus and his consort, Melinda, still bore the traces of their recent move-in. Boxes were piled in every corner, some half-unpacked, all marked vaguely if optimistically with words like *bath* or *hallway*. Max knew from experience that the labels had no bearing on the contents; that the box marked "kitchen" would contain books and the contents of a medicine cabinet and a woolen coat, but in the interests of verisimilitude and truth in packaging, it might also contain a single spoon.

"You go," a voice whispered at his shoulder. Melinda had caught up with him in the foyer. "I can't . . . stand . . . to look at him again." She flipped a switch at the foot of the stairs. It illuminated the landing above via an old-fashioned overhead globe.

Melinda gazed somberly at the handsome priest. She saw that Max's dark gray eyes were nearly opaque in the strange solo light.

Why had she thought of going to him first? She supposed it was that sense of calm competence he carried about him. In a crisis, you wanted someone like Max.

You also wanted someone who wouldn't judge too harshly.

As Melinda waited below, Max took the steps two at a time, the dog following. Max poked his head in various open doorways before finding the master bedroom toward the rear of the house. The door was only partially closed, and he easily slid his lean body into the opening. When he saw in the faint starlight a form sprawled on the bed, he closed the door on the dog to keep him out of the room. He reached out a hand to operate the light switch by the doors. Years of training and instinct had him pulling down the sleeve of his jacket to cover his fingertips as he did so.

Thaddeus lay facedown on top of the bed clothing, which remained neatly tucked in on that side of the bed. The body was fully clothed in a shirt and trousers. It looked as if he had fallen at a forty-five-degree angle to the low mattress, so that the toes of his shoes rested on the floor, an awkward balancing act. A slight redistribution of the deadweight would have sent him toppling to the floor.

Max crept over for a closer look. Thaddeus's face was turned toward the windows, which opened out onto a small balcony overlooking the garden in back. Max could see his blank expression clearly, but to be

sure, Max placed a hand against his neck, fingers touching the area behind Thaddeus's ear. No pulse. Max removed his hand and, as he did so,
noticed the dark stain. Blood? In the glaring overhead light—it was on a
dimmer stitch, but Max had turned it to full blast—it was a confused
impression, but something dark and moist was on his fingertips.

He stepped outside the room, again carefully shutting the door behind him, and made the call directly to the private line of DCI Cotton.

CHAPTER 7
You Again?

"You again?" said Cotton on seeing Max at the door of King's Rest.

"It sort of goes with the territory," Max said, shrugging as he stepped aside to admit the DCI from Monkslip-super-Mare.

"Right," said Cotton. "I suppose calling the police in an emergency has gone completely out of style. Around here, they've learned to call in the vicar first. Of course."

"I *did* call you," said Max.

Despite the early hour, Cotton was immaculately dressed and with not a blond hair out of place. He strode into the room as if he were there to show off the latest in men's fashion. He carried the leather briefcase—so omnipresent, it seemed welded to his side—in the way most women would not set out without a pocketbook. What was in there, like the actual contents of Her Majesty the Queen's handbag, might never be known. His only concession to the hour was that he wore a turtleneck and slacks instead of a suit and tie. He carried a jacket hooked dashingly from his thumb and thrown over one shoulder, like a politician on a hand-shaking, baby-kissing mission. Unlike many politicians, Cotton was one of the handful of men whose integrity Max had always found to be unfailing, his moral compass unwavering.

"Why not call Musteile?" he asked now, spinning to face Max.

Max looked at him stony-faced as he waited for Cotton to answer his own question. Constable Musteile was the local bobby, a silly man held in near-universal contempt by the villagers for his inflated sense of self-importance. He had recently somehow gotten himself issued a bulletproof vest, which provoked great hilarity in the village as he rode about on his bicycle, the ridges of the vest ostentatiously visible beneath his tight shirt. He was the type of official for whom the slogan "Question Authority" had been created. Fortunately, the generally peaceful village of Nether Monkslip gave him little scope for exercising his worst tendencies. Musteile's attempts to hold Neighborhood Watch meetings so villagers could report suspicious incidents had become noisy social occasions complete with wine and appetizers, and a peeved Musteile had canceled any further attempts at portraying Nether Monkslip as a hotbed of anything resembling crime.

Besides, no one would report anything short of the apocalypse to Musteile if they could help it.

"Well, okay, you're right," admitted Cotton. "Musteile is the last man you'd want on the job. It would be like asking the village idiot to investigate. Why HQ puts up with him, no one knows."

"Oh, I think they do," said Max.

"Right again! He sucks up to the higher-ups, that's why, casting himself as the simple man of the people keeping the crime rate in check: They have only to look at the low crime statistics to see what a fine job he's doing. They're very big at HQ on presenting themselves as being in touch with the local farmers and herders and so on, although most of the brass would run a mile if presented with anything that didn't have a saddle or a sail attached to it. As if there were anything like real crime going on in these parts to begin with. Well, except for the occasional murder . . . Uhm . . . I mean to say, there's not a lot for Musteile to do, in the normal run of things."

"I'm not sure this is murder," said Max. "But . . ."

"But you're not satisfied. Right. So show me."

And they walked up the stairs leading from the showy stone hallway, which seemed, as Cotton commented, simply to cry out for tapestries and battle-axes. Max led the way toward the master bedroom door, behind which lay the supine, extinguished form of Thaddeus Bottle.

They stood looking at the body, Max hanging back in the doorway. Cotton took in the framed photo on the dresser.

"Married?"

Max nodded. "It's his wife who found him. I left her in the kitchen with a cup of tea."

"Fill me in."

"Well, let's see. Thaddeus Bottle is, or was, a character actor—a stage actor, primarily—who dabbled in writing plays. He also did some work in film, I gather." Max watched Cotton closely as he told him this. Cotton's background included having done his homework—when someone had remembered to put him in school—late at night in his hippie/rock star mother's dressing room, waiting for her to come off the stage. It had been part of the chaotic and peripatetic upbringing, being the child to a woman not unlike the Patsy Stone figure in *Absolutely Fabulous*, that had made him long for nothing so much as stability in his life. He was one of those men for whom bringing order out of chaos was a personal necessity—a question not of honor so much as of survival—and his reaction to an untidy upbringing had been to enter a profession where order was the, well, order of the day. Fortunately, he was very good at it.

Cotton especially noticed furnishings and fashions, the props and decorations of a man's or woman's life. Max's working theory was that Cotton's only nod to the flamboyance to which he had been exposed in childhood was this awareness, and his own sartorial choices.

Right now, Cotton seemed to be taking the news of Thaddeus's arty career in his stride, so Max went on. "He and his wife moved into the village about six months ago, maybe a bit more, causing quite a flutter of excitement."

"You were immune to the fluttering?" Cotton asked, picking up on Max's dry tone.

"I knew who he was, but in the vaguest terms. Those who follow the arts more closely than I seemed at least to recognize him on sight."

"Did you get any sense of what kind of man he was? Offstage, I mean?"

Max thought carefully before speaking. "He was rather full of himself. He also seemed to me to be awash in a sea of insecurities. The two things so often go together."

"They are all insecure," said Cotton. "Actors."

"Even the nice ones?"

"Sure. Especially the nice ones. They're the ones who get trampled to pieces repeatedly. You're saying he wasn't nice?"

"Not to his wife." Realizing he'd just unwittingly chucked Melinda into it, Max added, "Not to anyone, really. You'd have to have more awareness of others to be nice to them, and Thaddeus struck me as having been born without that side to him." Max glanced over at the body lying on the bed, maintaining its precarious balance, half on and half off. If there had been any hope for Thaddeus's coming to an improved understanding of his fellow man, that hope was finally extinguished now.

Cotton paused, considered.

"You really think it's another murder? Here?" Cotton, looking around him, swept out an arm to indicate the entire village, as if they stood not in Thaddeus Bottle's ornate Versailles-style bedroom but in an enchanted clearing where no harm could ever befall them. Fairies and green elves would soon appear, crawling out from beneath the toadstools of Raven's Wood.

"I'm not sure," said Max. "There's an odd bit of bleeding at his neck, as if he'd been stabbed, but it's quite a minor wound, and I wouldn't think deep enough to kill him. I'd feel better if your doctor took a look, though."

Cotton shook his head somberly. "Please God, let it not be a murder—not again. Even equine crime in the area has fallen one hundred percent since the Monkslip Horse Watch was established. Roger Mathews had his tack returned to him—a thief with a guilty conscience; wonders never cease. We've gone from less than no crime to *this*—to some sort of killing spree."

Since he seemed to be peering closely at Max, as if searching him for concealed weapons, Max felt compelled to say, rather defensively, "Well, don't look at me. I feel exactly the same way you do."

"It's like you're a magnet or something," said Cotton. "Since shortly after you came to live here, people have started dropping like flies. . . ."

"It's pure coincidence," said Max somewhat testily. "We will probably find that the seeds of this crime were sown long ago and far away. If I were you, I would start by talking with every actor appearing for the past thirty years in a performance in London's West End. Then I'd talk to every director, stagehand, and fellow playwright. Thaddeus Bottle was hardly a candidate for the Nobel Peace Prize. He was quite a contrarian individual, opinionated and brusque to the point of rudeness. Ask anyone." *And* he called me "Rev" after I'd asked him not to, thought Max, but he didn't add this aloud.

"Oh, we shall," said Cotton. "Ask anyone, I mean. Meantime, Max, I'd appreciate it if you'd give me some insight into Thaddeus's relationships in the village."

"You're quite sure I'm not a suspect?" Max asked drily.

"Of course not. You're simply a magnet. Or perhaps some sort of catalyst. Go on, now. Dish."

"Let's do this downstairs, shall we?" Max turned and began walking away, with Cotton following. They reached a small front room below, a formal sitting room. It had a door that could be pulled shut. Melinda was nowhere about, but presumably she was in the kitchen, staying put, as she'd been told to do.

"Apparently, the man was notorious—had made his presence felt in a remarkably short time," began Max. "I don't like saying it, but since the spouse is always the first suspect . . ."

"You think she's a likely candidate for this misdeed."

"*If* she could pull herself together long enough to plan such a crime, yes. Personally, I don't think she could. But certainly, with Bottle's off-handed treatment of her, she wouldn't be human if she never reacted to his abuse in some way. I gained the impression that her drinking may have been an attempt to drown out the voices suggesting she'd be better off without him."

"Why do you think she stuck around?"

"That, you'd have to ask her. She is many years younger than he is, or was. Attractive in a—oh, I don't know. In a sloshing about sort of way. Provocative low-cut dresses, flashy costume jewelry, very high heels—it's a wonder she didn't break her neck in those. It all seemed designed to prove something—heaven knows what. That she was attractive to someone, I suppose. Or maybe it was some pathetic attempt to get her husband's attention. In which case, she had her work cut out for her. Sad to say, Thaddeus seemed to keep all his attention in reserve for himself. He was a man for whom the word *humbug* was invented."

A flourish of flashing lights outside the window announced the arrival of Cotton's team. He had alerted them after talking with Max on the phone. It would be highly unlike the priest to involve him without good reason, and so Cotton had acted on the assumption foul play would need to be investigated.

Cotton went to get everyone sorted on their various tasks. He returned shortly—they didn't need to be told what to do.

So while all the photographing and examining of the body were taking place upstairs, he and Max went to talk with Melinda, Thaddeus's widow, in her extravagantly padded, tufted, and embroidered sitting room at the back of the house. Max, taking a seat, felt he might sink and disappear into a quicksand of puffy fabric. The room opened off the kitchen, and it was obvious this was where the real living took place, not the more formal room at the front. In pride of place over the mantelpiece was a flat-screen television.

"I'm so sorry for your loss, Mrs. Bottle," said Cotton. The words, while too commonly used by someone in his line of work, were spoken with sincerity.

"Thank you," she said. "But I don't understand—why are there all these people in my house? It was a heart attack or something, wasn't it?"

"There were," said Cotton smoothly, "some indicators we need to look into. It may mean nothing, but obviously, if your husband did not die of natural causes, it—"

"It must have been a professional killer," said Melinda, interrupting. In the next moment, she seemed to realize this abruptness was not fitting, that the occasion called for befuddled sadness, and she made a show of using a tissue to dab at the corner of one eye.

Professional killer—a term Max had always found somewhat bizarre, as if such people had their own logo, newsletter, and Web site, or maybe a secret handshake and Masonic-like rites of initiation. Maybe a bowling team.

Cotton looked skeptical but had learned to dismiss nothing as ridiculous until it could be proved to be ridiculous. Melinda stood and began drifting about the room in a distracted manner, actually bumping into a small side table, as if to suggest her distress made it difficult to navigate. She picked up a photo of herself and her husband. It happened to be a wedding photo of the pair of them standing before a registry office, Melinda, the bride, in a pastel dress, clutching a bouquet of spring flowers.

Melinda's disorientation seemed real enough, but Max wondered at the cause. Heartbreak and grief didn't seem to be in the cards, but a sense of bewilderment and worry would be normal given the circumstances.

"What would make you say that?" he asked her. "About the professional killer? Did your husband have any connections with underworld figures?"

"Well . . ." she said, and paused to moisten her lips. She had sharp little incisors, almost as if she'd filed them to a point. She sat back down on the tufted sofa across from the men. She said, much as if this were a topic she'd been dying to bring up, "I wouldn't be a bit surprised."

"But you have no evidence for believing someone with a grudge might take the opportunity to, well, get even," said Cotton.

"Not *evidence*, no. But . . . he was not always as popular offstage as he was onstage, if you know what I mean." She seemed again to remember the occasion called for at least a show of grief, and, plucking another tissue from a box on a side table, she dabbed tenderly at one dry eye.

"Was there drug use? I mean, did he use drugs, or hang about with people who did?"

"No," Melinda said decisively. "He thought drugs were bad for the complexion—aging, you know—and he'd never touch them. He took a prescription drug for his heart, like many men his age, but he wouldn't go near anything illegal. In the theater, though, you're around the occasional drug user—all the time, really. I mean, the type of person who uses drugs recreationally. It's just part of the, you know . . . the creative thing they do."

"I see," said Cotton. None of this sounded like the sort of thing that could be construed as a drug-related episode gone wrong. An image of an actor showing up in full Kabuki-style makeup to avenge some imagined wrong or another flashed through Cotton's mind. An actor angry with Thaddeus for upstaging him or her.

He glanced at Max, who seemed to be grappling with some puzzle of his own. What now? Cotton wondered. He didn't have long to wait.

"I wonder," said Max, "why he didn't cry out if he were in trouble?"

Melinda shrugged. She didn't have an answer for that. It was odd, because Max had the inescapable sensation she had been expecting the question. As Max let the silence lengthen, she finally said, "Maybe he did and I just didn't hear him. It's a big house. I was asleep."

Max paused again before trying his next question. What he wanted to ask was whether she and Thaddeus had been getting along.

"Was there anything else that might have been weighing on your husband's mind?" He kept his face neutral, his voice calm. He might have been asking her to recommend a good chimney sweep.

He again let the silence draw out. One badly timed word and she would clam up. Trust, Max knew, was as intricately built yet fragile as a spider's web. Once, when he had been part of a hostage-negotiation team, a coach sitting next to the primary negotiator had sneezed. Since the sneeze had been clearly audible in the background, they'd had no choice but to admit to the kidnapper there was someone else listening in. The incident had stalled negotiations for days.

Trust was always at the heart of these situations, and trust slowly accrued over days or even months could be lost so quickly, sometimes forever.

The bluntness of Melinda's eventual answer surprised him. "There was very little on my husband's mind, if you want the truth, beyond his immediate needs and wants."

Cotton, who had begun to stroll about the room, abruptly stopped his forward motion. He had been scrutinizing the contents of a glass-fronted cabinet full of expensive-looking gewgaws, thinking what deplorable taste these people had. Suddenly, he turned to Melinda, all ears.

"There was trouble between you?"

This earned him a squawk of protest, followed by a heated denial. "Not at all. I just knew him well. I'm simply saying he could be, like most actors, self-involved."

Cotton nodded understandingly.

"Had anything unusual happened lately, to you or to your husband?" Max asked her. "Anything at all? Any change in routine, for example?"

"Not really," she said. "Well, if you're including the *really* trivial things, I mean, one odd thing did happen, but it's not worth mentioning."

"Go on," said Cotton.

"It's just been on my mind, you see," said Melinda. "I'm sure it's not relevant. It's that I lost a pair of earrings a few weeks ago. Thaddeus had given them to me as an engagement present, actually. They weren't worth a lot, but they were pretty. Antique—a sort of stylized design. Art Deco. Quite unique. It was a bit odd. I suppose the clips came loose and I lost them. They were my favorites, apart from my butterfly earrings."

Max, no matter how he tried, could not see how to elevate that to the list of unusual happenings, but he filed it away for future reference. He had, after all, asked her to remember even small things that had been out of the ordinary.

"A bit unusual to lose both at once, wasn't it?" he asked.

"I was carrying them in my purse for a while. I'm not used to clip-on earrings, and they can start to hurt. So maybe they got caught up in something else in my purse, like a handkerchief, and I dropped them without realizing. That's what I thought at the time. But is it important?"

Max shook his head. "I don't see how."

She turned expectantly to Cotton, as if hoping the questioning might be over now, but she was to be disappointed.

"So," said Cotton. "Your husband decided to retire to Nether Monkslip? It's hardly a mecca for those in the performing arts. Why here?"

"First of all, he didn't retire, exactly." Lazily, she scratched one thin arm with her long red fingernails. She was still wearing the extravagant white negligee and robe, looking like a thirties film star, and Max wondered if the ostrich feathers, still a bit droopy with moisture, tickled her skin.

"No?" Cotton asked.

"He announced he was leaving," she said. "When no one begged him to stay, he started talking about moving here. Downsizing to a simpler life—you know the sort of thing. The next thing you know, he was talking about getting in some chickens and things—thank God nothing more came of that idea. But he was hoping to finagle an interview with a reporter and he thought a back-to-nature angle might entice her. I tried to tell him he wasn't the ruddy Prince of Wales—imagine how much he welcomed *that* opinion."

Cotton's raised eyebrows took in the fancy-schmancy chairs and lamps and other appointments in the room and he wondered, if this was supposed to be the simple life, how complicated their life must have been in London.

"The parts simply had dried up, you see," Melinda explained. "And requests for rights to produce his plays dried up about the same time. The stuff he'd written was all rather dark, unhappy, and Pinterish, but unlike Pinter's plays, Thaddeus's gloomy twaddle had gone out of style. It happened suddenly, really, which was upsetting for him. As well as embarrassing, once he'd made his big announcement. He *had* to leave, you see. He'd closed out his other options. The West End no longer was returning his calls."

She sounds as if she's apologizing for Thaddeus, Max thought. As if she's excusing the man's behavior, which, from what Max had seen, was really inexcusable. His career failures had probably been both preventable in some cases and unavoidable in others, but what was nearly certain was that they'd had nothing to do with Melinda. She'd been simply handy as a shock absorber. He'd seen it too many times in marriages where a change of circumstance, particularly financial, created stress for fair-weather couples. The Bottles did not appear to be hard up, not judging by all the froufrou, but Thaddeus had struck him as the type of man whose entire ego, and how he defined himself, would be caught up in his career. With diminished prospects for a career, the ego took a beating. And so, sometimes, did the wife. Max made a mental note to talk to Melinda on her own and in private.

"I see," said Cotton. "But, why here? It's not exactly a well-known area."

"Oh, didn't I say? He was the son of the village saddler—of course, that was yonks ago, when his father lived here, and when people kept saddlers in constant business. I mean before everyone drove cars everywhere. Long gone now—the father and his shop, of course. And his mother. This house is where his family lived, you know—Thaddeus's family. Of course, it was mostly torn down to build all this."

Her hand swept out, Marie Antoinette showing off the Petit Trianon.

"Nice," said Cotton. "Your husband had no wish to continue in his father's business then? As a young man, I mean?"

Melinda looked at him as if he were mad even to ask. The hand holding the tissue, which had been raised to dab at her eyes again, was stilled in mid-flutter.

"Thaddeus knew nothing about that sort of business," she said. "He wanted from an early age to be an actor. From the way he told it, he got out of the village the first chance he got."

"Which was when?" asked Cotton.

She was picking at one of the feathers on her robe and didn't seem to have heard him. Max thought she might be in a state of mild shock. Over her head, he gave his own head a little shaking motion. Cotton caught his meaning but ignored him for now, apart from softening his voice by a notch as he repeated, "Which was when? You say your husband got out of here at the first opportunity."

"When?" she repeated. "He was eighteen, maybe nineteen. He went to study drama, didn't he? He wasn't going to follow in his father's footsteps. And who could blame him, really? It was a business he had no interest in, and it was largely a dying business anyway. What used to be the village saddler's is now a shop selling handbags and belts made of recycled materials. I've had my eye on a satchel they've designed. It's really quite pretty. . . ." She seemed to realize she was rambling off the path and resumed her plucking at the robe.

"And then he had some success on the stage," Cotton prompted.

"Yes," she said. "He really was marvelous in his heyday, you know. But then, somehow . . . He got older. Things just changed. His leaving hardly left a void in the West End; he could easily be replaced by any number of other actors. Thaddeus was hoping to be recognized in the Queen's New Year Honours list—for services to literature or some such. I can't imagine who or what put such an idea into his head. So far as anyone is aware, the Queen had no idea Thaddeus was alive. I think he was getting senile, personally."

"Really?" Cotton asked, again interrupting his perambulations around the room. "What makes you say that?"

"He had memory lapses, especially when he'd just woken from a nap. He'd often be confused, disoriented. It went beyond misplacing the car keys and things. There would be these big . . . sort of blanks . . . in his thinking."

That was quite common as people aged, Max knew. He looked around him from out of the folds of his puffy chair, wondering, Could there be a reason beyond sentiment that Thaddeus wanted to move to this house? Did it conceal a crime? A skeleton? Some event from his youth?

Or was it just his ego at work? Much more likely, that explanation: the triumphant return of Thaddeus Bottle, to a bigger house than his parents had been able to provide for him.

One question among many remained unanswered for Max—apart

from the question of who had killed Thaddeus. "You're still in your nightclothes," he observed. "How did you change from day wear without noticing your husband on the bed?"

"There's a dressing room off the bedroom," she answered promptly. "I never went into the bedroom itself. I just changed into something comfortable and then went back downstairs to watch the telly."

More than two hours had passed. They heard the sound of many pairs of feet clomping down the stairs, followed by more pairs of feet. That large herd, thought Max, would be the photographer and forensics team leaving, followed by the police doctor. Cotton slipped in and out of the room, collecting reports, while Max sat on, keeping Melinda company.

Max wondered if Thaddeus was being taken away now. He would have to leave soon himself (thankfully under his own steam). But this was Sunday—for a vicar, a major day in the week, and he couldn't hang about.

Max recalled being at the scene of another death a few weeks before. He had happened to be on a home visit when the man, to all appearances nicely recovering from surgery, collapsed from what turned out to be a fatal blood clot. The clot had moved with swift and deadly precision toward his heart even as Max punched 999 into his mobile.

"Please, make him live," his wife had said. She'd said this to Max, she'd then said it to the ambulance attendants when they arrived, and she'd repeated it like a mantra as the emergency crew worked frantically to restore the spark of life to her husband. Max could see it was already too late.

The woman's eyes had darted between Max and the attendants the whole time. To whom had she been directing her plea? Not to God. Not "*let* him live," but "make him live." As if to say, You're the professionals: Do something, medical or miraculous, or both. *Do* something.

Looking at Melinda now, he wondered: Had she loved Thaddeus

like that, perhaps at some level that was like a faded image of the original fondness, gratitude, or attraction she once had felt for him? It didn't seem possible, but certainly her sadness and confusion seemed genuine, if somewhat overplayed. Max chastised himself—no one knew what went on between two people in a marriage, or what was the glue that held them stuck to each other.

As they waited for Cotton to return from another consultation with his team, Max's thoughts drifted inexorably to Awena. In his undercover days, Max had on several occasions pretended to be married. The pretense had helped him avoid tricky situations where he was being invited to party with the bad guys. He'd often been tested but had found that establishing the rules early on made his later refusals believable. The worst criminals had instantly understood when he said he loved his wife, a fact that had astonished Max every time it happened. They would not have believed him if he'd claimed ethical scruples, of course, but love was the great universal, even for men who dealt in piping the sewage of terrorism into the country.

No "civilian" woman he'd dated had ever had an inkling he worked for MI5, a reality that had struck him with full force on the death of Paul, his partner. Talking to a girlfriend about his life, telling the truth, would have been to breach the code that Max had sworn to uphold. The reality was that with Paul gone, he had had no confidants, no peers, no one who knew anything of him beyond what appeared on the surface.

Part of Max's recruitment process, once he had been talent-spotted by one of his Oxford professors, had been to undergo EPV, or "enhanced positive vetting." It was the highest level of clearance, and it had included questions about his private life of the most intrusive nature imaginable. Questions about his sex life had predominated. He'd been a very young man, and not all that experienced in the ways of the world, or the scrutiny might have been unendurable. He might also not have passed the test except for that relative inexperience, he realized now.

There hadn't seemed to be a great deal of point to that interview, and Max had come away from it wondering if female recruits were subjected to the same intense scrutiny of this area of their private lives. Somehow he'd suspected not, but he couldn't have said why that was so.

This questioning had been followed by further examinations by all manner of MI5 types, male and female, and psychologists—ditto. There had been written tests and endless interviews, designed to fulfill what purpose, he had never been sure. Testing his consistency, most likely. His ability to tell the same story, over and over again.

Max thought back to his time at Thames House, the home of MI5. Those who worked there called it "the Ice House," because its predominant color scheme consisted of whites and pale blues and grays. There had been lots of glass, he remembered—sheets of glass everywhere. A real house of mirrors, it had been.

In his later years in the service, Max had rarely been inside the building—it wouldn't have done for him to have been seen going in and out the front door. The back entrance was as closely guarded a secret as the Queen's dress size. It had been a world of codes and drops and bombs and things not as they were, but as MI5 wanted them to be perceived.

Max had the patience and watchfulness of a spider, as one of his superiors had written in his personnel file, but he lacked the venom. This was not, it had been added, meant as a criticism, but as a description of the usefulness of his personality to the service. People trusted Max, even crooks. MI5 had others to provide the venom.

Max, after the murder of his colleague Paul, had been looking for the soul pipe that would allow him to escape the sordid underworld he had inhabited as an MI5 agent. And he had found Nether Monkslip.

At least he'd thought he had escaped that world.

Cotton poked his head in the door and signaled for Max to join him in the hallway.

"The doctor agrees with you," he said once they were safely out of hearing. "There's something fishy here."

Max nodded somberly. Here we go, he thought.

"I'm going to ask your help again, Max. You know these villagers. You know Melinda, even, better than I do."

"You're taking it as given it's Melinda?" Max asked. "That she had something to do with this?"

Cotton shook his head. "Don't know, now, do I? But you know the people who know her, and who have interacted with her and Thaddeus over the past months. I'm just asking for a little of your . . . unique insight."

Max hardly bothered to feign reluctance. It never seemed to fool Cotton anyway.

When he had been with MI5, he had felt as if he were protecting the entire world. Defending it, even helping save it from destruction. His scope of influence had been broader than in Nether Monkslip: very broad indeed.

He rarely admitted to himself that sometimes he missed those days of glory—or vainglory.

Now, with the death of Thaddeus Bottle, he was once again being called on to defend a very small corner of the realm. It felt familiar. It felt right.

"I could probably squeeze in a visit or two," he told Cotton.

CHAPTER 8
Routine

Max, having two village churches in his care in addition to St. Edwold's, had a full Sunday schedule. On returning to the vicarage, he showered and shaved, then quickly prepared a boiled egg on toast to go with his black coffee. He stole a glance at the headlines of the *Globe and Bugle* and saw that Kate and William had once again pushed the rest of the world off the news radar. The Duchess of Cambridge must have gone shopping again. Perhaps it was as well—the daily diet of wars, plagues, and riots could use some leavening every so often. Max sent up a prayer for the couple's continued happiness and, while he was about it, for world peace as he waited for his egg to boil. Mrs. Hooser had left him a small paper bag full of mushrooms, a departure from her usual caloric offerings; the rain must be helping to bring them out in Raven's Wood. He fried them in a thimbleful of olive oil. After breakfast, he would set out in the Land Rover for Middle Monkslip and the small church of St. Cuthburga.

It was as he was leaving that he found the sheet of paper with the Bible quote. Someone had slipped it through the mail slot in the front door, folded in half.

Max read "He shall suck the poison of asps: the viper's tongue shall slay him."

He recognized the quotation as being from the Book of Job. Underneath it was typed, in a separate paragraph, ". . . with their tongues they have used deceit; the poison of asps is under their lips."

He thought that last was from an epistle to the Romans. The typing had been generated by a computer printer, using a Gothic-style font, and printed on A4 paper, the ordinary kind to be found in any office-supply store.

He turned the paper over. Nothing on the back. Nothing out of the ordinary about it apart from those thundering Bible quotes.

Well, he thought, the references to poison certainly confirmed his suspicions. Too late now, but in the unlikely event there were prints, he used his shirttail to hold the letter by one corner. Then carrying it into the kitchen, he retrieved a plastic food-storage bag from a drawer and slid the page inside. He rang Cotton and asked him to send a PC over right away to pick it up.

"This is nice," said Cotton. "The killer is going to spell it out for us, is he?"

"Or she. It's unsigned, of course. That would make your job a little too easy."

"For a change. But the whole thing seems like a double bluff to me."

"How do you mean?"

"You nearly said it yourself. This kind of poison-pen letter—if you'll excuse the pun—this kind of letter is usually a woman's weapon. You know that as well as I do. Unfortunately, so does half the population— anyone who has seen a crime show on the telly knows we'd suspect a woman first."

Max was nodding; he'd had the same thought. "Certainly. But notice that this isn't exactly a poison-pen letter—at least not in the usual way. The target of the letter, presumably Thaddeus, is already dead. And it's not the 'I saw what you did' sort of thing sent to a living person, with an implied blackmail threat. It was sent to me. This is almost, if not an apology or a mea culpa, a rationalization. To be precise, it is the killer—or whoever sent the message—explaining why Thaddeus had to die. I think we have to say this letter came from the killer. I mean, who else would send it other than, perhaps, an accomplice? Thaddeus, the writer is telling us, was a wicked man. Not just an unpleasant and vain man: a wicked one. A liar. The first quotation is from the Book of Job—one of the more unsavory passages. It also talks of vomit and bowels and so on."

"Puh-*lease*." Max could picture the pained expression on the fastidious Cotton's face. "These Bible authors really had a way with words, didn't they? Well, as I say, it could be a double bluff. A man hoping we'll think it's a message from a woman."

Max was busy wondering why the missive had been sent at all. Most killers who went in for this sort of thing were hoping to be caught. There were ways to track down where the letter had come from, apart from fingerprints. Perhaps the killer didn't realize it, but computer printers had their own unique identifying characteristics. Once a suspect was in view, the police would need a search warrant to do a comparison test against the suspect's printer, but if they found a match, the evidence would be nearly irrefutable.

So there was something just that bit mad and reckless about sending such a message. It seemed an unnecessary risk for the killer to take—apart from anything else, it was just possible that Max's correspondent had been spotted at the vicarage door, leaving the missive. It spoke volumes about the killer's state of mind. Max spoke these thoughts aloud to Cotton.

"I agree. We've already been moving fast—the lab has orders to prioritize the samples taken at the scene. But we'll have to move faster in talking with the villagers."

•   •   •

Preoccupied as Max was by Bible passages and the death of Thaddeus, there was one incident that morning that drew him away from disturbing questions surrounding the finding of the body and into the present of his pastoral duties. It happened as he was leading the service at St. Cuthburga, which service he sang, exuberantly and slightly off-key, blissfully unaware of how much his parishioners enjoyed these *Britain's Got Talent* performances.

It was a full house. Tom and Marie O'Day, a handsome and well-suited couple who were mainstays of the community, sat in the front row, singing the responses with matching energy. The Tailors' two-year-old was learning to talk and chose the middle of Max's sermon as the time to hone this new skill. Still, Max had officiated at the Tailors' wedding and took vicarious pride in the vocal result, which result he had also baptized. The rite of baptism was one of his pleasanter duties as vicar, although he had been peed on several times and poked in the eye once by a walnut-size fist.

Mr. Baker, a new widower, had what sounded like a serious cold, and he harrumphed and coughed his way through much of the service. Max made a mental reminder to call on the man at the first opportunity, knowing how easily people in mourning succumbed to serious illness. The most annoying of platitudes was that God never sends you a burden you cannot bear. That simply wasn't true. Max had seen many people broken on the wheel of chance, and the Bakers' marriage had been an extraordinarily close one. But he also had witnessed that the people who survived were rewarded down the road in some wholly unpredictable way—with a sudden windfall, loving grandchildren, treasured friendships, or some other compensating factor that seemed designed to illustrate the mysterious ways of their Creator.

With part of his mind on what he had seen and heard that morning at King's Rest, he began to pace through the service as if going for his personal best. He forced himself to slow down and focus on the meaning of the words he was saying—words that generally acted as a balm to his soul.

Then Mr. Brainard dropped the collection plate, causing a scramble to retrieve the coins that rolled down the aisle. All in all, it was one of Max's more chaotic services.

As he administered the Eucharist, he could not help but notice a young girl as she swayed up to the altar rail behind her parents. He wasn't sure of their names but thought they might be the Brandywine family. The girl was wearing a mere suggestion of a skirt and a low-cut blouse that barely covered a shelflike bra she wouldn't actually need for a couple more years. She was in full makeup and perhaps twelve years old.

Outside St. Cuthburga's after the service, the men and women gathered in time-honored fashion, stopping to greet and shake hands with the vicar at the door. The women, Max had noticed, had started wearing hats again, strange confections of feathers and lace that sometimes covered one eye, and with matching pocketbooks and shoes.

Max finally managed to take aside the parents of the girl as their daughter flirted loudly with whatever portions of the local male population, young and old, drifted past. The father was a portly middle-aged man, beaming with the sort of half-witted geniality of the born enabler; the mother was of approximately the same age, wearing a tight-fitting costume she had somehow poured herself into, and a shellacking of tangerine makeup.

Max exchanged the standard pleasantries and then quietly said to them, "What your daughter is wearing today—I feel it's unsuitable attire for church. You and she are, of course, most welcome to attend services whenever you like, but she needs to be dressed appropriately. What she wears outside of church is, of course, up to you."

He was thankful to be spared their denials and any pretense they didn't know what he was talking about.

"You're a prude," the mother said.

Max, who felt he'd slept with a large percentage of the female population of London in his time, said, "Hardly."

"Yes, you are," put in the father, loyally taking sides.

Remembering his recent night at Awena's, which had ended in the wee hours, Max repeated, "Hardly. I'm not asking that you shroud your daughter head to toe in some medieval religious costume. I'm asking that you guide her in dressing in a manner appropriate to the occasion. She is dressed appropriately for a disco or a nightclub." Or perhaps a night on some oligarch's yacht, he thought, but did not say this aloud. "She was not dressed appropriately for a house of worship, joining others in showing respect for her Savior, theirs, yours, and mine."

They stared at him uncomprehendingly.

"You will need to teach her that, as those wiser than I have said, 'to everything there is a season.' She is precisely, I would suggest to you, at a time in her life when she needs to hear the occasional, the reasoned and calm and rational 'No.' And the answer to her inevitable 'Why not?' has got to be 'Because I am your parent, I know more than you, and I say so.'"

There was a flicker in the father's eyes that told Max he was making a bit of headway there. Less so than with the mother, who, he suspected, placed—misplaced—a high premium on her daughter's sexual attractiveness as being a reflection on her own.

"You're just worried about what the men will think," she said.

"And you're not? As her mother?"

As there was no answer to that, she simply regarded him warily from her small greenish eyes, made smaller by being encircled with thick lashings of black kohl.

"I'll be complaining to your bishop, then," she said.

"That is, of course, your privilege. He has raised four daughters, so I think you may find he agrees with me." Max added more gently, "Men need women to help set the boundaries—not the other way around. Just as she needs you to do the same for her."

He left them looking in equal parts mystified and outraged by his presumption. From experience, he knew they would not come back to the church for a while. They would repeat the tale of their conversation to anyone in the village who would listen, and with any luck, the reactions of the people they spoke with would exert its own pressure. He could see he was not the only one to notice the girl's Las Vegas showgirl attire. When the parents did come back—and he was certain they would—it might be without the daughter, which in itself would be a sign that something he had said had penetrated. Deprived of her weekly outlet for seducing the local swains, the daughter might eventually accede to her parents' request that she tone it down a bit.

He felt the inclination to deliver a further little homily to the daughter herself, but he stifled the idea as overkill, for the moment. Instead, he attended to the usual weekly business around the church, setting up appointments with various parishioners needing his attention. Then he put his old Land Rover in gear and drove away.

The entire incident had made him think of Melinda, who so clearly had no identity or resources beyond her attractiveness, an attractiveness that in her case depended too much on a fast-disappearing youth.

How far, he wondered, would that lack of self have taken her in a wish to break free of her overbearing husband?

Back at the vicarage, he phoned Awena. Her cooking class continued through the weekend, as many of her students had full-time jobs outside the home. He doubted she'd heard the news about Thaddeus Bottle but was surprised—why was he surprised?—to learn the tendrils of the Nether Monkslip grapevine had stretched to reach her at the cookery school of Denman College.

"Tara phoned me," she said. "Melinda was a regular customer of the yoga studio and Tara has been quite concerned about her."

"In what way?"

"In every way. Her weight, for one thing. Her mental state overall. She is far too nervy, and far too thin. Tara was trying gently to wean her into the holistic frame of healthy mind, healthy body."

"That's good. She doesn't seem to have a lot of friends here."

"She's friendly with some of the women in the class. Gabby Crew from the salon and the estate agent, Bernadina Steed, are often in the same class with her. How is she doing now—Melinda?"

"Not really well. She's in shock, I'm sure." Max, remembering that Melinda had lain next to a corpse in bed, thinking it was her living husband, appreciated how utterly disconcerting that would be.

All of that supposing she hadn't herself been the one to turn her husband into a corpse.

They talked awhile longer, and then Max had to rush to take the next service, this one at St. Edwold's. He started to sign off, hesitated, and said, "I love you." How odd that sounded, coming from him. And how completely true. "Please hurry back."

"And I love you, Max," she said. "I don't suppose there's any point in telling you to not get too involved in this investigation. Let Cotton do his thing."

"Of course," he said. "I'll have just a few conversations about the village. That's all."

As he was ringing off with Awena, the bells of St. Edwold's sounded outside the vicarage window. Automatically, Max checked his watch and gave it a little shake. Then he realized Mr. Stackpole, the sexton who maintained the church building, had slipped up. More likely, because he didn't hold with all this tampering with the God-given time, Mr. Stackpole was delaying getting around to making the adjustment needed to "spring forward." The church bells were automated these days, since the demise of peasants willing to ring the hour. They ran off of some ancient, precomputery mechanism that had to be reset and programmed by hand.

All of which reminded Max of his upcoming appointment with his bishop. He would have to travel to Monkslip Cathedral, the seat of the Bishop of Monkslip, and have what was certain to be an awkward conversation in the bishop's palace. Max was sure that, given the current situation, he'd get much the same advice from his bishop as he was getting from Awena: Stay clear of the investigation.

But there were other topics Max felt were of more importance to discuss than his involvement in the investigation. His burgeoning relationship with Awena, for one. People might make mild jokes about her mash-up of vaguely neopagan, druidic, and Wiccan leanings, but to Awena, of course, this was no joke. Any belief system looked at dispassionately seemed a bit mad—even, he had to admit, his own. How to bring this into the conversation with the bishop was beyond him.

And should he even mention the weirdly reappearing image on the wall of St. Edwold's? It was little Tom Hooser who had noticed the resemblance to the face on the shroud of Turin, one day blurting out the likeness to a full congregation. And Tom, Max recognized, was no doubting Thomas: To him, the face was quite real and it was the face of Jesus, which face he recognized from seeing the shroud on a BBC documentary. Tom had several times repeated this assertion, usually in the middle of the most sacred and solemn part of the church service. Max had desperately wanted to shush him from the altar, but of course he could not. Generally, his sister, Tildy Ann, would elbow him or stomp on his foot and that would resolve the matter until the next time.

Would the bishop want to hear about the image? Surely not. Besides, it would be taken care of by the roof repair, for clearly the image was just a water stain. Repairs would get under way once the village was safely past the time of the spring showers.

Max decided that the next day he'd start his investigation of the Bottle case. His attendance at tomorrow's meeting to discuss the children's Easter egg hunt was not required, and he found he was glad to avoid this particular chore this time. Of all the topics to evoke strong feeling, this was possibly the strangest. The hunt had "always" been held, or so some maintained, in the St. Edwold's churchyard, among grazing sheep. There had arisen a faction that held this practice was too morbid for the smallest villagers. Thaddeus Bottle, Max recalled, had been among the most vociferous of the traditionalists.

Max felt a slight tinge of guilt at dodging this particular bullet, and vowed to make up the lapse at the first opportunity. There would always be another committee in need of mediation.

He left the vicarage and walked to the church vestry to put on his vestments for the service.

Subject: NEWS!

From: Gabrielle Crew (gabby@TresRapidePoste.fr)

To: Claude Chaux (Claude43@TresRapidePoste.fr)

Date: Monday, March 26, 2012 7:42 A.M.

Claude—Forgive me for not writing yesterday, but you will understand when you read this: I awoke Sunday to the news that Thaddeus Bottle had been murdered—at least the police have been called in, so it clearly is not being treated as a natural death. More to come on that subject "as it develops." I am not yet completely part of the village grapevine, but it would appear the media will be taking an interest in our small community, and I will be closely following their updates. I'll e-mail you the links to anything of interest.

I read somewhere once that Her Majesty's government reads all our e-mails. Did you know that? It should make us all feel important. One wonders how they have the time, but I suppose they have machines that scan everything for them, looking for key words like *bomb* or *kill.* I should ask the vicar—he's a former MI5 agent. At least that's the rumor that goes around about him. He never talks about it. That wouldn't be his style at all. So modest, so blindingly handsome—if only I were thirty years younger! But then, there's not a woman in this village who hasn't thought something along those lines. There was a lot of competition before Awena came along and scooped him up, apparently without even trying.

You'd think a man like that would be bored in this little village where nothing ever happens (usually), but he seems quite content, precisely like a man who has found his true vocation at last. A bit like me, really—I found my niche late in life. It helped that I inherited my abilities from you and grandmother, for there was little call for a hairstylist in Sierra Leone. Clean water and food were the priorities.

Today's paper contained an article about the origins of British Summer Time. An article on Saturday would have been more useful to help prepare one in advance, but we are in the land that time forgot, literally. Anyway, it seems that during World War II in England, they set the clocks ahead for summer, but they didn't set them back when summer was over. This threw everything out of step until finally they got it sorted, in 1945.

The more governments get involved, the bigger the mess.

Off to yoga class now, where the talk will no doubt be all about what happened to Thaddeus. I doubt Melinda will be there, but you never know.

Love, your Gabby

CHAPTER 9
All Things Bright and Beautiful

Monday, March 26

MI5 had, if nothing else, provided Max with a strong sense of purpose. He had begun to fear he might have lost the almost incandescent awareness that had consumed him in the days when every lapse in his attention to detail might mean a life lost. But at his core he remained vigilant, alert to nuance—mostly by nature, he had come to realize, and only partly by training.

Now, the priesthood had provided him with a sense of purpose, if of a different kind.

And Thaddeus's death, he realized, provided a nearly perfect intersection of the parts of his MI5 life he had missed with the instincts and intuitions he had honed as a priest. The things happening in Monkslip were like fault lines beneath the surface, biding their time and waiting silently to destroy.

If there were any way to stop the damage, he intended to.

Following Morning Prayer, and guided by yesterday's phone conversation with Awena, he walked over to the Goddessspell shop. So many of the women seemed to know one another from that particular nexus of village life, it seemed as good a place as any to start his asking around (he still hesitated to use the word *investigation,* even if that was what it was).

And from what he knew of the shop's schedule, one of Tara's yoga sessions in the back room should be just about wrapping up.

Goddessspell held everything magical, including, as far as Max was concerned, Awena herself. Her absence from the shop when he walked in, setting the bell over the door jangling, reawakened Max's sense of a gap in his personal universe. Several times a day, he'd turn to say something to Awena, or his hand would reach for the phone, and the realization she wasn't there or couldn't easily be reached left a frustrated void in his soul. He'd started saving up little things he wanted to tell her, rehearsing them over in his mind.

Max marveled anew at how quickly he had fallen into the most significant romantic relationship of his life. They had been friends for several years, and Awena was someone in whose presence he always had felt comfortable. She was easy to talk to, she tended not to judge him or others, and she was inclined to keep her mind trained on the same things that mattered to him. On the "bigger-question picture," he supposed he would call it.

If she did judge, it seemed to him she never judged harshly, even if she did appraise with astonishing accuracy.

The night of her holiday party in December, the night of the Winter Solstice, he had fallen irretrievably in love. He'd been drawn to Awena for a very long time, and was only just then willing to take a chance and act upon this attraction. He'd just returned to the village after an upsetting incident of murder at Chedrow Castle, a case that he'd helped Cotton sort out. While the distance from Nether Monkslip and from Awena had not been great, it had at the same time seemed endless, and he had come to realize the one person he needed to talk with, to sort things out in his mind, had been Awena. Thus so stealthily had she become his confidante. Thus so irreversibly had he realized his need for her—not just as a friend but as a partner and lover. Her face had become as familiar to him as his own in the mirror: her dark hair, with its prematurely white streak at one temple, her face soft as rose petals, her stately demeanor. And while temperamentally there might have been differences between them, he knew the differences were beneficial to them both.

Inside the shop, Max peered through the beaded curtain at the back, to be greeted by a sea of undulating derrieres of varying sizes and latex coverings, all pointing more or less skyward in what had to be a down-dog pose. Max didn't entirely understand the need for organized group exercise—he ran, biked, or walked almost everywhere, alone or with Thea for company. But he suspected there was a lot more female bonding going on in these classes than would have been the case in a male-equivalent class, where such activities tended to devolve instead into high-stakes competitions.

Delicately, he withdrew and began looking around at the merchandise in the shop. There were crystals and stones and chimes, candles and incense, herbs and oils, soaps, and bundles of sage—smudge to purify the air. There were shawls and cushions and bells, and jewelry and books and relaxation CDs, and little statues and emblems representing different beliefs: Pagan, Goddess, and Wiccan; Buddhist, Hindu, and Christian. Everything in the place sparkled; everything enchanted, appealing to all the senses. The hand could not resist reaching out to touch the different baubles and crystals, and the mind could not fail to be calmed by the little prayers of hope and affirmation. Max himself owned several of the music CDs of Eastern and Western chanting.

Through his mind ran more of his conversation with Awena on the subject of how Melinda had become a fixture at the yoga class.

"I've also had a word with her," Awena had told him, "because I thought her working out was getting to be obsessive, and I was trying to steer her toward the meditation classes. Even yoga, done the wrong way, too vigorously, can damage the muscles and ligaments. Besides, Melinda was becoming emaciated, even by Hollywood standards. And who was she trying to impress? Her husband, easily thirty years her senior? It was all out of balance."

"I saw that for myself," said Max.

"Tara called it 'appeasement,'" Awena concluded. "She wasn't trying to impress Thaddeus, but appease him, or so Tara thought. He's a bully, that man."

Max decided it might be safe now to steal another look at the yoga class. Now they were on their backs, legs feebly waving, like dying insects after a visit from the exterminator. The likeness was particularly pronounced in the case of Melinda, with her sticklike legs sheathed in black. He could see now that Gabby was also part of the class. She was having as much trouble as the others with this pose, which the lithe Tara illustrated with the ease born of years of practice. But then, Gabby had twenty to forty years on most of them, too. Viewed in that light, she was holding her own with women half her age.

In a few minutes, the class ended, on Tara Raine's *"Namaste."* Tara emerged first from behind the curtain, her face serene but flushed, the freckles highlighted against her lightly tanned complexion. She wore a tie-dyed T-shirt over peach-colored yoga pants; her hair was curled into a bun at the neck and held in place with four butterfly clips, their wings opalescent. When she saw Max, she bounded across the room, greeting him with a smile and a light hug, exuding good health and karma. Tara greatly approved of Max as a suitable partner for her friend Awena.

Other women began to file out from the yoga studio. Max realized they were all there, the ones he wanted to talk with: Lucie Cuthbert and Bernadina Steed and Gabby Crew. They began to gather around him, all, like Tara, looking flushed and rejuvenated by their exercise.

And by something more, Max realized: Sensing his mission, they were finding the chance to speculate wildly about the murder too good to resist.

"I should run," announced Gabby. "I have an emergency updo to fit in this morning, Melinda's coming over for her regular appointment, and I still have to shower." But she made no move to leave.

Tara said to Max, pointedly, although Max could not fathom what the point might be, "Melinda gets her hair done nearly every day."

"Every *day*?" Max, knowing nothing of what women required to keep them looking their best, felt he was wandering into foreign and potentially hostile territory. "That seems a lot."

Tara said, in a low voice, "Not if you're Melinda. It's all in keeping with her personality. I've heard it called a 'toxic quest for perfection'—that was Jane Fonda, I think. And that's what it looks like—toxic. The constant exercise, the perfect makeup, the focus, focus, focus on wardrobe. I'm worried about her weight. She's too thin but doesn't seem to realize it." Now Tara made a shushing signal, one finger against her lips. "She's still in the next room."

Just then, the subject of the conversation unfolded herself from where she had stayed behind, doing extra-credit poses: Melinda Bottle, the grieving widow. Although, Max realized, there were worse ways to mourn a sudden loss than by practicing yoga.

She greeted Max with a wan smile and, wrapping a drapey brown shawl across her bony shoulders, she nodded absently to the others before leaving. The bell over the shop door clanged with finality behind her. Gabby Crew followed her out, perhaps to offer an encouraging word.

Once they were certain Melinda had gone and would not be returning to retrieve some forgotten article, Lucie and Bernadina quickly got down to brass tacks.

"You are investigating the death," said Lucie Cuthbert with her typical forthrightness. "You think it is a murder, don't you?" There was concern on her face and a furrow in her brow, but also a sparkle in her eye—one with which Max was getting to be too familiar. Homicide was the great leveler—*every*one was interested in murder, particularly one that had taken place practically in their midst. That Thaddeus had actually been in her house, having a meal at her table, probably added much to the frisson. Bernadina Steed gazed up at him, the same look of anticipation widening her made-up eyes and parting her glossy lips.

They were *excited* by the murder, Max realized. Not an unusual reaction for those whose lives seldom were touched by the harsher realities of life and death, but still . . .

Max wheeled out the usual platitudes ("It's too soon to call it murder"), knowing he wasn't fooling Lucie, and knowing she knew.

"The lab hasn't returned all the results yet," he said. "We can't know until then, and it would be wrong to speculate."

Lucie and Bernadina exchanged glances, then turned to look at him. "Hmmph," they said. Lucie, religiously brought up, could not quite bring herself to tell the vicar to cut the crap, but it was a close thing.

"If there is anything you noticed that night at dinner, however," said Max, "you never know . . ." His voice trailed off vaguely, hopefully.

It was all either of them needed in the way of prompting. They again exchanged glances, and somehow during the exchange, without moving a muscle or so much as blinking an eye, Lucie gave Bernadina the go-ahead signal. The women of Nether Monkslip mobilizing for an intelligence-gathering mission were an awesome sight to behold. They probably had received their marching orders from Miss Pitchford, who had recently been sidelined to her cottage by a minor injury to her foot. The frustration of not being in the center of operations must have been almost more than the poor woman could bear.

"Well," said Bernadina breathlessly. "He was rude, didn't you think? He was just really out of line with her. With Melinda."

"Um-hmm. Anything else? Anything concrete that you noticed that he said or did?" asked Max, quickly relinquishing his hold on the pretense that none of this mattered to him apart from idle curiosity. He, too, was "on a mission from God with a full tank of gas," as the Blues Brothers would have it—an MI5 hound on the scent.

Another telepathically significant glance was exchanged. This time, the torch was handed over to Lucie. She inched closer, as if about to impart the secret ingredient in her recipe for chicken stuffing.

"There have been rumors," she began. "About Melinda."

Max waited. It was a bit like watching the slow drip of a water tap after the pump has been primed. And here, at last, out it came.

"There is a man involved, Father Max," said Lucie, the words tumbling, and her accent becoming more pronounced, in her haste. "No one is quite sure who it is, and one does not like to say unless one is positive. But *cherchez l'homme* and you may find the bottom of this."

She looked pointedly at Max, as if expecting him to whip out a pencil and notebook and start jotting all this down.

Bernadina, practically hopping from one foot to the other, jumped in.

"I think I know who it is, but of course I couldn't possibly say." This virtuous silence lasted less than three seconds. "The thing is, I may have been instrumental in introducing them. I didn't mean for anything to happen, you understand. It's just that when Thaddeus asked for a recommendation—well, you see, with me being in the business and all, it was natural I—"

Here Lucie cut in, "It's Farley. We think it's Farley."

It was not a name with which Max was familiar.

Lucie elaborated: "He lives in Staincross Minster and he's an architect. Farley Walker is his name."

Max nodded. "That's right. I've seen him in the village—rather, I've seen his sports car."

"That is him," said Lucie. "A shiny red sports car, very expensive. He's quite well known in these parts. People looking for someone who understands renovations and the restoration of old buildings go to him. We consulted with him when we moved out of our rooms over the shop and into our new house."

"Not only Thaddeus but also Melinda asked me for a reference," said Bernadina, thus somehow absolving herself of all blame in the murder that surely must have resulted from this innocent introduction. "They both did."

"What makes you think there was anything between Melinda and this Farley person?" Max asked them.

A scoffing noise erupted from both Lucie and Bernadina. Really, men could be so thick at times.

"One just *knows*, Father. It is impossible to hide *l'amour en fleur* from a woman, particularly, if I may be permitted to boast, a *French*woman." Here a Gallic sniff as she looked down her nose, as if to demonstrate her bona fides in these matters. "Melinda, who was leading a dog's life with old grumpypants—the world's greatest writer and actor, to hear him tell it—had in recent months just cheered up no end. Oh! *Mon Dieu!* The signs were clear."

"But you're just guessing it was Farley—*if* there were anyone. There's no evidence it was he. Or even that she was interested in anyone but her husband." And he thought, I need to check this out before the gossip reaches the ears of Cotton and his team. What if the women have it all wrong?

The women shook their heads in unison this time at Max's stubborn refusal to face facts.

"Why don't you go and ask her?" said Lucie.

Max thought he probably would do just that, wondering very much what sort of answer he'd get.

But: "Now, that's funny," Max heard Tara say as he turned to leave. "Who would steal that?"

Max looked over to where she stood. Engaged in organizing trinkets on one of the wooden shelves, she had held herself apart from Max's conversation with the other two women. Now she was holding up a little display of herbal sachets made of some shimmery blue fabric. "I know there were five sachets in this basket a few days ago—I noticed because we were running low, and I meant to tell Awena when she came back. Now there are three, and I haven't sold any. How odd."

It *is* odd, thought Max. Nether Monkslip wasn't immune from crime—God knew—but pilfering and petty theft were mercifully rare.

"Kids," said Tara. "We do get them in here, attracted to all the sparkly stuff. I suppose when my back was turned . . . Anyway, Father Max, when you talk with Awena next, tell her I miss her."

CHAPTER 10
Three for Tea

Max retraced his steps of Sunday morning, walking out of the village proper and past the train station, on his way to ask Melinda about the architect's place in the scheme of things.

But as it turned out, he didn't have to ask.

When he'd talked with Melinda early Sunday, Max had promised he would again stop by the house with information regarding services for Thaddeus at St. Edwold's, once he had checked his calendar. Again walking up the graveled path to her door, this time in broad daylight and at a leisurely pace, Max was met by the sight of a flashy red sports car parked askew in the circular driveway, as if the driver had been in a great hurry. Max stopped to admire the sleek red lines, the chrome, the shiny hubcaps. It was the same car he had seen around the village—it would be impossible to miss—and of course the women at Goddessspell had just reminded him of its existence. The architect to whom it belonged seemed to have wasted no time in calling on the grieving widow.

Max knocked on the door rather more loudly than was necessary: He felt the pair might need a little time to sort themselves out before anyone could make it to the front of the house. The Melinda Bottle who answered the door was looking flushed and disorganized and—no question about it—happier than when Max last had seen her. She had changed from her yoga togs into a jumper over a tank top and jeans, and her feet were bare aside from the bright pink polish on her toes. From somewhere deep in the house, the dog, Jean, barked.

Melinda pushed back the heavy dark hair that fell in messy ringlets over one eye. "Oh," she said.

Max explained his mission with regard to services for her husband. He added gently and with an Oscar-worthy subtlety, "I see Farley is here."

"Hello, Father." The brash male voice reached him from around the corner, coming from the direction of the front sitting room. The voice was followed into the extravagant hallway by a man of middle years—he was perhaps in his early forties, but on first meeting he looked younger, having the physique and the sun-kissed glow of an athlete, perhaps a rower. He first shook Max's hand, then smoothed back his own shiny dark hair, nearly a match for Melinda's shade. He straightened the handkerchief in his jacket pocket, pulled his matching tie into line, and smiled.

"I see the village grapevine has alerted you to the situation," said Farley. "Or are you honestly here on other business?"

"A bit of both," admitted Max.

Farley smiled, not in the least bit embarrassed or put out. "I would say, 'This isn't what it looks like,' but in fact, it *is* what it looks like. Actually, unless you are wholly lacking in imagination, what you see before you is exactly what it seems."

"I do see," said Max. "And I wonder . . . I wonder if I might have a word, since you're here?"

Farley looked over at Melinda, who lifted her eyes to his. Farley quietly took Melinda's hand. She was alight with happiness, her thin frame aquiver like a whippet's, and she probably would have agreed to any suggestion so long as it came from Farley. Smiling, she threw her left arm wide, gesturing that they should follow her, and then fairly skipped toward that large living area at the back of the house (what Max thought they would call a "family room" in the U.S.).

As they followed her down the wide hall, a hall fit for a coronation, Farley said to Max, "Mel and I have . . . formed an attachment. Lying about it now would only make us look guilty, given the circumstances— what's happened with Thaddeus and all. It was Bernadina Steed who introduced us, actually. I was sent over to advise, ended up doing a few minor repairs while I was here, and . . . well. I'm good with my hands, you see. I mean to say—um. You know. But I hope we can count on you to be discreet, Father?"

Max shook his head. "No, you can't, actually."

"I thought vicars had to be, well . . ."

"Tactful?" said Max, finishing for him. "It's a murder investigation, and that's always a game changer. You can count on me not to gossip needlessly, but withholding what I know to be relevant to the investigation isn't possible. I'm sure you can understand why, when you think about it. Besides, I shouldn't count on someone else in the village not knowing about this already and telling the police. In your shoes, I would tell the police straightaway, before they find out for themselves."

"This has nothing to do with Thaddeus's death. You have my word," said Farley. Melinda, who had stopped and turned, waiting for them to catch up, nodded earnestly.

"You have our word," she said solemnly.

Well, that's all right, then. Thinking the police might need more than their word, he peered at them both, taking in Farley's matinee-idol looks and putting to account his flashy lifestyle. Appearances, Max thought, might be deceptive. They so often were. Certainly this pair seemed ideally matched, which Max could not have said of Melinda and her so recently deceased husband. Melinda was close to Farley in age, similar to him in looks, and they seemed to have similar tastes, something Farley confirmed when, gesturing toward the grand hallway, so out of place and proportion, he said, "I'm helping Melinda decide what to do about Bottle Palace here. I think"—and here he shot her a fond look—"I think she's at last willing to agree with me that the house would be worth more if the modern part were demolished or vastly revised to fit the intention of the original builder, however many centuries ago he set those intentions. I'd plump for demolishing the thing."

"And I've told *him*," she said sweetly, "the house was completely Thaddeus's idea. I knew the Jekyll and Hyde nature of the place would be a challenge, to say the least. But as it turned out, interior decorating was the least of my worries. The later addition barely meets code. We've had a hundred workmen in and out of here trying to make it habitable."

"I understand the house had a particular meaning for your husband," said Max.

"Yes. It's pathetic, really. He was returning in triumph to the scenes of his childhood. This was basically a ramshackle farmhouse when he lived here as a child—nothing special about it. But with the later addition it became—to him—a most desirable property, because it was *big*. You don't have to be Freud to figure that one out. He had made it at last, he was rich—at least by the standards of the area—and he wanted to be sure everyone knew it. He was really a city boy at heart, so this rustication didn't really suit. But Thaddeus was determined and at first, at any rate, he was happy with the decision." She thought a moment and corrected herself. "With *his* decision. I like it here. I've adapted"—and here she tossed a coy look at Farley—"but I wouldn't have chosen it for myself, by myself."

"Was there a reason for that, do you think? I mean, had someone treated him badly, that he felt he had to show off his success?"

Melinda shrugged inside her oversized jumper. "He never said, if so. I think it was just his nature. I remember thinking, many times: Big fish, small pond. He liked to impress, Father. Needed desperately to impress. And in London, there were fewer people anymore who even knew who he was or who he had been. Particularly among the younger generation. I'd say his fan base there was approaching zero. So Nether Monkslip fulfilled a long-held fantasy. Please have a seat."

They had been standing as they talked. Now she pointed to a low sofa ranged before the brick fireplace. The sofa looked like it could easily seat ten people. Max opted instead for the matching side chair, which sat at a ninety-degree angle. The loving couple nestled in the corner of the sofa nearest Max. On the low table before them was a tray holding a teapot and some biscuits and chocolates.

"The tea's gone cold, I'm afraid. Shall I get some more?" Melinda asked.

Both men shook their heads, but Farley leaned over and picked up the plate of sweets, offering it to Melinda. She gazed longingly at the exquisitely decorated biscuits with their swirls of white and dark chocolate. Those have to have come from the Cavalier, thought Max, recognizing Elka's yin-and-yang specialty biscuits. He was astonished to hear weight-conscious Melinda say, "Well, maybe just one." She actually took two.

Wonders never cease, Max thought. Out of the critical gaze of her husband, she was eating again. He half-expected her to look around to make sure Thaddeus wasn't watching. The transformation was complete. But—what had she been willing to do to throw off that yoke?

"Do you know," Max said to Farley, "I think I would like some tea after all. And I would like a private word with Melinda about the final arrangements for Thaddeus. Would you mind . . . ?"

Again, Farley proved himself impervious. He smiled and, picking up the teapot, took himself out of the room. Max waited until the sound of his footsteps receded, then said to Melinda, "I can only let you make your own choices, but I don't think it is particularly wise for Farley to be here. It's bound to cause talk and raise suspicion, complications you won't need. You do understand—the police are going to be looking for answers. DCI Cotton is an honorable man and a decent cop, but even good cops make mistakes. Especially when presented with clichés."

"I don't see why I should pretend," said Melinda. "I am in love with Farley. And he with me. *And* by the way, I had nothing to do with Thaddeus's death. That was just . . . unfortunate timing. I was going to leave him anyway."

The resemblance to a pouting four-year-old was near perfect. Max, thinking Thaddeus probably found the timing unfortunate also, merely said, "Don't hand them your head on a platter is all I'm saying. Play it cool. *Be* cool. The spouse is always the main suspect, the first person police look at. Cotton wouldn't be doing his job unless he looked very closely at you, at what you do, and at what you've been doing." Because he wasn't certain her instinct for self-preservation was at an all-time high, he added, "If they learn Farley was part of this scenario, which they are nearly certain to do, he could be in trouble also."

That did the trick. For the first time, in her concern for Farley, Melinda seemed to realize the precariousness of the entire situation. She really was one of the most other-directed people Max had ever met. Max found himself hoping she wasn't trading one toxic attachment for another—her relationship with Thaddeus had been anything but healthy. If Farley proved likewise to be the sort to take advantage of a pliant nature, well . . . only time would tell. The best Max could hope for now was to extricate her from suspicion in having anything to do with Thaddeus's death—assuming she was innocent.

"Now, before Farley gets back," said Max, "tell me everything you know, or think you know, about what's been going on here."

CHAPTER II
Hot Water

"Since you think it's so important, I'll tell you that Farley and I hardly ever—you know—got together, really," Melinda told Max. "There weren't that many chances. We met on Saturday nights, when we could. That was the only time we could guarantee any extended time with each other. We stole other opportunities sometimes . . ." Melinda gave Max a shy teen-ager smile. "So you see, it wasn't that big a deal—Inspector Cotton will have to realize it wasn't like we were meeting up all the time."

"It's more likely Cotton will think that the fact you had to ration your time together so strictly was an added motive for murder."

"Oh," she said. "I hadn't thought of it that way."

"Start thinking that way, Melinda," said Max. "Now, Thaddeus had been married before, you said."

"That's right. His wife was French—that's why his accent stayed in such good form. We met not long after she died. I was—well, I was still married, but only just. I fell head over heels when I met Thaddeus. Yes, you can look surprised—he was much older. But that had nothing to do with it. We seemed made for each other. At first."

"Go on," Max said.

"I'm not sure what all you want to know. I discovered he was a real actor. And by that, I mean he acted nonstop. He was never 'off.' It's very hard to live with, that is. You never know what you've got. A comedian one day, a tragedian the next."

Max nodded. During his time with MI5, he had had to disappear into a role, sometimes for months on end. It was no wonder he had felt his psyche was fragmented by the time he left the outfit. Did actors, on leaving a play or movie, feel the same way? A more troublesome question was whether that was why they were attracted to role-playing in the first place. Was it a symptom of something in their upbringings that made their characters require some assembly?

"What else can you tell me?" Max prompted.

"Well, he was adopted, and I always thought he was insecure because of that. The people who adopted him already had children of their own—a reversal of the usual process, where childless couples adopt and then find they're expecting one of their own.

"Insecure," mused Max. "Passive-aggressive, would you say?"

She considered this diagnosis. "No," she said at last. "No, he usually skipped right over the passive part and went straight for the jugular."

"I'm sorry," said Max. "That must have made things difficult for you."

She acknowledged the sympathy with a slight shrug. "I can tell you one troubling bit of scandal from his past," she said. "His first wife was thought to be a suicide. I believe the story was that she was driven to suicide, and absolutely I believe it now. I have often felt the same way. There was no escape from him. And the thing no one tells you is it takes money to leave a marriage."

Max assumed that meant there had been a prenuptial agreement.

"Yes." She replied, without embellishment, to his question on this topic. But she was not through talking about Thaddeus's first wife. "She was rich, you know. I wasn't, particularly. That must mean he loved me at one time. Don't you think?"

Max had no answer for that. Did she really care what Thaddeus had thought? Farley's being in the next room spoke to the opposite reaction.

"I should tell you something," said Melinda. "Those earrings I told you about when you were here with Inspector Cotton . . . those engagement earrings I lost?"

"Yes?"

"I think I may have been with Farley when I lost them. But I couldn't—you do see, don't you? I couldn't tell the detective that."

Max sighed.

"You're going to have to tell him now. You're going to have to tell him everything."

She just looked at Max.

"But this couldn't have anything to do with what happened to Thaddeus," she insisted.

"That doesn't matter. *Every*thing. Do you understand, Melinda? No matter what happens, the only thing that can save you here is the truth." And that, thought Max, applies whether she's guilty of this crime or not. The lies piled upon lies would only hurt her case, if it came to pass there was a case built against her. And against Farley, for that matter.

There was the trace of a sulk, and Max made as if to leave, as if to wash his hands of her.

"Oh, all right," she said. She held up her hands in surrender, and she sighed. "It's been so lonely for me here," she said, as if to explain her behavior. "Even though people have been kind—invitations to join the book club and so on."

Ah, the book club, thought Max. The Nether Monkslip Book Club—not to be confused with its offshoot, the Writers' Square, with which it ran somewhat in tandem—recently had selected *Sister Carrie* for discussion, in the mistaken impression it concerned the travails of an

Anglican nun rather than the arguably more interesting travails of a kept woman, chorus girl, and, ultimately, theater star. The Reverend Max Tudor suspected Suzanna Winship might have been behind the choice, but that could not be proven. Nonetheless, it did have, for Suzanna, the happy, if unintended, effect of offending old Mrs. Clark to such an extent she had resigned "forthwith," in writing, from the club. ("Does anyone but a solicitor say 'forthwith' anymore?" Suzanna had asked the group, reading aloud the note in the spidery handwriting, her eyes aglow with delight.) Max had spent many frustrating hours drinking gallons of tea and trying to woo Mrs. Clark back, for in truth she was a lonely old soul, a condition no doubt owing to her general prickliness, and the book club had been one of her few social outlets. Believing Max when he repeatedly assured her the selection of *Sister Carrie* had been an innocent mistake, she had finally been won over, "but with grave reservations," all of which were iterated in another open letter to the book club. Suzanna had been sternly forbidden by Max to read aloud from this letter. Meekly, she had agreed to Mrs. Clark's return, but could not help adding that Mrs. Clark could return "forthwith."

The book club next had tried reading *Beowolf,* a tale most of them got a third of the way through, exhibiting all the careless pleasure of mourners at a funeral, before abandoning the effort. It was an experiment with Great Books quickly discarded in favor of the new bio of a prime minister's wife. Mrs. Clark had been outvoted this time.

Farley returned to the room just then, and Melinda turned instantly to him, as though he had come with a fire ax to rescue her. Their attraction seemed to be mutual; Farley, putting down the replenished teapot, sat down and solicitously took her hands in his.

Max felt any useful information from Melinda would dry up in the face of her waning attention. She only had eyes for Farley.

Max said his good-byes to the spellbound pair.

CHAPTER 12

Word on the Street

Tuesday, March 27

The next day, DCI Cotton left a message for Max with Mrs. Hooser, saying that the preliminary test results had come back. Would Max have a moment to meet him for a ploughman's lunch at the Horseshoe? The police had set up temporary quarters in upstairs rooms there to conduct their investigation. This message Mrs. Hooser had delivered, heart pulsing with curiosity beneath her old-fashioned housedress: What test results? Swearing her to secrecy about Cotton's message, but with faint hope she could live up to her promise for even an hour (she was already untying her apron, no doubt preparing to head out to purchase some "forgotten" item like a bottle of Fairy washing-up liquid from the little shop attached to the post office), Max dialed the DCI's mobile number and arranged a time to meet.

Before he left, Max pulled a gray jumper over his head. It was warm against his skin and carried a faint trace of Awena's scent. He straightened the clerical collar that showed above the crew neckline, checking his appearance in the mirror. His dark hair remained stubbornly wayward, but hair products only seemed to make it worse. Besides, Awena claimed that tousled look was all the rage now.

He ran downstairs and gave a shout-out to Mrs. Hooser, on the million-in-one chance she was still in the kitchen. He was just pulling open the front door when he spotted another page of A4 paper on the rug beneath the mail slot. This time, he picked up the missive with gloved hands.

He read, "We are orphanes and fatherlesse, our mothers are as widowes." This was followed by a different quote, also from the Bible: "They slay the widowe and the stranger: and murder the fatherlesse."

From the antiquated spelling, Max surmised someone was copying from the 1611 King James version. He repeated the steps he'd taken with the previous message, retrieving from the kitchen a clean plastic bag to slide the page inside. He set out again to meet Cotton, turning the quotations over in his mind, and making a slight detour up Church Street to the High, sweeping a proprietary glance over St. Edwold's. The stone church might have been there since the dawn of mankind, so ancient and immovable did it appear, as if held together not by mortar but by some magic Nano glue. There was comfort in thinking that long after he himself had gone, St. Edwold's would stand. As he passed beneath the tower, the church bell announced the hour in its jubilant way.

Good. Maurice had finally brought Nether Monkslip into line with British Summer Time.

Max at times worried his church might become redundant—repurposed or abandoned, as so many churches in the UK had been. St. Edwold's was a jewel in a perfect setting, and Max felt it had to be preserved, and not just as a beautiful and historic structure. He wanted to make St. Edwold's as vital to village life as it had been in centuries past, and for people of all faiths. St. Edwold's could once again be the place where the community came together for support in times of joy and sorrow.

Several trees in the churchyard were budding in a crayon-y shade of green, impossibly neon bright against a blue sky—but it was a sky graying at the temples. For a storm was churning, carried in on the waves of the Channel a few miles away, and the preview of coming attractions was this gray-sheen backdrop in the distance. Fallen raindrops from the last cloudburst sparkled like fairy lights in the trees and bushes. It was still what he thought of as "hot-water bottle" weather: The bottles may have been put away in preparation for spring, but many were now being brought out again, just in case.

Max spotted a car parked on Church Street that he hadn't seen in the village before. On closer inspection, he decided the car might belong to a journalist, for it was a scruffy-looking conveyance, missing a hubcap or two, its seats brimming with a hodgepodge of clippings and papers stuffed every which way, and spilling out of boxes. His heart sank, and just then a BBC News broadcast van with a satellite dish on top drove by. This could only be in honor of the murder. Wouldn't Thaddeus have loved the attention?

Nether Monkslip, Max realized, would have to endure another season of being the media's latest darling—not so much because of Thaddeus's fame, which was already a dying star in the ever-expanding Kardashian-style celebrity firmament, but because the idyllic village already had a recent murder to its name. Fortunately, most of the more elderly members of the press chose not to report, but to hang out at the Hidden Fox or the Horseshoe, waiting over a pint for the news to reach them. It was the aggressive, ambitious young whippersnappers, as Miss Pitchford called them, who provoked the most outrage. One had followed Sandy Sechrest down Beggar's Alley at the time of the "Unpleasantness at the Harvest Fayre," as it had come to be known, shouting questions, practically stepping over the threshold into her cottage, until the normally agreeable woman turned and threatened to call his editor if he didn't leave her alone. "Like he'd care," the reporter had replied.

Fortunately, Max knew he could rely on the proprietor of the Horseshoe to allow Cotton and himself to have a private conversation in the snug, away from prying eyes and recording devices.

Several of the villagers were out and about. There was Elka Garth, struggling with an awkward tray of baked bread for delivery. Her son was, as usual, nowhere in sight, so Max stopped to help her as she opened the boot of her car. A man Max recognized as one of the owners of a nearby farm went by with a large wooden tray of lettuces. Max saw Gabby Crew approaching, dressed warmly for the day, heading in the direction of the ancient alleyway that housed the Cut and Dried salon. She delayed him with a smile.

"This weather!" she said, dabbing at her forehead with a handkerchief. "You don't know what to wear, do you? I start out dressed for winter and then by the afternoon I'm roasting."

Max smiled, nodded, and started to move on, but quite evidently Gabby had something more on her mind than the weather. Finally, she asked, rather shyly, if she could stop by the vicarage for a chat sometime in the coming days.

"I'm not an Anglican," she said. "But I'd like your advice. Does it matter that I'm not a member of St. Edwold's?"

"Of course it doesn't matter," said Max. "Anytime—I'm glad to help if I can. And I think you'll find the entire village is part of St. Edwold's, regardless. It's just part of the fabric of the place."

He was struck by the memory of Gabby's odd behavior in changing the seating arrangements at Lucie's dinner party. But, running late, he didn't ask what was bothering her, afraid she might launch into the whole story there and then. It was a dodge he would later come to rue. She didn't look particularly worried, just hesitant, squinting as she looked up at him, as if deciding how far she could trust him with her secrets. It was always like this in Nether Monkslip—Max couldn't walk down the High without being asked several times for his opinion or advice, although there were those kind souls who assumed he must be deeply contemplating his next sermon, and thus was not to be bothered. In the case of those who did approach him, it was nearly always on a matter so minor, he couldn't believe people couldn't figure it out for themselves. In fact, they could; he had come to realize they often just wanted him to confirm what they'd already decided.

And so Max explained to Gabrielle "Gabby" Crew that he was late for his luncheon appointment and began to pull away, with every outward sign of reluctance.

"Why don't you ring the vicarage when you're ready?" he said. "It will save you a trip if I'm not there."

She smiled and nodded, and stood beaming after him, adjusting her gloves. The vicar was *such* a kind young man.

Max, now walking faster to keep to his appointment, thought that Gabby, despite her friendly nickname, and underneath her surface amiability, was rather a thoughtful and observant woman. There was something fixed in that upright posture of hers that might reflect her thinking. He had worked with many such people in MI5. They were invaluable because they were unwavering in their commitment: Unflappable human beings were rare. Max thought he might like a word with her privately about Melinda and the situation in the Bottle household, for he doubted Gabby would have missed anything . . . well, anything *amiss* there.

He passed the Cavalier Tea Room at the foot of Martyr's Bridge, where the water ran fast beneath, a ripple of silver in the sunshine. Elka Garth must be baking hot cross buns for Easter, he thought. The aroma was so powerful, he found his steps slowing momentarily. It was an aroma that evoked for him powerful memories of childhood, like Proust's madeleine.

Easter always fell on the first Sunday after the first full moon after the Spring Equinox—as Awena loved reminding him, it was yet another Church celebration inextricably tied to the ancient, often astrologically based rituals of long-vanished religions and civilizations. Even the colored Easter eggs in the annual children's hunt were pagan symbols of fertility. Very few, least of all the children, thought it strange or macabre these "pagan" eggs were always hidden in the ancient St. Edwold's cemetery, with its moss-covered headstones and tilting Celtic crosses. It was simply a place full of good hiding spots. He remembered Thaddeus had agreed with him on that.

Across from the Horseshoe, a few cars were parked with haphazard abandon near the railway station, as if their owners had been abducted by aliens rather than been in a hurry to catch the next train. Given the oftentimes-erratic departures and arrivals at the whim of the conductor, this haste was probably not unseemly. There was Easter shopping to be done in Staincross Minster, which put extra demand on the renovated old train, a train that had featured largely in what DCI Cotton had taken to calling "Max's last case."

Max now came upon Suzanna talking with Elka, who had stopped and rolled down the window of her car for a chat. Suzanna had binoculars slung around her neck and seemed to be aiming them down the High Street.

"Why are you wearing a trench coat?" Elka was asking as he approached. "It's not raining."

"I'm on the case," said Suzanna. As Elka looked puzzled, she added, "It helps me think like a detective. You know, get in the mood. Play the part."

"And what has your role-playing brought you?"

"Well, nothing so far. I saw Miss Pitchford go into the post office, so she must be on the mend, even though she was hobbling a bit. Mrs. Barrow had trouble using the Cashpoint machine again—you know how she is; she won't let anyone help, thinking they're trying to rob her, so a vast and seething queue always collects behind her. Other than that, it's been really quiet around here. People are sticking close to home."

"I should think so," said Elka. "People are frightened. There's a maniac on the loose."

"Suzanna," said Max, "with all due respect, you need to leave this to DCI Cotton and his team. It's a dangerous situation, and if you are putting yourself in danger, you'll only add to his burden."

"Nonsense," said Suzanna briskly. "Whoever killed Thaddeus—and very good riddance, by the way—has nothing against me."

"That's not how it works, Suzanna," said Max. "If you do see something the killer thinks you shouldn't have seen, you could become the next target. You do follow that, don't you?"

"I read detective stories, Father Max. I know how these things work."

Max was tempted to demand she hand over the binoculars, but he realized not only had he no right to do so but that it would be a pointless exercise. Suzanna, relentless, would always find a way.

CHAPTER 13
At the Horseshoe

The Horseshoe, like many such old English pubs, was divided between a saloon and a public bar. Max found Cotton in the saloon, a handsome room with windows darkened by the smoke of centuries, blackened beams crossing the ceiling, and gleaming brass against the whitewashed walls.

There sat Cotton by the door, resplendent in his bespoke suit, a starched shirt like gray armor against his chest, and a nicely contrasting tie. His blond hair had been smoothed in place, a reproof to Max's own efforts in that regard, and his gray-blue eyes shone with the passion tempered by intelligence that was fast earning him a superstar reputation on the force.

He greeted Max like the old friend he now was, asking first how Awena was doing.

"Good good good," said Max quickly, too quickly, making it clear this was a subject he wasn't willing to pursue.

"Well, good," said Cotton. *So,* he thought, I'm not supposed to know the obvious about Max and Awena. Alrighty then. Far be it from me to parachute blindly into those waters, however warm and tranquil they may be.

"Well, kemo sabe," began Cotton. "Let's find a corner away from prying ears, shall we?"

They had a word with the landlord and were given a coveted spot in the snug.

Once they were completely settled in with jackets stowed, Max tossed the sheet of A4 paper, encased in plastic, on the table. "Delivered the same way," he said.

"Another one?" said Cotton. He read aloud "'We are orphanes and fatherlesse, our mothers are as widowes.'"

Max said, "The first quote is from Lamentations. The second quote is from Psalms. I didn't stop to look up the exact verse for you. The first quote is talking about the suffering following the destruction of Jerusalem by the Babylonians. I don't recall the exact date, but it was about 600 B.C."

Carefully, Cotton put the paper in its plastic casing into his brief-case. He exhaled mightily in frustration. "Well, that's clear as mud. Are we to look for a Babylonian suspect, then?"

"I would look for someone who feels they have been oppressed, someone who feels he has lost everything. Someone without hope for justice who has thus taken justice into his own hands. That last was just a guess, but we do have Thaddeus's corpse to explain, and it's too great a coincidence I would suddenly start getting these thundering quotations from an anonymous correspondent."

"They surely have to be from the killer. Agreed."

"And there is that hint of recklessness in using the same method of delivery. Although the vicarage is just that bit sheltered from prying eyes that the person wasn't taking a huge risk. Besides, I have visitors all the time, as well as people dropping off a note rather than disturb me by knocking. No one who saw the delivery being made would question what they saw for a minute."

They were interrupted by the landlord's daughter, come to take their order for lunch.

"It's like this," Cotton resumed when once again they were alone. "The police surgeon—Wouters—agrees the coroner should have this case brought to his attention. That's about the most I can get out of him 'pending further testing.' In case we're wrong, you know, he doesn't want to be accused of sounding the alarm for no reason. But that wound on the victim's neck—well, it's damnably hard to see why Thaddeus Bottle would have stabbed him*self* in that way. It doesn't look like something you could do to yourself accidentally. Furthermore, Wouters says there is a foreign substance in the wound. He's running further tests, but it's not a usual substance."

"He's thinking poison, of course."

Cotton mentioned a name.

Max was taken aback. "That's rather exotic, isn't it?

"Not in this shrinking world. As it happens, Wouters has come across this once before. We shall see if he can confirm his hunch."

"Was there a weapon found?"

Cotton nodded appreciatively, giving Max the benefit of his laser-like gray-blue gaze. "No. No, there wasn't. And that's part of what cinched it for Wouters. And for me. There should have been a weapon found by the body. We'll have to have proceedings at the coroner's court, a mere formality to identify Thaddeus Bottle as the deceased, to have the pathologist's report read out, and to request an adjournment pending further police inquiries."

"That will really get the press's attention, an adjournment," said Max. "We've already got the BBC and at least one enterprising local fellow here."

"That guy from the *Globe and Bugle*. Right. I thought I saw his car earlier. What a slob. It's a wonder he can find the steering wheel."

"Maybe you could give him a parking ticket."

Cotton smiled. "All this rot you read in the news about journalists and police on the take—I don't get it. I can hardly stand to brief the media for even ten minutes on a case, let alone take money from them for providing tips on celebrities. Of course, it helps that I don't know any celebrities. The one I did know, sort of, has now been killed."

But Max wasn't really listening. Cotton sat back and watched, amused, as Max ticked over the case in his brain. You could almost see the gears, watch the connections being made and the little synapses fizzing. It was like watching one of those enhanced computer graphic things on the telly.

Max was thinking: A stranger to the village, killed not very long after his arrival. Why? He was an old man. Maybe not a particularly nice old man, and hardly a crowd pleaser in his private life, but at least he posed no physical threat to anyone. Except, perhaps, to Melinda?

After a while, Max voiced some of his thoughts aloud, then added, "Unless . . . unless he knew something about someone already living here—about one of the villagers. Something that put the person in danger, so he felt he had to strike out to defend himself. As we've often said, there are few people living here anymore who are *from* here."

"Which means," said Cotton, "someone now living here recognized him from somewhere else—or he recognized that person. Could Thaddeus have been trying a spot of blackmail?"

Max hesitated. "I suppose it could be something like that. Definitely he seemed the type to enjoy the sense of power that can come from holding things over people's heads. Whatever happened, he must have been a threat to *some*one, and that led to his death."

"No one we've talked with claims to have known him well, although there seems to have been no love lost between him and the members of the Writers' Square. Frank Cuthbert called him a 'philistine,' and he could barely bring himself to be even that polite. I gather Thaddeus was rather hard on one of the other members, and they all stick up for one another. No, unless you count the occasional insomniac who caught Thaddeus in one of his old movies on the telly, no one claims to have really known him."

"Avoided him, rather," said Max. "Yes, I can see how that would be true. He was arrogant. But crafty with it. Arrogance usually goes hand in glove with stupidity. Have you noticed? And I don't think he was stupid."

"We've done some looking into his background, of course, and I was on the phone earlier to his agent. I'm not sure the agent was all that fond of him. Call me crazy, but that's the impression I got. One thing he said that really struck me. He said of Thaddeus, "He wanted to be a famous actor, and anyone who got in his way, even unwittingly, became the enemy.""

"He was also a playwright," said Max.

"Yes," said Cotton. "According to the agent, he was not a bad playwright, either. But nobody recognizes playwrights anymore except perhaps for Tom Stoppard. I say 'anymore,' but no one has ever recognized the playwright. It was the recognition Thaddeus craved, and for that you need to be on the stage or in film, not behind the scenes."

"I promised Melinda I'd have a word with someone who can speak at the service for Thaddeus," said Max.

"Did you now?"

"Yes. 'At the behest of the widow' sort of thing. It seems the desire is for the splashiest funeral possible, but Melinda is worried no one will trouble to be there unless someone, preferably a professional, starts drumming up publicity for the 'event.'"

"Good luck with that. Altogether I gathered from the agent that Thaddeus went through life leaving in his wake a surge in the demand for apologies—apologies that never arrived, it need hardly be added. But if you're asking my permission, by all means speak with the agent—I'll put in a word for you if you'd like. You'll find him forthright in stating his belief that Thaddeus was a thorn in everyone's paw, but he has offered to help in any way he can."

Max nodded. "One thing I noticed at the dinner party," he said. "Thaddeus is probably not from England originally. Am I right?"

Cotton nodded. "He was born in France, where he was christened Thaddee Landry. The 'Thaddeus Bottle' came later, with his adoption. A lot of people from around here have roots going back to France. How did you know?"

"His French was too good, for one thing, although Melinda did mention his first wife was French, which would help explain it."

"And for another?"

"He made a reference to *the* New College at Oxford. Most people born and raised here and claiming to know firsthand all the theatrical movers and shakers and professors of theater would know to leave off the word *the*. It is called simply New College."

"You're quite right. He was adopted by the Bottles when his parents were killed in a car accident. This was early in 1945. The Bottles were distant relatives. I guess they wanted to thoroughly anglicize the boy."

"Interesting, that."

Cotton waited for enlightenment on what was interesting, but none was forthcoming, so he said, "I've searched the house—King's Rest. Or rather, my team did so—a thorough search from top to bottom. Technicians: fingerprint people, blood people, all the usual lot."

"Nothing of interest?" Max asked.

"Unless you count some really execrable artwork, which includes a velvet painting in one of the bathrooms, there's nothing much to draw our attention," he told Max. "They've taken away the hard drive from the computer in his study to have a look at its contents. At a cursory glance, they won't find much but some overblown prose and some pretty hilarious attempts at a science fiction book, much of it repurposed Ray Bradbury. But it was old stuff Thaddeus hadn't accessed for a while."

"Isn't it possible he was writing something that portrayed someone in an unflattering light?" Max asked. "A character based on a real person?"

"If so, it must date from some time ago," said Cotton. "And if you're thinking that could be a motive, well, from what I saw, he wasn't exposing anyone's embezzlement or anything of that nature. We didn't find any recent writing, or anything that suggested to me that what he was writing was based on a real person. Do writers do that anyway?"

"You could ask the local writers' group, but I should think most real people translated directly into text would not be all that interesting to the wider world—not unless they're well known to the broader world in some capacity, like queens and prime ministers."

"Oh, I don't know," said Cotton. "I think Suzanna Winship's life might make a fascinating read. Anyway, I've got a uniform with literary aspirations looking at all of it. We'll see if he finds anything suggestive."

"That would be PC Detton, correct?"

What a memory the man has, thought Cotton. PC Detton, a struggling scriptwriter, was responsible for some of the more colorful police reports handed around the Monkslip-super-Mare police station. He had written some of the reports in the Chedrow Castle case, in which Max had been involved a few months previous.

"I need your help on this more than ever, Max," said Cotton. "We've got a new prosecutor, and she's already putting pressure on me to nail Melinda for this."

"It would be nice if she waited for some evidence."

"She's ambitious."

"Nothing wrong with that."

"She's also an idiot."

"An ambitious idiot. Problem."

"Yes. Whenever someone in law enforcement puts career advancement first, integrity second, we're all of us in trouble. We might as well roll up the flag and go home. She also has a tendency to think in clichés, which I find maddening. She's decided that Melinda must have killed her husband because, A, Melinda was in the house and, B, she was married to

Thaddeus. Those are the two items that make me think Melinda would not have done this, at least not in such a way that the spotlight shines brightly on her alone. She's not the sharpest tool in the box, but she'd know not to poison her husband and then hang around waiting for the poison to take effect. She could have doctored anything she liked in the house and then left town for a while. Poisoned the brandy. Hired a hit man. Anything but involve herself so directly."

Just then, a shuffling noise alerted them that a waitress was bringing their meal. They got their drinks and serviettes sorted, and waited until they were sure she was out of earshot. Then Cotton said, "Does anyone in the village know Melinda particularly well?"

Max took a small bite of his buttered bread and cheese, shaking his head. "Not sure. I could ask Awena when I see her."

With finely calibrated irony, Cotton said, "What a good idea. No rush. Whenever you happen to run into her will be fine."

Max had the grace to blush ever so slightly, but still he didn't cave. Cotton had to hand it to him.

Cotton looked at him, the handsome priest who had set aflutter the hearts of every maiden and matron in Nether Monkslip and surrounding villages. Church attendance had skyrocketed, and Max had been the re-cipient of countless gifts of hand-knit scarves, socks, and jumpers, most of them multicolored and of an indescribable awfulness. Cotton assumed Max donated the items to the poor. The local soup kitchens must be a riot of color these days.

Max looked back at his friend. His alert, kinetic, fiercely intelligent friend, whose interest in order and justice matched Max's own. The new prosecutor was going to be a problem for Cotton, Max knew, if Cotton's marching orders suddenly became all about making the numbers look right—closing the case, throwing a bone to the press, all with a high-handed disregard for the truth. More than one innocent prisoner had swung by a rope made from the threads of a prosecutor's ambition. A single honest cop or two couldn't thwart that kind of systemic corruption.

"The trouble is," said Cotton, taking a thoughtful sip of his ale, "we don't have a lot of forensic evidence to go on. No fingerprints or hair samples that shouldn't have been there, for example, or that can't be accounted for by the usual visitors to the house."

"We'll get there," said Max with calm assurance. "Slate is easily cut into slabs if you know where to place the chisel. It opens up and peels off in layers, just like this case will do."

"I'm glad you're so confident."

"Not confident so much as . . . determined," said Max. "We have to clean up this mess—this latest mess—for the sake of all the villagers."

"Drain the swamp," said Cotton.

"Yes. That's precisely it. This village seems to be attracting something—I don't know how to say it. Something dark and dank and—and very *old*."

"The village is said to be the site of a long-ago murder," said Cotton. "I've always wanted to know more about that."

Max nodded. "We go for centuries without a murder, and now this. We're practically awash in a crime wave."

"Remind me. What murder was it, back then?"

"I don't have the details. It was up on Hawk Crest. I think that's how Nunswood got its name. It must have been a nun murdered."

"Sounds like there's a story there."

"Oh, yes. No doubt someone in the Writers' Square will get around to investigating it one day. Trouble is, if it's Frank, he'll get half the facts wrong."

"Poetic license."

"Writing without a permit, more like. Anyway, we've got to stop *this* crime wave in its tracks, to mix my metaphors, and the only way to do that is to catch whoever killed Thaddeus."

Cotton, who still thrilled to that "we" whenever they were discussing an investigation, nodded solemnly. He had rather come to count on Max to see the connections most people would miss.

CHAPTER 14
Picture This

The two men sat for a long time, going over the case, lingering after most of the pub's lunchtime patrons had departed. The pub owner issued an order to his staff to let them be.

Cotton reverted now to a previous thought, part of a conversation he'd had earlier at the station with his assistant, Sergeant Essex.

"Since Thaddeus was more a stage actor, we know little about his private life. Anyone in television or movies would get more press."

"I doubt he'd be pleased to hear that," said Max.

"We've managed to sniff out some gossip about his life before Melinda. The agent was very useful in that regard."

Max was nibbling on a slice of apple. "Oh?" he said.

"Thaddeus's money came largely from the life insurance policy he had on his first wife, not from his career as a playwright."

"He talked as if his career was a great success financially," said Max.

"Well, he was a bit of a phony."

"More than a bit," agreed Max.

"I keep forgetting you had the advantage of knowing the man in real life."

"I wouldn't call it an advantage."

"Point taken."

"Still, that sort of bamboozle—it's just a bit on the dishonest side," said Max. "It's not major crime. It's more indicative of the type of man he was—that ego would shine through so much, it was difficult to see the soul beneath the bombast."

"Here's where it gets interesting, I think," said Cotton. "Melinda claims not to have known the source of his wealth was not his career, but his wife's life insurance policy. He had a policy that gave him four hundred thousand pounds on her death."

"Could anyone be that naïve?" Melinda, he recalled, had said the first wife was rich.

Just then, the bereaved widow happened to be passing by on the High Street, wearing white jeans, short black boots, and a slouchy black jumper. She carried shopping bags in both hands. Both men watched as, framed by the window, Melinda lightheartedly skipped over a puddle.

Max turned back to look at Cotton. "Well," he said, "let's assume for the moment, then, that she's telling the truth. It doesn't really matter, does it? He was wealthy, relatively speaking. Prenup or no, she probably would have received enough to live on in a divorce settlement."

"If he died, however, she'd inherit the lot," said Cotton.

"I just don't see her as clever enough to pull this off and get away with it."

Outside, Melinda, switching her umbrella from one hand to the other as she juggled her shopping, dropped one bag in the puddle. Instead of an outburst of annoyance, her giggle could be heard. Is she *on* something? Max wondered. He could perhaps ask Bruce Winship if he'd given her something to calm her down. If so, he'd overdone it.

"Why not?" Cotton asked. "She's getting away with it so far. There is no proof she did anything but live in the same house as the murdered man. Her fingerprints, for one thing, are useless as evidence. Even if there were incriminating fingerprints, which there are not."

"Right. And no murder weapon. And even if there were a weapon left in the bedroom, her prints on it might not mean a lot."

"Max, however we dress it up, Melinda is the obvious suspect. She was right on the scene and he treated her like dirt under his feet—so I'm told by everyone, including you."

"You didn't see her that night when she came to the vicarage to fetch me. She was completely undone."

Cotton, who was thinking, You are such an old softy, Max, said, "I saw a woman pretty well pulled together, ostrich feathers and all."

"By the time your lot arrived, she'd composed herself. Maybe she took a tranquilizer to calm her nerves."

"It's most foolish for people to talk to the police when they're sedated. We want them in the raw, as it were, anyway."

"I'm sure," said Max. "Even so . . ."

"Then there's this business with the estate agent. With Bernadina Steed."

"What business with Bernadina Steed?"

"Ex-lovers," said Cotton. "She was a former lover of Thaddeus Bottle. Don't tell me you didn't know?"

Max, remembering back to the dinner party, thought of the body language. Bernadina and Thaddeus had stood too close together during the before-dinner drinks. And later there'd been that certain awareness of each other's presence. . . .

"I guess I knew without knowing," he said. "Something seemed to be going on. You're sure it was an 'ex' situation?"

"So Bernadina says."

"I wonder if they were planning a rematch. They seemed friendly enough."

Cotton said, "I never quite believe anyone who claims to be just good friends with an ex-lover. Human nature doesn't work that way. If you were as friendly as all that, you'd still be together, wouldn't you?"

"One does have to wonder how much his wife appreciated this warm friendship with Bernadina," said Max.

"I don't think she cared. She had Farley to keep her warm."

Max sighed. "I can't help but wish she'd been discreet about that— half the village seems to have been on to them—but I've urged her to be frank with you now. You'd have found out anyway." He sighed again. "What messes people create for themselves."

"It keeps both of us in business, at any rate," said Cotton. "Where would the world be without policemen and priests? Anyway, our actor and playwright may have been lured to Nether Monkslip by the estate agent, Bernadina—it's one theory. She, however, claims 'all that' is in the past and they'd entered the 'just good friends' stage."

"She told you this?"

"Actually, I learned it from Annette Hedgepeth at the Cut and Dried. There are no secrets at the Cut and Dried. Abandon hope of a private life, all ye who enter there."

"There's nothing suspicious, is there, about the death of Thaddeus's first wife?" Max asked. The bread and cheese were gone, and he was left with an enormous slab of onion on his plate. Somehow that didn't appeal, and he pushed the plate to one side.

"No. Straightforward—nothing to arouse suspicion. Cardiac arrest."

"We might have thought the same about Thaddeus's death," Max reminded him. "Maybe we were *meant* to think that. For a man his age, that would be expected."

Cotton nodded, concentrating on finishing his meal. There was a paper rack near their table, holding several of the more recent tabloids and a few magazines, no doubt reading material left behind by patrons. Max's eye was caught by an old issue of *Glossamer Living* magazine, the same copy that was in a stack on his desk at the vicarage. One of the headlines across the front held the words NETHER MONKSLIP—FOODIE HEAVEN, which was no doubt why the magazine had caught his eye. He reached out and plucked it from the rack, turning to the page indicated on the front. There he saw a photo of the new White Bean restaurant. It was an indoor shot, a crowd scene—photographed to make the place look more crowded and popular than perhaps it had been that night. Max held the page closer, for something a bit odd had caught his eye: He could see a waitress at the back, holding a tray, and glaring across the room. Max followed the line of her sight: She appeared to be looking at a table that held four people, and she was staring with unguarded contempt at someone at that table for four.

"Look at this," Max said, holding out the magazine so Cotton could see. "That's Thaddeus and Melinda. That's the backs of their heads anyway. I'm sure of it."

"Hmm," said Cotton. "I believe you're right. Who are they with?"

"Lucie and Frank Cuthbert. Their faces are a bit blurred, but it's them. Look at the waitress, though. See the look on her face."

But was it Thaddeus she was looking at? His wife? Lucie and Frank? There was no way to tell. The waitress looked stricken. No, more than that: She looked really, really angry.

Heads nearly touching, the magazine sideways on the table between them, the two men looked at the photo together.

"Is it important? We could get lab analysis done, facial recognition, yada yada," said Cotton. "We've started spotting a lot of criminals by the shape of their ears, would you believe it?"

"There's no need for all of that. It's a photo of Thaddeus and Melinda; I am certain. Notice the earrings she's wearing—very distinctive.

They might be the pair of earrings she told us she lost. And his hair—even from the back, that can only be Thaddeus."

Cotton held the photo up to his nose. "Okay," he muttered at last into the magazine. He set it down and looked at Max. "You're right. So why is the waitress looking at him like she'd like to slice him up and offer his entrails as the main course?"

"We can't be sure it's Thaddeus she's looking at."

Again, the photo went up to Cotton's nose.

"Have you thought about getting some eyeglasses?" Max asked mildly.

"The carrying case ruins the line of my suit," said Cotton. He put down the magazine. "Again you're right. She *might* be looking at Melinda. Just a small chance she's looking at the other couple—Lucie and Frank. She'd mostly see the backs of *their* heads from that vantage point."

"Right."

"Melinda could tell us the circumstances," said Cotton. "I'll ask her. Then I'll have a talk with the waitress."

"Her name is Kayla Prince," said Max, "and she's a St. Edwold's parishioner." Max hesitated. "Would you mind if I had a word with her first? Knowing Thaddeus, the topic might be a rather delicate one for her to talk about, and she might be more willing to talk about it with someone in a less than official capacity."

"You think they had an affair?" asked Cotton.

"Perhaps," replied Max with judicious hesitation. "Given that it's Thaddeus we're talking about, and that he clearly had a roving eye. But it could be almost anything, really—again, given that it's Thaddeus. There is an enormous difference in their ages, not that that ever stopped a man like him."

Cotton soon afterward gathered his things and took himself off to have Max's Bible quote sent to forensics, and then to have another word with Melinda. Max stayed behind a few moments, staring at the onion on his plate, thinking and planning his strategy.

"If your current way of seeing isn't working, open your mind to the opposite path" was one of Awena's sayings. Since something continued to bother him, he sat quietly for a moment, trying to pin down what it could be.

The pub owner, recognizing the signs, tactfully left Max alone.

CHAPTER 15
Grimaldi the Elder

Max eventually made his way out of the Horseshoe, his eyes blinking against the tentative rays of sunshine outlining gray clouds in gold. He walked over to the White Bean on River Lane. The restaurant was closed at this time of day, but he found the place unlocked. He pulled back the door onto a new world, a Nether Monkslip of the future, for the restaurant was as different from the huddled, dark Horseshoe as day is from night.

The place had been equipped with spaceshippy fixtures of gleaming stainless steel. Mobiles in artistically stylized shapes—gulls or fish—hung from the ceiling. Each table held a vase of dried herbs and flowers, their stems anchored by the white beans of the restaurant's name, the seeds functioning as a sort of gravel. The large open space was designed so the chef and his assistants were on constant display to the patrons while preparing the food, like people putting on a puppet show. From the doorway, Max could see that an enameled cast-iron pot stood bubbling on the cooker. He stood, he realized, at the vantage point from which the magazine photographer had taken his shot of the restaurant.

Max stepped inside, still taking in the place before calling out a tentative "Hallo." He recalled that the Parish Council meetings to gain permission to convert the derelict old cottage into the restaurant had been epic. In the end, the restaurant had won the fight, since experts all agreed that demolition was the only alternative.

Max had met the owner before, at what passed in Nether Monkslip for a glitzy, star-studded event: the restaurant's grand opening. He knew that the Grimaldi brothers came from Siena—the ancient Tuscan hill town of the she-wolf that suckled the infants Romulus and Remus. The brothers' names were Umberto and Fabio. Umberto, the elder, was the businessman, and Fabio was the chef. He was reputed to be a genius in the kitchen.

Umberto looked up from papers he was going over in the kitchen. He saw Max and acknowledged his presence with a nod and a smile, holding up one index finger to indicate that Max should wait.

Max took a menu to look at and sat down in one of the restaurant's booths. It was the same booth he and Cotton had just been peering at in the photo.

As the menu explained, in rather extravagant and slightly broken English, the restaurant prided itself on providing locally sourced food whenever possible. When food had to be shipped in, it came from not very far away, and it was of the finest quality Great Britain could offer. Relationships of trust and honor were established with local farmers, the menu explained. When corn was ground, for example, it was grown and ground just for the restaurant, and used in a polenta cake topped with white beans, roasted squash, garlic, and sage. Serving corn in a land that regarded it as feed for cattle was innovative in itself, Max realized. Overall, the Grimalidi's defining ideology seemed to be "Down with supermarkets and to hell with pub food."

On the menu also was escarole, sautéed in olive oil with garlic and hot peppers. He'd have to ask Awena about that, since he wasn't absolutely sure what escarole might be, although the description of how it was cooked was making his mouth water. There also were some recipes using pine nuts and olives, dishes Max thought might be borrowed from Liguria.

Spring veggies predominated at this time of year, of course, and chef Fabio had incorporated asparagus, scallions, artichoke, and first peas into the various pastas and risottos. For dessert, along with the expected gelato, the restaurant offered a cheese plate with West Country cheeses and cheese from Cheddar, as well as French cheeses that no doubt owed their origin to Mme. Luci Cuthbert's shop: It was cheating a bit, Max thought, but forgivable to add them to the menu.

The special that night was pasta with sage and butter, a Tuscan-style dish cooked with the garlic "in its shirt"—with the cloves unpeeled. It sounded wonderful, and Max immediately vowed to bring Awena here for dinner at the first opportunity. Hang the calories.

Somehow, Max had added weight with each murder investigation. He had just lost the half a stone he had gained during what he thought of as the Michaelmas murder. Then Christmas had followed soon after, and no one "did" holidays like the villagers, who on any day seemed to love nothing better than the chance to lavish attention on their vicar. They fed him cucumber sandwiches, scones, and chocolate cake by the trolleyful. And tea. Gallons of tea: Earl Grey, hawthorn, chai, Indian, Chinese. Sweetened with white sugar, brown sugar, artificial sugar—it made no difference. Without his daily run, he thought, he'd be as big as a house.

When Max read the food column in the *Telegraph,* as he more and more frequently did in a fantasy escape from Mrs. Hooser's more unspeakable cooking efforts, he marveled at the ability to describe the taste and texture of things in a way that stirrred hunger in the reader. It seemed to him among the most esoteric of arts, like building ships in bottles. The Grimaldi brothers, with their tentative yet colorful grasp of the language, had mastered the skill.

Just now Grimaldi the Elder, as the villagers called him, was making his way over to Max's booth. Umberto was probably forty-five years of age, and just graying at the temples. Muscular in build, he was shorter than Max, and with a bit of a paunch. He had a purposeful walk, like a man leaning into the wind, and what seemed to be a permanent five o'clock shadow—the few times Max had seen him, he'd had such a heavy beard that the lower half of his face seemed tattooed with a permanent dark cast. His nose had clearly been broken at some time in the past, and in profile he strongly reminded Max of Federico, one of the dukes of Urbino in the famous early Renaissance painting in the Uffizi Gallery.

Umberto sat across from Max and said, "So. What do you think of our little place, Father?"

"It's really very striking," said Max diplomatically. He was not always a fan of the modern, but this, he could see, was unique, interesting, and well done. "Unusual."

Umberto smiled; he had a somewhat wolfish smile. "We hired an architect to do the renovation. He was 'mirroring the aesthetic,' this architect person said. He would actually say things like that to me. 'Mirroring the aesthetic.' What in hell was that supposed to mean? I ask you. And then he would go on and on about panels, and tiles, and deliverables. And niches—he was very big on niches, this trendy lunatic. He said the goal was to be representational—of what was never said. An aquarium? He would show up with his rulers and his diagrams and his spreadsheets, and I swear to you, I wanted to kill him before it was over, just stab him through the eye. The bill for all of this, I need hardly tell you, was astronomic and well over the estimate, which was already laughable. They could build the Taj Mahal for half the amount."

"I see," said Max mildly. "This was Farley, was it?"

But Umberto was not yet done. "He said something that sounded like doing a 'full nose sketch,' and to this day I don't know what in fuck he was talking about. Yes, it was Farley. Farley Walker. And he talked about blond wood—he was big on blond wood, you can see." He waved an arm around him. "He advised us to have a roof deck over the river, and that is very nice indeed—yes, I agree. But then it became talk of textures and glass and planned elevations and viewpoints and space and transoms and skylights and frames to analyze the elements and creating tall panels to intersect with the borders and shadow lines, and I tell you, there was no end to this bullshit. I am going to start walking around with blueprints under my arm so when people see me immediately they will know how creative I am. *And* I will wear groovy sunglasses in case they miss the point. Now what was it you wanted, Father Tudor?"

"Call me Max, please. Or Father Max, if you must."

"I'm from a Catholic country. The Anglican ways are not so automatic for me. I'll try, but it will be hard to remember just plain Max."

Max smiled and said, "I love your country. Everything about it, beginning and ending with the food."

"I love it, too," said Umberto. "The food, the trees, the colors, the hills. The silver-greenish color of the olive trees is what I miss the most—isn't that strange? Here the bright green—it's not the same. I never knew how many shades of green there were before I came to England."

Just then, one of the blue-jeaned kitchen staff, a young man with cockatiel hair, walked by carrying a large tray of fresh vegetables. Umberto stopped him, grabbing him by the arm. Umberto picked up a head of lettuce and stared at it, eyeball-to-eyeball as it were.

"You call this lettuce? Where did this come from?" he demanded.

The young man squeaked a reply. "The Browns' farm."

The Browns—Lexington, Concord, and Bunker—were three siblings from the U.S. who had recently inherited a farm on the outskirts of Nether Monkslip. Max had not yet met them but, in the way of the village, felt that he already knew everything pertinent there was to know.

"I thought so," said Umberto. "Those three—unless they're growing marijuana out there, they're going to have their asses handed to them. The land is unforgiving if you don't know what you're doing."

And having delivered himself of this homespun prairie philosophy, he returned his attention to Max. The head of lettuce sat on the table between them, a silent witness to their conversation. It looked like a perfectly fine head of lettuce to Max, but, unlike Umberto, he did not feel qualified to pronounce on all things leafy.

Umberto, Max realized, reminded him of someone, and he realized it was Suzanna Winship, who likewise had a tendency to say whatever was on her mind.

"It must all be quite a sea change for you," said Max.

"It is, but we like it very much. It is hard to leave Italy, but until the finances are straightened out, we are doing so much better here. It is a shame. Not since the war, I don't think, has there been so much financial turmoil."

As with Lucie Cuthbert, Max noted, there was no other war—there was only the Second World War. Umberto said, "Do you know, my grandfather never would talk about the war. Basically, I think he managed to bullshit his way through the whole tragedy, saying yes to the Germans and, as soon as they were not watching, doing nothing, even stealing from them where he could. Many survived in this way. The risk was crazy, but all his life he would get this look on his face when the subject of the Nazis came up, like he'd swallowed sour milk. You knew it was better not to ask, but we have often wondered, my brother and me.

"Anyway, we Italians survive all of that, and now the euro. Bankers without guns are doing the damage now. We don't know how it is going to—how you say? Shake out? How it is going to shake out. For now, I think we've made the right move. Fabio—he's still deciding. He tells me I'm a dreamer. Well, I dream big."

"Why bother dreaming any other way?"

Umberto nodded. "And it helps that Fabio, he is a genius. He will bring us to fame, you wait and see. We may open a local produce shop in the cottage next door. Bernadina Steed is helping us with the purchase. Now, Father Tudor, you are here—why?"

"I was hoping, actually, to talk to one of your staff. Don't worry," he added hastily. "She's not in any trouble."

"This is about the murder, isn't it?"

"Well, yes, but how did you know?"

Umberto answered obliquely. Max had a feeling Umberto was rather good at that.

"She's a good woman. There is nothing to be said against her, but perhaps she is lacking in judgment."

"What do you mean?"

"I mean Thaddeus Bottle, but don't read that the wrong way. Kayla couldn't pluck a chicken, much less kill anyone."

Max mind traveled back to the expression on Kayla's face in that photo. The brief instant, captured forever.

"Of course you can talk with her," Umberto was saying. "I can't stop you. But I think if you are looking for the likely suspect, it would be more worth your time to talk with this Farley person. Mr. Trendy Pants."

"Really? Why do you say that?"

"Well, nudge, nudge, as they say. That's *amore*."

Did the whole village know, then, about Melinda and Farley? And did that mean Thaddeus had known?

"I try to speak no ill of the dead, but Thaddeus was . . . a demanding person." This hesitation seemed an unusual deviation from Umberto's unusual forthright manner. "Rude. Full of himself." Having gathered steam, Umberto spat out a word in Italian, then translated it into something milder. "He was a jerk."

Just then, the woman Max had recognized from the photo as a parishioner of St. Edwold's, Kayla Prince, came up to the table. She set two cups of coffee before them, clearly following prior instructions from

Umberto. Tan, trim, attractive, she bore more than a passing resemblance to a much older Pippa Middleton.

After she left, Grimaldi said, "She won't last long. She's too pretty to be stuck out here in what is essentially nowhere. And what is more, she knows it. She makes no secret that she's saving her money to live in London. But she may be aiming a bit high."

"She comes to St. Edwold's with her mother."

"Her mother is the only reason she's having trouble leaving—the mother has a dicey heart."

"Dicky," corrected Max automatically. "A dicky heart. Yes, I know." He took a sip of his coffee. "Could I talk with Kayla alone for a minute? I know she's probably busy. It won't take long."

Kayla sat across from him five minutes later, taking Umberto's place. She was her usual friendly self, if a little wary. The magazine Max had been looking at with Cotton was spread before them on the table. Max pointed at the people in the photo, who had been sitting where he and Kayla sat now.

"This is the man who was just murdered. And his wife."

Kayla peered closely at the picture.

"Yes."

"Do you know the couple they're with?"

She nodded her head yes. "The man who was murdered and his wife—they sometimes brought people from London. Friends of theirs. But that looks like Frank and Lucie with them. Anyway, I didn't wait that table."

"How do you know Thaddeus and Melinda came from London?"

It wasn't meant to be a trick question. Thaddeus had been well enough known in the village that most people would know where he was from. But she blushed, and stammered, "I don't know, do I? Look, Father, I really don't see—"

"What it has to do with anything? You're right—it is probably of no moment. But you are in the photo, and your face . . ." He stopped, looking straight at her. "The expression on your face is . . . unusual. You're looking at Thaddeus, aren't you? And it's difficult to understand what he could have done to deserve such a look, just having a meal in a restaurant with his wife and friends."

That Lady of Shalott look: She wasn't just stunned. She was—perhaps *revolted* was the closest word. And angry. Perhaps above all, angry with herself.

"I think . . ." said Max tentatively, "I think you had some sort of relationship with him." It was too easy to see how it could have happened. Kayla was looking for a way out of the village. Thaddeus had been a potential conduit to a world of glamour, even of stardom. She wouldn't be the first person to look for a shortcut to fame. He realized for the first time that Melinda might have fallen into the same trap.

Kayla stood up from the table, and Max thought she was just going to leave and say no more. She would certainly have been within her rights. But she came back with a pot of coffee, and a cup for herself. Then the story came out.

"I met him the night of the restaurant opening. I was here, helping the caterer. One thing led to another. We didn't have—there was nothing between us, but I knew what he wanted. And I let him believe he stood a chance. That was wrong of me, Father, and I know that now. I should have told him to go to hell or I'd tell his wife. I've wished a hundred times I'd done exactly that.

"He promised to help me get a job in London, to get my name before the important agents and directors. Right. What he had in mind would get my name before them all right. He organized an introduction to some guy in London—he said. I actually went to London, and the address he gave me was a phony. The guy's name was phony. There was no such place in the West End. I guess he was hoping I'd be really grateful—

beforehand—and wouldn't think to check up on what he said—beforehand. He was half right anyway.

"I confronted him, and he had the nerve to laugh. He thought it was funny. 'You're only average,' he said, 'if that.' He told me I had no potential in the theater 'or anywhere else.'"

Ouch, thought Max.

"He added that I was too old, that I'd be a laughingstock. I was just reeling. I don't know why I just stood there and took it, but I did. Part of me believed him, you see. You always believe the bad things about yourself, don't you? Anyway, what I couldn't believe was that he would have the nerve to show up here, after pulling that on me, but somehow I think he'd gotten wind there would be a reporter from *Glossamer Living* at the restaurant that night and he was hoping someone would take his photo. Didn't I nearly split a gut laughing when I saw they had taken his photo all right—from the back?"

That was it? Max wondered. A tawdry little ploy from Thaddeus—a ridiculous and cheap attempt at seduction that had failed. And when it failed, he was happy to send her off, wasting her time on a wild-goose chase. It seemed like a petty revenge, and, on reflection, probably just the sort of thing Thaddeus would do. If the woman had come across with what Thaddeus wanted, then, maybe, he'd have arranged the introduction he'd used as bait, but even that was doubtful.

They talked awhile longer, but Kayla had shut down now, and he got no more from her.

What is she not telling me? Max wondered. Was she lying about how far had she allowed intimacy with Thaddeus, decades older than she, to progress? For who would be able to find out the truth, now that the man who had tricked her was dead?

Somehow, Max didn't particularly want to know the details. But her revulsion for Thaddeus now was real enough. Real enough to kill over? From the look on Kayla's hardened face, the answer was yes.

CHAPTER 16
Poetry and Prose

The members of the Writers' Square had convened an extraordinary meeting. It was merely an excuse to discuss developments, thinly cloaked by Frank's claim that he'd been having problems with a plot point—*plot point* being a professional term he'd picked up from a rejection letter he'd received, in which it was claimed his work needed one.

Gabby had been invited to join the group, but not without opposition from Frank. Suzanna had broken the news to him just before the meeting started.

"But she's—" Frank began.

"She's what?"

"Well, she's a hairdresser, and . . ."

"And you're what—a brain surgeon? What difference does it make? We need to mix things up in this group, and she said she'd be willing to give it a try. Shush now. Here she comes."

Suzanna and Elka had already explained the rules of the group to Gabby. She would have to read her work aloud—there were no exceptions to this rule. Suzanna thought she would balk at this, and she did.

Only by bringing Elka onto the case was Gabby finally persuaded she would be in good company, with a patient and receptive audience. Elka wasn't sure how true that was, but she sensed an aloneness that clung to Gabby and wanted very much to include her in village life. It was an aloneness with which Elka was too familiar.

So at Tuesday's extraordinary meeting, they made the usual rounds of the group, each member reading aloud from a work in progress, or discussing what they were planning to try their hand at next. Frank began reading the same passage they had heard at the previous meeting. There was some objection to this, and he said, dropping all pretense, "Does it really matter? We're here to discuss the murder, aren't we?"

When it was her turn, Gabby cleared her throat and in a quiet voice that had them all leaning in to hear, she began to read.

> *I look for you in every flower.*
> *She said mums were your favorite*
> *But I knew that wasn't so.*
> *Nothing showy would do.*
> *Something sturdy, plain, and white would be*
> *Your plant du jour . . . .*

As Gabby had read on, they had a sense they were hearing a unique voice, untrained, plain, and raw but transparent in its desire to communicate heartfelt emotion. Whether poets could be trained was a large question, but the members of the Writers' Square registered that their low expectations of Gabby's abilities as a poet had been colored by her sex, age, and occupation. Not all were as embarrassed as they might have been by this realization, but all felt somewhat chastened.

> *. . . A tall stem,*
> *Against the blue sky*

A blossom
White as a nun's cowl,
Devon cream and white cliffs.
White as a shroud.
When we talked
Each morning
There would be
A vase of tulips between us.

It was, they knew without being told, a poem of loss. Frank's face masked an expression of surprise as Gabby continued to read. He'd been expecting something more along the lines of a limerick.

Adam, possibly the most cerebral of the group, felt the impact of the poem as a quickening of his breathing, and a pounding of blood he imagined he could feel as it left and entered his heart. Having never had such an experience, and having no words to describe it, he shifted uncomfortably in his chair as he waited for the reading to end. Gabby at last looked up, blushing at her own boldness and fearing the others' judgment.

Finally, she became aware of Elka staring at her.

"That was beautiful," whispered Elka at last.

"That's nice," said Suzanna, less easily impressed. "What's it called?"

Gabby hesitated, realizing: "I hadn't put a title to it."

"Who's it for?"

Again the hesitation. Clearly, Gabby was not used to the spotlight and was wriggling under the novelty of being the center of attention. She tugged nervously at the cuff of her sleeve. "I suppose I was writing it to my husband, to Harold. So, 'For My Husband,' I suppose. That would do as a title. He would have liked that."

"That's nice," Elka said again. She seemed to be fixed on this simple thought. Gabby was known to have been widowed. "It's nice you remember him that way." Elka's own husband was gone and best forgotten, having left her to raise their son, a monumentally tough job, about which she held remarkably little rancor. Her son was the center around which planet Elka wobbled.

"It's every bit as good as anything Thaddeus Bottle ever wrote," said Adam. Frank nodded.

The mention of the great playwright formerly in their midst sparked an immediate detour in the conversation. They quickly moved from theories of who might have wanted to kill Thaddeus (everyone) to a critique of the man's work.

"Of course it's not the same thing," said Frank. "It's two different sets of skills entirely, acting and writing."

"I wouldn't agree," said Adam. "Look at Shakespeare. Actor and dramatist."

"Well, Shakespeare was *Shake*speare, wasn't he? Everyone else is just everyone else."

"Ah, gentle Shakespeare," breathed Adam. "How I'd love to interview him over a pint of ale."

"What would you ask him?"

"I'd ask him for his autograph, for a start," said Adam with a laugh. "He left only five or six signatures. None of his plays or poetry survives in manuscript. Noah says the dream of his life is to find such a manuscript inside one of his antiques over there at Noah's Ark—the pages perhaps used as lining for a drawer or trunk."

The faraway look on all their faces at the thought of such a find was dispelled by Frank.

"Perhaps we should set our sights a bit lower. Suzanna, what else do you have to read for us tonight? A little light romance?"

If Suzanna was perturbed by the "less than Shakespearean" implication behind Frank's word, she shrugged it off. Suzanna was aiming unapologetically for the Jackie Collins crowd.

"I'll just get some more coffee before I begin, shall I?" she said. "Be right back. Elka, you brought biscuits again, did you?"

Elka nodded. "Lemon."

"Ah, good! I skipped dinner to be here on time."

"I can't think of anyone more qualified to write a memoir than Suzanna," said Elka when Suzanna was out of earshot.

"Me, either. But," Adam added hesitantly, "I thought she was writing a romance?"

"I'm not sure in Suzanna's case there's a great deal of difference." This from Frank. "As I understand it, apart from her vicar book, she's been working on a tell-all about her more rackety days in London working for that now-defunct newspaper, a tale thinly disguised as fiction. At least I think it's disguised."

"Oh my. Could we be sued by someone?" wondered Elka.

"Just for being in her writing group? I doubt it."

Adam had another thought. "She's not writing about any of us, is she?"

"I don't think so," said Elka. "She says, 'Nothing interesting ever happens here in Brigadoon.'"

"That's not true," said Frank. "We have murders, don't we? And there's a definite chance Royalty may visit the village soon."

A rumor had been spread by the *Globe and Bugle* that an HRH or two were staying with friends nearby. This rumor seemed to be the incentive for numerous shopping excursions by the villagers into nearby Monkslip-super-Mare, the colorful seaside town nearest the estate of the stately friends. Sadly, there had been no reports of a live sighting. It would appear the Duchess of Cambridge no longer had time to shop for her groceries at Waitrose.

The Royalty buzz had somehow become entangled with an earlier rumor involving an equally unlikely visit from the Archbishop of Canterbury. Given Nether Monkslip's reputation as a place of healing and spirituality—this due partly to the menhirs on Hawk Crest and partly to the abbey ruins—the rumors combusted like heat and flammable gas, taking on new life with the theory that the mystically inclined Prince Charles would be drawn as if by magnet to the area, with HRH Camilla, however reluctantly, in tow.

The villagers were content in the case of the archbishop to let the man come to them, rather than that they should find cause to seek out His Grace. As Elka Garth had been heard to comment, the archbishop, unlike HRH Camilla and—God knew—Catherine, always wore the same old outfit.

Suzanna returned. Tonight she wore a tailored men's-style shirt and a skirt fitted like cling film to her wide hips. Her blond hair gleamed and her brown eyes sparkled in the firelight. She was holding aloft a circular plastic item decorated with beads.

"What *is* this?" she asked. "An IUD?"

Elka looked up. "It's a stitch marker, dear. One of the knitters must have left it behind. It looks like one of Miss Pitchford's."

A local knitting circle led by Lily Iverson, the resident expert in all things woolen, also used Adam's shop as meeting space. Sometimes one member would take turns reading aloud while the others clicked softly away with their needles; generally, they just chatted, taking occasional sips of their wine. Miss Agnes Pitchford had been working for months on something white that might have been a ship's sail.

"Oh," said Suzanna. "*Not* an IUD, then. Anyway, I've just remembered what happened at the second-but-last Christmas office party before the 'dark Satanic mills' folded," she said. "I can't tell you the details—I've got to save *some*thing for the book—but it involved the photocopying machine and a reindeer antlers headband. Of course, this was just after my divorce, so allowances must be made."

She looked around at her audience. Gabby looked particularly taken aback. The rest of them were used to it.

"What? We *were* on deadline."

Frank, who despite his better judgment had read the paper until it folded, was thinking Suzanna's story explained so much—the typos, the missing paragraphs, the page numbers out of order.

Suzanna said, "I'm just getting to the part where my boss finally left to 'explore new opportunities,' as it was announced in the trade press. That is trade-press speech for rat deserting a sinking ship, not to be confused with rat walking the plank. At least he didn't say he wanted to devote more time to his family. I knew his wife. She would have been appalled to have him underfoot all the time."

"This was just before you came to Nether Monkslip, wasn't it?" asked Elka. "Your job at the paper?"

"More or less," said Suzanna. "It seems like another world now. The memory of the days when I toiled among the other ink-stained wretches is fast receding."

"Do you ever hear from your ex?" Elka asked.

"My ex-husband? God, no. The last I heard, he was starting some sort of adventure company. Perhaps he and the new girlfriend will be eaten alive by rhinos. Or maybe he'll get his ass permanently wedged in a crevasse while he's leading a potholing expedition down a cave. Either way, I'm not going to lose any sleep over it."

Yes, thought Elka. The arrival in the village of Umberto Grimaldi was doing Suzanna a world of good. She had seen them talking together in the village more than once.

Elka glanced at her minutes of the meeting, which she had begun to notice were very short on meaningful content. "Should I mention the murder at the Bottles'?" she asked.

"Of course!" said Frank. "Everything is material. Just make sure you get the apostrophe right." Once they had agreed on the name Writers' Square, there had been endless discussions over where the apostrophe should go, before or after the first *s*—or, more daringly, if an apostrophe was even needed. Then, at Frank's insistence, it had become

Writers' □, to make it all incandescently literary. After further debate, this was shortened, for publicity purposes (for when, said Frank, they had something to publicize), to W□. In speech, for the cognoscenti, it was "the Square," as in "See you at the Square at seven." Frank, in particular, liked to toss this phrase about in public, hoping to be overheard.

The apostrophe debate had at last tapered off, only to be resurrected when Waterstones, the famous bookshop, dropped the apostrophe in its trading name and logo, provoking indignant howls from the Apostrophe Protection Society, headquartered in Lincolnshire. "It's just plain wrong," the society's chairman had been quoted as saying, little knowing he was reigniting the debate among the habitués of the Writers' (née Writers) Square (née Circle).

"See?" Frank had said. The existence of such a society had been to Frank a beacon of hope for civilization, like evidence of intelligent life on Mars.

"But if we get a Web site, the apostrophe will have to go, along with the little square," said Adam. "At least in the Web site address."

"You will have to pry the apostrophe from my cold, dead hands," cried Frank.

"That can be arranged," said Adam, who was also toying with writing a murder mystery, and felt that Frank was looking more and more a likely victim. Adam might be an artsy and gentle spirit, but, like anyone, he had his limits.

Still, he looked now at his fellow writers with something like proprietary pride. Gabby would make a nice addition, he thought—Elka had been right. The ranks of the group had shrunk from about ten members at its zenith to the current five, absent Awena. One former member, a terrible cook, had been writing a cookbook. Another had been writing a self-help book, although her personal life was a shambles. These two, luckily, had quit early on. The cookbook author, when asked by a doubtful

Elka whether she had tested her recipes, had replied, "No! Of course not. The publisher has people who will do that for me."

Elka had looked around the group for confirmation. "People?" she'd asked at last.

"Yes. Publishers have test kitchens and things."

"Somehow, I wouldn't count on that, dear."

"Yes, they are far too busy making sure the apostrophes are in the right place," Suzanna had said, not daring to meet Frank's eye. But Frank had been beaming at the support from an unexpected quarter.

"Undoubtedly they are," he had said.

Subject: Melinda

From: Gabrielle Crew (gabby@TresRapidePoste.fr)

To: Claude Chaux (Claude43@TresRapidePoste.fr)

Date: Tuesday, March 27, 2012 9:48 P.M.

Claude—The death of Thaddeus Bottle is on everyone's mind. Father Max showed up after yoga class yesterday, asking questions. Clearly murder is suspected.

There have been several murders in the Monkslip area recently, and the good Father has been "on the case" each time. You can see he's distressed, as though this were somehow all his fault. He's that kind of person, Father Max.

Annette at the salon is decidedly unnerved, but she's not alone—people, after all, come here to get away from crime.

My first meeting with the Writers' Square was earlier tonight, and I think it went well. It was an "extraordinary" meeting because they usually meet on Thursdays. (They used to meet on Saturdays, but too many social occasions intervened. As Suzanna says, "I might have a date again one day. Who knows?")

But this change created a problem for Melinda Bottle, and that is what I wanted to tell you about. You see, she confided in me that Saturday was the only day of the week her "friend" Farley could easily get away to meet her. So Melinda simply kept telling Thaddeus she was going to a Saturday Writers' Square meeting, hoping for the best. She was bound to be caught out eventually, but she was getting reckless and she didn't seem to care. She can be rather a silly woman. I don't know if what she feels for Farley is love; I think in Melinda's case, infatuation will always take the place of affection.

I went to see her this afternoon. The police and other

officials had left her alone for the moment. She was not taking it all in, and finally she said the doctor had given her something to calm her down, and she'd doubled the dose, which explained the trancelike state she appeared to be in.

Poor Melinda. She is just now tasting her freedom and she doesn't quite know what to do with it. Her shock is physical *and* mental, even given that they were married only a few years. Even an unattractive personality can be comforting to have around every day—it depends on what you grow used to. And, of course, she'll have the money to keep her warm. She told me they had mutual life insurance policies, something he'd talked her into years ago. I just hope she gets a grip soon.

Thaddeus Bottle. He could so easily have died from an accident, or a mistake, or from age, and the death of a nicer man might have attracted little notice, but the fact that it was Thaddeus—a famously unpopular character—meant the authorities would be paying closer attention.

And Father Max, who misses nothing, desperately wants to get to the bottom of this, to make his little village whole again.

My e-mails to you are becoming my diary, as I don't dare tell anyone what I know. People confide in me because they know I don't gab—despite my nickname.

Thank you for being there, as always in my heart.

Ever yours, Gabby

CHAPTER 17
Bishop's Palace

Wednesday, March 28

Max's dreams were disturbed and varied that night, his mind ransacked for every fearsome moment he'd ever lived through. One final dream began as he sat on a beach, relaxed, warm, and content, his eyes shut against the sun. The scent of the sea and of suntan lotion surrounded him. Slowly, he became aware of a person taking the spot next to his; he heard the snap of an umbrella being unfurled, and the rustle of sand disturbed, and a can of soda popped open. Much later, his dreaming self opened its eyes and saw beside him the man in the strange blue sunglasses who had haunted his days since his friend Paul was murdered.

In the dream he thinks of Melinda, lying in bed next to a corpse.

The man turns his head and smiles at Max and it is a smile of mockery, revealing teeth black and rotting. It is the face of the devil, of course Max knows this. But still Max wants to see the eyes behind those sunglasses.

Then in the relentless logic of dreams, Max realized he was dreaming of a beach only because it provided a setting for a man wearing sunglasses. And that struck him as significant, fraught with an importance he didn't understand. Was Paul's killer sitting on a beach somewhere even now, happy and enjoying his freedom?

Vestiges of the dream stayed with him as he finally surrendered to dawn and consciousness. In the half-light world between dreaming and waking, he struggled to remember the vivid but disappearing details.

With a sudden spurt of anger, Max thought he'd give anything to see the man caught and punished.

*Any*thing.

So it was in a distracted and tired state of mind that he made the early-morning drive to see the bishop in his palace. His thoughts clung more to the night before than focusing ahead on what he suspected would be an important interview.

The weather had shifted yet again, unseasonably warm for March. Nearly everyone he saw had pushed their sleeves up or had found a favorite colorful short-sleeved dress or shirt in the closet; nearly every window was open in every cottage. The change was striking, for the recent winter temperatures in England had been far below the norm. Nether Monkslip, generally spared the worst, had felt the nip, as well.

Less than two hours later, Max turned off the motorway and followed the signs into the center of the old cathedral town; before long, the palace came into his view, perfectly framed in the windshield of the Land Rover. He had forgotten until he saw it again how imposing the place was, how austere yet magisterial; it overwhelmed the viewer, as it was meant to do. If not for the traffic, Max would have pulled over to stop and gaze in awe along with the tourists. Most unusually, the palace, adjacent to the equally magnificent cathedral, was walled and moated and drawbridged like a fortress, these belligerent touches being remnants of a feud centuries before, when hot oil and molten lead were still standards in the arsenal of weapons. Now swans floated serenely on the still waters of the moat, and rang a bell when they wanted food. Entry to the grounds was through a gatehouse; once one was inside, the gardens of the palace grounds bloomed in beautiful contrast to the area's violent past.

Max found a parking spot for the Rover and set out at a jog to keep his appointment. Passersby smiled at the sight of the running priest.

The bishop, a ginger-haired, comfortable-looking man in his sixties, was dictating a memo for his secretary into a small microphone. He was grappling, as always, with some of the more vexing issues of the day as the Church of England emerged, blinking in its molelike way, into the twenty-first century.

"We must wholeheartedly embrace the gay community, clasping it—wait. Make that: We welcome the gay community with . . . Wait. Wait. Make that: We welcome the gay community. Full stop."

The bishop cleared his throat.

"Erase all that and let's start again," he said into the machine. Even as he did so, he could picture his long-suffering secretary in the outer office heaving a monumental sigh. "Opening paragraph," said the bishop firmly. "The ordination of women, while not embraced unconditionally in the beginning, has become for many a beacon of common sense, an ethical torch lighting the way to an inclusive vision for mankind and womankind. Correction. Make that: womankind and mankind—good. After so many centuries, we simply could no longer skirt the issue. Wait. Make that: We could no longer avoid the issue. As we enter the twenty-first century, we embrace . . . uhm. We love . . . uhm . . . In Christ, we love *every*body."

Max, meanwhile, having found his way to the bishop's private rooms, had been bidden by the man's secretary to wait in an outer chamber. After refusing the offer of coffee, Max merged into the darkness in the corner of the room, dark-haired and dressed head to toe in black, aside from his white collar, which caught the light like a fallen halo. The area had been set up for visitors with a low, worn velveteen sofa and chairs and a large, square coffee table. On offer were an array of religious magazines and newsletters, each one of a stultifying dullness worse than the last. Or perhaps, Max thought, he was simply too keyed up about the upcoming meeting to focus on the meaning of the text. He picked up one magazine and saw the headline: THE TOMBOLA AS CHURCH FUND-RAISER: AN OVERVIEW. No, he decided. Overall, it was the content, not his fragmented attention span. He chose to sit, hands folded, actively cultivating a sense of inner calm, even as his mind tried and failed to predict the upcoming interview. Perhaps he should take one of Awena's meditation courses on offer at Goddessspell.

It was fifteen minutes before he was summoned into the presence. Still not time enough to have sorted out what and how to tell the bishop. He didn't expect a grilling, but the summoning to the inner sanctum was unusual enough that *something* must be up.

Max's innate honesty was struggling with the more mundane problem of how to construct a coherent narrative out of all that had befallen him since taking up his duties in Nether Monkslip. Murders, police investigations, and his deepening relationship with Awena, just to touch on the highlights. Difficult to predict which of those topics would upset the bishop more.

At last, his name was called. The secretary led the way into the room, announced Max, and closed the doors behind him with a muffled thunk. Max pasted on a confident smile and strode across the large room toward the bishop's desk, then stood and bowed his head in a respectful nod. The bishop, turning off his microphone, greeted him cordially and waved him into a plush-covered seat.

Max liked the bishop. The Right Reverend Bishop Nigel St. Stephen, often called by the media "The People's Bishop," was a bit of a politician, a bit of a hearty hail-fellow-well-met sort of person, but any man in his position had to be. He had to remain smooth, unruffled, and steadfast, however buffeted he might be by trends and fashions, and Max felt that overall the bishop's concern was not for himself and the impression he might be making, or the legacy he might be leaving behind, but for the welfare and survival of a Church he evidently cherished.

In person, he was no different from any other busy executive, apart from the way he was dressed—in an antique costume that included a pectoral cross suspended by a gold chain. His clothing was in contrast with most of his office furnishings, as if he were an actor in a historical drama who had mistakenly wandered onto the deck of the *Starship Enterprise*. His desk, with its impressive-looking computer, was free of the usual nest of wires and coils, and it had a huge flat-screen monitor. In addition to the computer were a laptop and a zippy little mobile phone. As Max had entered, a ream of paper had shot soundlessly and with lightning speed from the printer connected wirelessly across the room.

What kind of computer was it? Only Lizbeth Salander would know. Suddenly, Max was in the grip of computer envy. His bulky little PC back at the vicarage, with its viper's nest of cords and its hiccuppy printer, was the best St. Edwold's could afford, and his software, with its humble offering of colored fonts, looked very limited indeed compared with this space-age show-off. Max reminded himself that he really used it only as a word processor, unlike the bishop, who effectively commanded a small empire from this office.

A large photo of the bishop's handsome wife and cherubic daughters had pride of place on the credenza, beside other mission-control equipment. Each daughter's face had the same look of jovial mischief as her father's, as if they were all in on some enormous prank.

On the drive over, Max had already decided to wait before telling the bishop about the face that kept reappearing on the wall of St. Edwold's. It would be most unwelcome news, and very hard to explain. The image, Max still reasoned, might simply disappear with the roof repairs.

Max thought the bishop might one day be calling him on the carpet because of Awena, but he was almost positive that day wouldn't be today. In his mind, Max had decided if it came to that, if absolutely forced to make a choice, he'd leave the Church. Briefly, he closed his eyes in a spasm of distress, willing the thought away. Surely it wouldn't come to that?

At each service, Max made the same announcement: that all were welcome to participate in the life of St. Edwold's. That included Awena Owen. That included anyone, in Max's book. If he were to be told the Church could not encompass a good soul like Awena's . . .

Awena's spiritual beliefs were perhaps outside the mainstream, but the fact she had beliefs at all in the day and age made her, like Max himself, a bit of a freak. Awena was one of the most religion- and creed-blind people he'd ever met. Labels simply didn't matter to her, nor did they apply to her.

His attraction to Awena had led him willingly to the point where he might again have to make life-altering choices. Theirs was a perfect attraction of mind and body that he knew could be gifted only once in a lifetime, and then only to the very blessed few. His past celibacy had not been intentional, God knew, but the unintended consequence of his status in the village, combined with the fact he'd met no one to whom he was attracted who was "suitable." Suzanna might fill the first bill as being ridiculously attractive, but never the second.

The same could be said of Awena's suitability, of course, but for very different reasons. He tended to summarize Awena this way: She sang in the St. Edwold's choir because she had a beautiful voice and loved to sing, not necessarily because she believed every word she sang. Her singing touched all who heard her because when Awena sang, she was clearly elsewhere, and not tethered to earth as they were.

Max wanted to tell the bishop about Awena, even though he knew it wouldn't be easy. He had come to realize he was more and more on the horns of a dilemma. He couldn't just cohabit with her. His religion and, in particular, his position within his religion forbade that. More to the point, he didn't want—could not even countenance—a casual and informal relationship with Awena. He wanted with all his being to marry her. What kind of repercussions that would have with his Church and its leadership he couldn't begin to imagine.

There was also the fact that he had not actually asked Awena to marry him. It was just understood that was where they were headed.

For his part, the People's Bishop was actually quite fond of Max—not least because, since his advent, St. Edwold's, a small and obscure church that had been in danger of having to close, as so many old churches in Britain had had to close, was now positively thronging with regular attendees. Indeed, there seemed to have been a surge in the demand for not only weddings and baptisms and confirmations and all the usual but also for Morning Prayer and other services where drawing a crowd was next to impossible these days.

The credit for all of this could be laid right at Max's door—the bishop knew, because the bishop had made inquiries. The bishop, in fact, operated not unlike a medieval potentate, sending out spies to get the lay of the land and report back to him. In this way, the bishop had learned that the people of Nether Monkslip trusted and liked Max; the women could be said to adore him.

Then there had been the recent and quite unexpected windfall, a benefaction of money left in a will and earmarked for the repair and maintenance of the roof of St. Edwold's. That in and of itself had been a miracle, as the sum had been quite substantial.

Yes, taken in all, the bishop had every reason to be quite fond of Max. If Max seemed to have a tiny independent streak, a way of doing things his own way on occasion—that seemed a small matter that could easily be brought under control if needs must.

In fact, the bishop was a man remarkably free of the petty jealousies that could beset men and women when presented with a hierarchical career path. Beyond simply liking Max, he believed furthermore that big things were in store for the handsome vicar, and the bishop had privately thought more than once that Nether Monkslip might offer too small a stage for a man of Max's leadership abilities and star qualities. Since he seemed nicely to have galvanized the local populace into unprecedented feats of church attendance, and in record time, just imagine what he could do on a larger scale, in front of a microphone or a television camera, perhaps? Max, in fact, had the potential to be a superstar. He was even a candidate to wear the purple cassock of a bishop one day.

Yes, thought the bishop, as he beamed at Max now, he had always been somewhat lenient because of Max's ability to pack the pews. But at what point did a charismatic leader tip over into dangerous territory and become a renegade priest? A wolf leading the flock astray?

Meanwhile, the independent-minded if potentially wolfish Max gazed wide-eyed at his bishop, trying to decide if and where to begin. The bishop's hair showed his Scottish origins, with the traces of bright ginger now mixed with gray. His face was red above the purple cassock. Max stared at this Technicolor vision, still running the various possible topics of discussion through his mind, and wondering if he should bring up any of the various subjects himself.

He need not have worried. The bishop, as always, wrote the script. Max, now having been invited to sit, was there as his audience.

"I was fascinated to read the media coverage of the events at Chedrow Castle," said the bishop. "That was such a nice photo of you on the front page of the *Globe and Bugle*. I rather wish you had filled me in at the time?" The bishop ended on a hopeful note, a wistful note of longing for a perfect world, rather than a note of anger.

"Yes," said Max, much relieved by the tone. "Fortunately, much of that interest has died down. It was quite a scandal for a while because of the prominence of the family, but now . . ."

Max was feeling thankful the bishop didn't yet seem to know about Thaddeus Bottle, and that he might yet be able to drop that into the conversation with less of a splash than hitherto. Of course, this meeting had been scheduled long before the occasion of the actor's death, so—

"So," said the bishop. "I hear there has been another unusual death in your village."

Were there spies in Nether Monkslip—apart from Miss Pitchford's nest of agents, of course? Max doubted very much the bishop kept the elderly spinster on speed dial, but one never knew. . . . Max's mind began to race at warp speed. *Don't ask. Don'taskdon'task'don'task.*

"Actually, said Max, "that is correct. There has been another incident. It might be an accidental death, though. There is a slight possibility—"

"Good, good! Accidental—I mean, terrible tragedy and all that, but we simply can't have you linked to another crime in the media's—well, the media's mind, for lack of a better word."

The bishop seemed to notice for the first time the stricken look on Max's face.

"It's not another murder, is it?" he asked.

"Uhm." (Sigh.) "It looks as though it may be."

"This makes three occasions of murder." The bishop held up the three fingers of his right hand, almost in a sign of benediction, and also as though Max had not yet learned how to count. "That woman in Nether Monkslip, and the Chedrow Castle tragedy, and now this. This actor and writer person."

Max said again, "That is correct."

"Poor soul. Well, nothing to do with us." And the bishop clearly prepared to breeze on. He tapped together the edges of some papers on his desk. Max felt he'd dodged yet another bullet. That the whole interview was an exercise in dodging bullets. Then the bishop stood and turned toward the window, which had been at his back. From there, he could see the looming tower of the cathedral, its spires puncturing the fat white clouds.

With the exquisite timing for which the man was famous, the bishop turned, just as Max was beginning to relax, and said, "We can't have any more of this, Max. Whatever is going on, you have to get to the bottom of it. Root it out, as it were. With your special skills, you should be of invaluable assistance to the police. I wonder," he added softly, after an appraising glance at Max. "I wonder . . . Has it ever occurred to you God may have brought you to Nether Monkslip for a purpose? For *this* purpose?"

Max could think of no reply. It seemed to him a highly doubtful hypothesis. On later reflection, he would find he didn't much care for the idea, for didn't it mean more people might be murdered in Nether Monkslip?

"I need hardly add, however," the bishop continued, "that if any of this interferes with your pastoral duties, I want you on the horn to me immediately. Do I make myself clear?"

Max, who was struggling to keep a hold on his emotions and not break into a sunbeamy, happy smile, said with straight-faced solemnity, "Of course, Bishop. Absolutely no problem." He didn't add "thank you," because he feared that would have sounded suspicious somehow. The bishop, far from giving Max a dressing-down, had just given his permission for Max to continue assisting Cotton in his investigations. Max could hardly believe his luck.

"Just try to stay out of the news from now on, would you, please?" The bishop moved away from the window and resumed his seat behind the desk. He folded his hands before him on the shiny surface and said, "Was there anything else you wanted?" There was the merest suggestion of a pursing of the lips.

Well, *you* were the one who called the meeting, thought Max. But having been giving this latitude, a grateful Max felt he had to come clean on at least one other topic. He owed the man that much. And it might forestall problems down the road.

"Bishop," he said, "I think I should tell you. I've met a woman, someone very special."

"Good, good!" said the bishop. "'It is better to marry than to burn,' and all that. Still, that is wonderful news. Congratulations. I don't know what I would have done all these years without my Sheila at my side."

"I mean, she's an unusual woman. She—"

"Well, of course she is! You're an unusual man, aren't you?" said the bishop, cheerfully dismissive.

"Thank you, but . . ."

Something in Max's tone made the bishop look at him alertly, head tilted. "She is an Anglican, isn't she?" But this was said jokingly.

Max gave a little sigh of relief. Here he could tell the truth and nothing but the truth. "She was baptized an Anglican, yes. But she's since adopted a more . . . spiritual and inclusive approach to religion. She . . . she is a member—well, sort of a member—of a different religion."

"There's nothing wrong with that," said the bishop. "That's a story I hear every day!"

"Actually," began Max, "her religion is a bit unusual." How to phrase this? His mind utterly resisted using the term *neopagan*, as if the gentle and people-loving Awena were steps away from reverting to cannibalism. To the Romans, *pagan* had meant country dweller, and it was not necessarily meant as a tribute.

The same problem with *druid,* which conjured up images of crazed, inbred villagers setting fire to a wicker man. "You see—"

"Anyway," the Bishop of Monkslip went on, with a complacent smile, "people are brought back into the fold when we set an example. It takes time. As Queen Elizabeth the First said, "I have no desire to make windows into men's souls.""

"Very wise she was," Max murmured, adding, "Wouldn't it be a messy world if we could see into men's souls?"

"Rather! Much better not to know and hope for the best," said the bishop. "As I say, people come into the fold when in their hearts they decide they want to."

"I wouldn't actually count on that," began Max. "She's very much her own—"

Just then, the phone rang, a shrill sound in the quiet room. The bishop turned and held one hand hovering over the receiver. "Now, if you'll excuse me, I have to take this call. All the best, Max. You will invite me to the wedding, won't you? Good-bye!"

And Max, having been given the bum's rush, stood and waved his farewell. The bishop was already deep into his phone conversation.

CHAPTER 18
Absent in the Spring

The subject of Max's conversation with the bishop was at that moment in the summing-up phase of her class on "Cooking and Healing with Herbs." In honor of the season, Awena Owen was kitted out in a bright daffodil yellow dress trimmed at the hem and sleeves in brocade of deep pink and coral. A bronze belt of woven fabric girded her waist. Over this Renaissance glitter she wore, however, a plain muslin apron, as she had just finished demonstrating how to bake onion bread spiced with tarragon.

Awena's life, when she wasn't occupied by running the thriving Goddessspell shop, consisted of things like soaking beans, waiting for bread to rise, and collecting and drying herbs. She also kept a beehive in her small back garden, and knew how to calm the bees by talking to them. Nothing she touched failed to attract devotees to the natural, back-to-land movement that had recently seized the public's imagination, the principles of which Awena had always espoused. She had made a start on writing a cookbook, but so far she was happier doing and demonstrating than writing and testing recipes. Besides, the book she had in mind, which combined how and when to grow according to the seasons, along with how to harvest and prepare, was so ambitious in scope, she doubted she would find the time to write it.

And then there was Max. Although she easily maintained a balance in her life, time spent with Max increasingly filled her calendar.

She turned to face her audience from behind a cooking range set into the center of a wooden counter. Behind her were two built-in ovens and a wall of cabinets and drawers containing every conceivable need for the modern kitchen.

Awena had packed as much as she could into a short course and was delighted by the enthusiastic response from the class. This reaction pleased her on a number of levels: She was teaching something she wholeheartedly believed in—a return to natural foods and a respect for the curative forces of nature, including leaving well enough alone. And that it was a Women's Institute course was important to her. The WI had done much for people around the world, feeding, clothing, and caring for those in desperate circumstances. That the university repeatedly had invited her back to teach an advanced course was a source of much personal pride; being able to share what she knew she regarded as the highest privilege.

"During the time of harvest," she was saying, "we can begin to see the vast array of the earth's bounty. And now we've reached the time of Persephone, the goddess of spring, who is the personification of everything that grows. It's time to think about planting dill, parsley, and chervil. Grow these herbs from seed—transplanting distresses them psychologically. Just as it does us humans."

There was the mildest titter from the group at this, but they understood what she meant, and they hung on her every word. Most of them were taking extensive notes as she spoke. Awena, inheritor of the druidic tradition of honoring every growing thing as literally a gift from the gods, was in her element.

"Remember that herbs love to be in the sun, as we all do. Too much sun, though, is good for no one. And we all need to breathe. For example"—and here she held up a bunch of something that looked like weeds—"I found these in the local market in Denman." She shook her head mournfully. "Imported. How much of the potency is left in a once-living creature that's been stuffed into a hot and humid and airless freighter to reach your table? And herbs are so easy to grow. . . ."

She went on in this vein, well past the time when the class was scheduled to end. She was still answering questions when one of the school's administrators popped her head in and pointed, eyebrows raised, at her wristwatch.

One of the women, who turned out to be affiliated with the BBC, stayed behind to ask if Awena would consider creating a show for television.

It was another hour before Awena could set off for Nether Monkslip. She had one errand to run, one appointment to keep, and then, at last, she could see Max again. She rehearsed in her mind how to tell him her news.

Back in Nether Monkslip, Awena walked toward the beauty salon, where a crowd had gathered.

For there was much to discuss. The villagers at times of crisis or excitement would congregate like crows, instinct drawing them, depending on the time of day, to the post office, the Cavalier, or the Cut and Dried. Of an evening, they might assemble at one of the pubs.

They spoke at first in hushed voices, for in the days following the murder the villagers had been particularly gentle with one another. Subdued, all of them. Well, nearly all, Suzanna missing the genetic marker for discretion and quiet, sober reflection.

For now, the grapevine with its many branches had taken root at the Cut and Dried, where the subject momentarily had worked its way back around to the relationship between Awena and Max, now in full bloom.

"I wonder what the sex is like," mused Suzanna, her voice carrying to the farthest corners of the room. Several heads turned.

"Suzanna. Really." This was Elka, shocked to her fingertips every time she thought she had gotten used to Suzanna's remarks.

"What? You don't look at people sometimes and wonder?" Idly, Suzanna plucked a little bottle of bright red nail varnish from the display at her side and assessingly held it up to the light.

"No."

"Never?"

"Never. Well, almost never."

"Hmm." Suzanna, replacing the bottle, seemed to be struggling to take in this unprecedented worldview. "To me, it's just one of those vexing questions in life, like whether the Queen has a passport."

"Maybe that's what she has in that handbag she always carries."

"With a photo of herself draped in ermine and wearing one of her crowns." Suzanna laughed. "Yes, that's just possible."

"Seriously, Suzanna. Just because something comes into your head doesn't mean you have to say it aloud," Elka observed.

"I don't much see the point in having an opinion otherwise."

"You might just try using the stop key on occasion."

Suzanna looked as if she might consider the possibility, but Elka didn't hold out much hope. Asking Suzanna to censor herself was about as effective as a team of Arab League monitors asking to be shown around the uranium-enrichment facilities. Suzanna, who had just been getting ready to tell Elka about her recent nighttime walk near the Bottles' house, decided to keep mum until her theories had solidified.

"I may have to come back another time," said Elka, glancing at her watch. "I've left Flora minding the shop."

Flora was a young woman who helped Elka outside of school. Honest but not hardworking, she could just about be trusted to ring up the cash register and bus the tables.

"Why not ask Clayton?" Suzanna inquired.

"Oh, I dunno. He gets bored pretty quickly."

There were various schools of thought regarding Elka's son, Clayton. One was that Clayton's behavior was a cynical, even creepy, mooching off of his overworked mother. The other was that Clayton had no control over his actions: He was just a bit slow-witted, as some are. The Major had tried to intervene by giving him odd jobs to do around his garden, a well-intended gesture, which, like all such gestures, had ended in tears. The Major, used to giving orders (even though the soundness of these orders was often questioned, and deservedly so), did have a tendency to try to boss people about.

And some held it was Elka's own fault for coddling Clayton. He was her only child and she'd raised him alone.

Suzanna thought all three of the above elements might be in play. "Have you ever asked your son to help you? Really asked?"

Such a novel idea, thought Elka. The answer is no, because he might refuse. Aloud and loudly and deliberately, he might refuse, not just passively refuse. And then where would I be if he left, but alone?

Suzanna returned to reading one of the gossip magazines that littered the shop. She was waiting for an updo, having been persuaded by Elka to give Gabby a try. Suddenly, Suzanna dropped the magazine in her lap in mock surprise and said, "I was just wondering what Angelina Jolie's theories of child raising might be and then as if by magic, *OMG!* magazine explores this very topic."

"You're joking, right?" said Gabby, stirring a bowl of hair color as if it were cake batter. She looked at the photo of the famous actress, oddly posed in a dark velvet dress slit up to there.

"Of course I'm joking. Angelina has a squad of nannies helping her and Brad with all those kids."

Suzanna, with her languid allure, felt she could run rings around Angelina in the vixen department, given half a chance and an unlimited clothing budget.

"Besides, Angelina is probably much too busy visiting holy yurts and Buddhist temples and things. Or is that Madonna?"

"What's a yurt?" Mrs. O'Day, from the neighboring village of Middle Monkslip, asked. The fame of the Cut and Dried salon was evidently spreading.

"It's rather like a circus tent," said Suzanna convincingly, although she wasn't entirely sure. "All the Hollywood types go there to open their pores and replenish themselves spiritually."

"I thought that was rehab," said Sandy Sechrest.

Elka, now glancing over Suzanna's shoulder, pointed to one of the photos in a red-carpet montage and said, "I love Rob Lowe."

"That makes two of you," replied Suzanna. "Give me Hugh Grant any day." Lowering her voice, she added, "Now that Max Tudor is otherwise engaged."

"Or Jude Law, for that matter," said Elka, the movie buff. "He reminds me of someone here in the village. I can't quite put my finger on it."

"DCI Cotton," said Suzanna and Gabby, Gabby calling over her shoulder from her station.

Elka snapped her fingers. "That's it! How could I have missed it!"

"Laurence Fox is no slouch, either," Suzanna added. "He can leave his shoes under my bed anytime he wants."

"Colin Firth!" someone shouted from across the room.

"That actor who plays Aurelio Zen!"

This prompted a heated discussion of the merits or lack of same of the various film, TV, and stage actors, a discussion that came close to veering into a shouting match because of the interference of the radio playing in the background, and because of the passion with which the women embraced their preferences in the romantic idol department. The BBC was covering a visit by the prime minister to the U.S., a story in which no one seemed much interested, and Annette Hedgepeth, the shop owner, crossed the room to turn down the sound.

It was then Awena walked in, keeping her twice-yearly haircut appointment. Given the recent topic of her relationship with Max, the conversation hit an awkward lull. Elka shot a meaningful look at Suzanna.

Awena looked around. The place was jammed with customers, with several women and one man—Frank Cuthbert—waiting for their appointments and several more having their hair worked on. Gabby's blue-white locks gleamed in the overhead light, and the floor was so littered with snips of auburn and gray and brown hair that Annette was kept busy sweeping up. Melinda was there also, Awena saw, wearing stacks of thin gold bracelets on each arm. In keeping with her personality, she jangled like the bells on a dray horse as she turned the pages of a fashion magazine. One woman sat shrouded in a black nylon cape and foils, looking as if she were waiting for someone to come and plug her in.

DCI Cotton, Awena learned, had just left.

"Grilled Gabby, he did," Annette said.

"He did *not*," said Gabby. "If I'd been in for a grilling, it wouldn't have been here, now would it? That man must have a police station *some*-where to go to, as much as he hangs around here. He talked to you, too."

"And I had nothing to say." Annette managed to imply she could have said so much, but the truth was, she was as baffled by the murder as anyone.

Suddenly, they both remembered Melinda was in the room, but since she sat right beneath the radio, which still broadcast unheeded from a shelf over her head, she appeared not to have heard the exchange.

Suzanna looked up at Awena—the sensual, voluptuous Awena, with her hair, long and black and glossy as a slice of anthracite, apart from that striking white streak at the temple. She isn't even *trying*, thought Suzanna, and yet she emits this—well, this *aura*. But Suzanna smiled, a genuine smile of renewed friendship, for she had determined to hold no long-term grudges in having lost the Max sweepstakes. For Suzanna, there would always be other prizes to be won. Prizes like Umberto.

Annette saw Awena and put down her scissors.

"You brought the salve? Fantastic."

Annette suffered from the beginnings of arthritis, and she swore that Awena's salve, comprised of ground cayenne and Cat's Claw, among other things, alleviated the pain of wielding scissors for much of the day. It wasn't a cure, but there was no question in Annette's mind that it helped.

"And here is some gotu kola, in case you cut your hand again," said Awena. "It can help with healing, and prevent scarring." The scissors were always extra sharp once the traveling knife sharpener had passed through town, and Annette's left hand still bore the traces of a scar. "You should talk with Dr. Winship about all of this," Awena added, "particularly if you're using anything else he's prescribed."

"Of course," said Annette. "Will do." She broke off as unusual activity at the front of the shop caught her eye. "Frank, what are you doing?"

"I'm alphabetizing the nail varnish bottles: Pagan Rose, Primrosey, Silverlight, and so on. It will make it easier for you to find what you want."

"I really would rather you d—"

Suddenly, there was a clatter. Gabby dropped the bowl she'd been using to apply color to her customer's hair, and Annette dropped the small jar Awena had just handed her.

"What?" said all three women simultaneously. BBC Radio 4 droned on in the background, now with news of the escalating euro crisis.

Gabby and Annette set about clearing up the mess. When they'd finished, Gabby tugged nervously at her sleeves, as if they chafed.

"Well, how clumsy can we get in our old age?" she said.

"Speak for yourself," said Annette. But there was humor in her voice. "You've been on your feet all day. Why not take a rest? I'll take over what you're doing when I'm done here."

"Thank you," said Gabby, clearly relieved. She consulted briefly with her client. "I was almost finished. But I do feel a little peculiar."

She inhaled deeply to settle her breathing. Awena and the others were reminded that Gabby was getting along in years.

"Thank you," she repeated. The rouge dotting her cheeks stood out against her suddenly colorless skin.

Subject: What to do?
From: Gabrielle Crew (gabby@TresRapidePoste.fr)
To: Claude Chaux (Claude43@TresRapidePoste.fr)
Date: Wednesday, March 28, 2012 1:46 P.M.

Dear Claude—I find my mind keeps returning to that misty winter morning in Raven's Wood. That morning when I knew what Melinda was thinking.

I had another recipe from Awena that I was anxious to try, this one for pasties made with mushrooms and lentils, and I knew a few mushrooms remained in the woods despite the cold.

I was lost in my own thoughts and so I almost literally bumped into Melinda: I heard a rustling of leaves and I looked up to find her there, carrying a wicker basket just like mine. That in itself was simply not her style, and I wondered how she knew to use a wicker basket to collect mushrooms, so the spores can escape and propagate the area. Someone must have told her, probably Awena, although anyone schooled in country ways would know it.

"I'm collecting mushrooms for our supper," she told me. I nearly laughed aloud at the thought of Melinda preparing anything not purchased, wrapped in cling film, from a supermarket in Staincross Minster. First of all, unless you know what you are doing, you can easily kill yourself: Many species around here that are safe to eat also resemble mushrooms that will send you to meet your Maker. You have to know the smell and color of the dangerous versus the safe ones, and that comes from the experience of being a countrywoman. I have always thought it wonderful that in France you can take your mushrooms to a pharmacist, where they are trained to identify which mushrooms are safe and which not. But that is the beauty of a nation that lives and dies by its food.

The poisonous Yellow Stainer, common to this area, may not kill you but it can make you very ill indeed, and if you are elderly—elderly like her husband, Thaddeus, for example—well . . . . Besides, what she had in that basket was not a Yellow Stainer. It was a death cap, and that is what Melinda was collecting. The death cap! A tiny sliver of which can be fatal.

In some shock, I pointed this out to her and she— reluctantly? yes, reluctantly—took the mushroom from her basket and threw it to the ground. I picked it up so some animal or another human wouldn't be poisoned by mistake. It was very odd behavior on her part indeed. Almost as if she planned to return to the spot once I had gone and retrieve it.

But this was months ago and nothing has happened since—well, until now.

All I had to go on even then was instinct. That guilty look on her face. I imagined that I knew what she was thinking. No—correction—I didn't imagine anything. I *know* Melinda was up to no good.

But the path to hell is paved with the bones of people who don't know when to mind their own business—at least I hope it is. I'm certainly not going to tell the police. Not the least of the reasons for my reticence is a complete distrust of the authorities, of any authority. This DCI Cotton seems like a sound man, but he has a case he needs to close, and he may be under pressure from higher-ups to do so.

Perhaps I can find a way to learn what the police are thinking. What harm could it do to ask around? It would put my mind at ease.

I am getting old now, nearing seventy. And there was I, hoping for peace in my old age!

As much as we think we have learned from living a long life, from long experience of making choices, it only becomes harder to know what is right. Max Tudor would say we see through a glass darkly, a dim reflection of the truth. And he'd be right.

I must get back to work now. But I think that writing to you, Claude, is what has kept me from going mad. Thank you for being there in spirit, in my spirit. Your presence in my heart is a late gift to me.

Love always, your Gabby

CHAPTER 19
Matters of the Heart I

Max had lit a fire against the chill that had crept into the afternoon, and now he sat at his desk, making notes for his sermon for Palm Sunday, a few days away. The smell of the burning logs was restorative, a much-needed tonic to the senses. Max had just officiated at the funeral of a middle-aged man in a neighboring village, a man who had almost certainly committed suicide after a long spell of unemployment. The cause of death officially had been accidental overdose, to spare his widow. It might even have been true. The doctor had made that choice, and Max had gone along with it. What earthly difference did it make now?

Not all that long ago, Max reflected, suicides were given roadway burials at a crossroads to emphasize their outsider status.

A television documentary program droned forgotten in the background. It had come on the air after a cooking show Max had found himself watching for no particular reason. He admired the skills involved in preparing a meal, and watching someone else do it was almost like having dinner without the work and the calories. It had taken him a while to realize that his meal-by-proxy habit had developed under the reign of Mrs. Hooser and her ghastly cuisine.

Thea slept before the fire. Done on one side, she had rolled onto her back to toast the other. She slept the sleep of the just, paws and nose in the air, her soft ears fanned out on either side of her head.

Max, wanting a drink, glanced at his watch. The sun wasn't yet over the yardarm. No doubt prompted by the day's sad duties, a memory of his old colleague Paul flashed through his mind, a memory brief but sharp, all the sharper for being so unexpected. But it was a memory of Paul alive, and laughing—they had been drinking together, watching a boat race, and Max had said something, presumably something amusing, and Paul had turned to him, startled into a great shout of laughter. The image came to Max now with the clarity of an old photo found in turning a page of a scrapbook. But with this image in his mind came also the scent of the cold breeze coming over the water, the cheers of the spectators, and the full force of the being that was Paul, alive in that startled laugh.

Max had tried very hard to crawl permanently into a bottle when Paul had been killed. It seemed the only possible, the only sane response. But even the taste of his favorite single-malt whiskey had become vile, and remained for a long time foreign to his palate.

Paul's death—the butchery that was his murder—had been the defining event of Max's life. He had emerged from what he recognized now as a clinical-grade depression and begun the halting steps toward recovery, a recovery that included a new capacity to measure life not in years, but in moments. Not too long afterward, by a circuitous route that included mindless wandering in Egypt, he had found himself reading theology, studying for the priesthood.

It wasn't as if his time with MI5, his time of being a young man, had been sacrificed in vain.

It was that it was someone else's turn, he had thought. *Someone else's turn.*

Maybe someone else would do a better job.

It wasn't as if he hadn't in the course of his career stopped guys who needed to be stopped—he knew he had. It wasn't as if he hadn't saved lives here and there—he knew he had done that also, and perhaps saved hundreds more he didn't even know about.

When he'd been recruited into MI5, he'd been enormously flattered, as if he'd been singled out for his brains, his looks, his breeding. How much had pride been part of his enthusiastic response? How much knowledge had he really had of what he was in for—how soon he would be crushed, compromised by the choices he'd been forced to make? He'd been twenty-one, for God's sake.

The age when the young everywhere were recruited to causes by the middle-aged, by the old.

There was a sudden shriek from the telly and he turned to see a creature being devoured by a larger creature. Too much reality, he thought, rising to switch off the set. Thea had rolled over in the instant, alert to predators.

He scooped up from his desk the pages he'd been working on, forcing his mind to his task, but he again found himself stuck for a conclusion to his Palm Sunday theme. Pacing the room, he picked up the book he had been reading the night before and just as quickly set it aside. A thriller didn't call to him when there was so much that was thrilling in his own cozy little world.

So he was in a somber frame of mind, and doing all he could to will himself out of it, when Awena appeared, metaphorically parting the clouds. There was a creak of the door opening into his study, and there she was, a bright flower against the room's dark paneling. Somehow she had slipped past the guard of Mrs. Hooser.

Ralph Waldo Emerson had said that nature always wears the colors of the spirit. So, thought Max, did Awena. Springtime yellow and pink were the choices for today's gauzy, sweeping gown, gathered high at the waist by a wide belt of bronze fabric. She wore thin sandals, which he knew without question were vegetarian, for Awena literally walked the talk. Her toenails had been buffed to a natural pink gloss.

Max scooped her into his arms and they kissed. After a long while, Max stood back, searching her luminous eyes, touching the face that glowed so pearl-like, the skin incandescent and soft.

He led her to the sofa, where she rested curled in his arms, her head against his chest. Both were filled with wonder and relief at finding the other sound and whole and unchanged. Slowly, they began to speak of the light nonsense that weaves lives together. How was the course received? Did he get a chance to look in on Mrs. Tribble as she'd asked? Would the rain never stop?

On they went, talking softly, catching up on each other's news.

Awena, of course, had heard all about the murder, but she knew Max would tell her what he could in his own way and time. And eventually, the subject drifted there, Max saying what little he knew as fact, and leaving out many of his suspicions.

He lifted the hair off the nape of her neck and then watched as it fell back into place, smooth as water.

"Your hair is beautiful," he said.

"I've just come from the Cut and Dried," she said. "Everyone was there. Including Melinda. She often is. And—you know, Max, there was this odd moment. . . . I'm still wondering what it meant. . . ."

"Oh?" said Max. "I . . ." And here he hesitated. Melinda's behavior and emotional reactions seemed to him to be all over the map, but his moral obligation was to avoid anything approaching gossip. Maybe the grief, so lacking when Max had talked with her and Farley, was finally seeping in. "I hope that's a good sign," he said at last. "That she was out and about, doing normal things."

"I'm not so sure," said Awena vaguely.

"What did you mean by 'odd moment'?"

"Oh. That had to do with Gabby and Annette, not Melinda. It's a bit hard to describe, but Gabby was working on a client and I think she may have seen or heard something that upset her. Or Annette did. Or maybe Annette was just reacting to Gabby, because Gabby dropped a bowlful of hair color, you see, and Annette dropped a jar about the same time. There was a lot going on—the place is hopping, with all that's been going on in the village."

"It's not like Gabby to overreact, I wouldn't have thought."

"Nor I."

"What did she hear? Or see?"

"Do you know, I thought about it on the way over here, and what she seemed to be reacting to was the BBC broadcast. But that makes no sense at all. . . ."

Max waited.

"BBC Radio Four was broadcasting the news headlines," Awena went on. "It was something about the prime minister and a visit to the U.S.—New York or Washington. He'd be attending a play and having some sort of fancy dinner. I'm sorry to say I didn't pay close attention because, frankly, it didn't seem important or even remotely interesting."

She sat up, pushing against Max's chest.

"Cotton seems to be following up a lead."

"Who says?" Max asked.

"The Greek chorus over at the salon, of course," replied Awena.

"I think we can agree on this: Everything said in this village gets distorted by the time it gets to the third telling."

"They are *so* excited to be part of an investigation."

Max was trying to envision Cotton attempting to conduct his investigation, exposed to a wave of chemicals, and to women—and sometimes men—with foil and clips in their hair, and with dye painted at their temples.

"Of course," said Awena, "it could have been the tattoo."

"What tattoo?"

"The customer Gabby was working on had a tattoo on the side of her neck. She was coloring this woman's hair, sectioning it off, and as she pulled the hair from the woman's neck, I saw the tattoo. It may have been that. Unless she heard someone talking about something that upset her. They were all talking at once—a lot of it was Hollywood nonsense."

Max said mildly, "Many people feel that way about tattoos, particularly people of Gabby's generation. They find them off-putting."

It was, he reflected, all one with the current trend of piercings and tattoos and other adornments, trends Max himself did not understand. It reminded him too much of slavery and branding, of prison camps. The next generation would probably go back to spats and pocket watches, or whatever would most startle or shock their elders.

"This was more than dislike. Gabby looked positively ill about the moment she saw the tattoo—drained of color."

Max thought back to the dinner party, remembering the look he'd seen, her face going rigid at the sight of the painting.

What was up with that? He could see no pattern.

A tattoo. A seascape painting.

He idly wondered aloud who would have known about the dinner party—known who was invited. It was the only thing out of the ordinary in Thaddeus's life, so far as he knew, in the days leading up to his death.

"I think everyone knew about it. I myself mentioned it in talking with Mrs. Watling at the post office."

That explains it, he thought.

Awena again nestled against him. "Oh, and Miss Pitchford was there also."

That really explained it. MI5 is the UK's domestic spy agency and GCHQ is its eavesdropping agency. To Max's certain knowledge, neither held a candle to the combined might of Miss Pitchford and Mrs. Watling, the local postmistress. It's not that either of them had too much time on her hands—far from it, in fact, for Nether Monkslip was home to the most industrious group of women Max had ever encountered— but that the pair were so plugged into the village doings that Max sometimes felt every heartbeat was being monitored as on an EKG. They operated out of various headquarters: the post office and local store, of course, and the beauty parlor. When their updates reached the local pubs at either end of the village, the men generally took over the news analysis and dissemination.

"What was it a tattoo of?" Max asked, circling back to the earlier topic.

Awena tilted her head, gazing at him from under her exquisitely arched brows. Max wished he had the talent to paint her portrait, just as she was at this moment, the firelight gleaming in her hair and eyes, casting the left side of her face into shadow.

"Nothing too rare or unusual," she said. "A dragon or serpent—a very elaborate design. But Gabby couldn't finish what she was doing, and she said she wasn't feeling well. Annette covered for her."

"Gabby is as strong as an ox," said Max.

"I'd have said so, too." Awena shook her head. "It really was the most enormous tattoo. Why do young people do that to themselves? I will never understand. I guess I'm getting old."

"Thirty-eight is not old. You think now it was the tattoo that bothered Gabby?"

"It had to be that or the prime minister's plans. Not likely, that. He often surprises us, but not to that extent."

"And it was a dragon?"

"I think so. Some mythical creature anyway. Breathing fire—you know the sort of thing. The flames sort of wrapped around the girl's neck. It was pretty, in its own way—colored in blue or black, with green and red highlights, is what I recall. Oh, and there were initials, letters, sort of intertwined with the creature's scales."

The Girl with the Dragon Tattoo, thought Max. Could Gabby have been put off by the image of something that didn't exist except in fantasy? Something from his MI5 course-work training flashed into his mind. A lecture on—what was the word? *Steganography?* A lecture that referenced Herodotus, of all people. The ancient Greek historian. And now Max remembered Herodotus had been mentioned in connection with the art of the hidden code, for Herodotus had recorded the story of a man who had shaved the head of his slave, then tattooed a secret message on the slave's skull. Once the slave's hair grew back, the message was of course hidden and the slave could safely be used to transmit a warning message of enemy plans to invade.

Steganography was still used by modern terrorists and very recently by Russian spies. Photos containing hidden text files were uploaded online, and then someone knowing where to look used special software to "coax" the words out. What appeared to be an innocent color photo of a flower, for example, might in fact have every five hundredth pixel changed to correspond to a letter of the alphabet. The human eye could not detect such a change, but of course a computer could.

During World War II, the Resistance used good old-fashioned invisible ink to send otherwise innocuous-sounding messages. A bill for horse manure could hide the plans for Allied troop movements.

He wondered: Could it be something like that? Gabby as a spy was hard to reconcile in his mind, but the hallmark of a good spy—as he well knew—was that no one ever suspected him or her.

"Did she appear to know the tattooed girl?" Max asked Awena.

Awena lifted her shoulders in a shrug. "She didn't seem to be a regular customer, no. In fact . . . hold on." Awena thought a moment, trying to bring the scene back into her mind. Then, slowly, as if reading from a teleprompter, she said, "The girl said she'd only just moved here. From Swansea, I think it was. From Wales, at any rate, judging by her accent."

Awena would know, thought Max. She was herself from Wales.

"Did she say how she'd come to be at the Cut and Dried? I know some people go to Monkslip-super-Mare for a haircut and make a day of it."

"I'm not sure this girl's budget would stretch to some of the places in Monkslip-super-Mare. I heard her tell Gabby she'd been recommended by a friend. That was a bit of a laugh, actually, but Gabby took it in her stride—she can do even the wildest haircuts and colors; that doesn't phase her. She's very modern in some ways—good at what she does. Anyway, I heard the girl say she lives in one of the council houses. Maybe Mrs. Hooser knows who she is. I don't know the girl's name, but I've seen her around the village, pushing a baby about in a pram. And Max—"

He interrupted her, intent on mining her memory while the images were still fresh. "You don't remember what the initials were, on the tattoo?"

"I don't, Max. I've been trying to remember. BRT? BRP? It wasn't a *word,* if you know what I mean, or it might have been more memorable. It was more like a license plate number. Whatever it was made Gabby jump—that's true, the more I think about it. She had all she could do to take a deep breath and continue with her work, or try to. Then she said she wasn't feeling well, and took Annette up on her offer of help. But she *was* feeling well. I mean to say, she had been fine a few moments earlier, and she was fine a few minutes later."

Awena added musingly, "Gabby is what Lucie calls *vieux jeu.* Old-fashioned, despite her ability to keep up with trends for her work. Not only in her mode of dress and her own hairstyle but in her worldview, too. There is purity about her; I suppose that is the way to express it. She sees the world clearly but wishes things were not as they are. It is surprising. That someone her age could still have that air of . . . of innocence."

Max thought that might be a condition much to be desired, although he could imagine the drawbacks, too.

Awena said, "I'm going to stop by later with some dried herbs Gabby wanted. I'll see what I can find out. She would tell me what's up, I think."

Max nodded absently. Then he said, "No." He screwed up his eyes, thinking hard about dragons. Absently, he added, "No, don't do that. We don't know what we're dealing with here. And until we do . . ."

Her fine clear eyes flashed, as she searched his face. "You don't suspect Gabby! That's too wild. What motive could she have?"

"None that I know of. And until we know the motive in this case . . ."

In her soft voice, Awena continued: "She is someone to confide in, Gabby. That is the quality she exudes. A good trait for a hairdresser. She might know quite a lot about what goes on around here that she isn't telling."

"Do you know," said Max, "I have never felt compelled to confide anything in my barber."

Awena smiled. "You just don't understand. Women go to the hairdresser's to focus just on themselves, even if just for an hour every few weeks or months. Men don't need that sort of outlet."

"Yes, they do. It's called a pub."

She smiled. "Okay. You win."

Max held her hand lightly in his own, then said, "You say Melinda seemed to be getting on?"

"Yes," replied Awena. "Too well, if you know what I mean. It is hard to imagine how those two ended up together, Thaddeus and Melinda."

"Isn't it just."

"I mean, do you feel overall that Melinda has or has ever had a great interest in the theater? In playwriting?"

"No. No, I shouldn't have said so. The *trap*pings of theater, perhaps. The clothing and the costumes and the opening nights."

"And the drama," said Awena.

"Perhaps a bit of that, as well." Max paused, then said, "I keep wondering: Could Thaddeus have known something he wasn't supposed to know? Is that why he was killed?"

"It's possible. By that criterion, half the village would be dead by now, though."

"True."

"Starting with Miss Pitchford."

"I'm afraid that's also true," said Max. "Thaddeus was 'from away,' so whatever anyone knows is probably from that time and place." A sudden thought occurred to him. There had been a time he himself had posed as a barber, helping MI5 collect DNA from hair cuttings to ensure they were following the right man, a double agent.

"Thaddeus had that glorious mane of hair," said Max. "Hair that had never turned gray. Was he a customer at the shop?"

Was he going off on complete tangents now? Max wondered. The image of Gabby collecting hair samples for MI5 was a nonstarter. But again, she might just be the perfect agent—the undetectable kind.

"His hair never was allowed to turn gray, perhaps," Awena said. "I've no idea if he was a customer. His hair color looked completely natural to me, but it can't have been—can it?"

"That goes with the actor's territory, that sort of vanity," said Max. "And with some politician's. They rely on their looks. It's only natural."

Still, Awena's comment gave Max pause to think. Most crimes could be traced back to the victim's disposition or character. Could Thaddeus's vanity have been a factor contributing to his death? And what sort of motive was that? His vanity had been annoying, nothing more. . . . Unless over time it had become the sand in the oyster. Max's thoughts kept coming back to Melinda, a woman living with such an irritant, day by day—and seeing a way out, in the shape of Farley.

Awena looked around the snug little room, then said, "It's so much quieter around the vicarage without Luther."

"I assume you mean the cat."

"The Bad Seed. Yes."

Luther, the church mouser, was back on the job after a temporary hiatus over the Christmas holidays. He was meant to be locked away in the vestry during services, but more often than not he was nowhere to be found when the time came for his incarceration. Max, glancing up toward the choir loft, would catch a glimpse of him through the railings, sitting quietly with his tail curled around his front paws, his green eyes following every movement of the service.

"He shows no sign of wanting to return to the vicarage. Mercifully, for Thea's sake. And mine."

"Ye-e-ess," said Awena slowly. "Not entirely domesticated is Luther."

An hour had passed without either of them realizing it. Looking at her watch, Awena sat up and said, "I need to get to the shops—I'm out of fresh food after being gone a week. Also . . ." She hesitated. "Also, I thought I'd pick up what bits of information I can. I doubt anyone will be in the Cavalier for a while yet. They're still under the dryer, most of them."

"Awena . . ." It was said with a warning note, the same sort of note he was used to hearing from Cotton, who both encouraged Max's contributions to investigations and worried about the consequences for Max, in equal measure.

"There are things the police will never hear," she said with quiet assurance. "Trust me on this. If you want to find out what is going on— and you do want to find that out, don't you?"

"Not at such a cost—"

"Then leave it to me. I *am* anxious to get home, though. I hope my herb garden wasn't completely destroyed by rain." She stood to go. He might not have spoken. At the door, she turned and said, "Whom do you suspect?"

Max answered indirectly. It was a trait of his that, she knew, drove Cotton quite mad. Awena was more accepting that all would be revealed in time.

"I suspect everyone," Max said. "But I have a question for you: What do you know about poisonous plants that grow in this area? What's locally available, in a poisoning sense?"

"Well, foxglove, to name one. It's a poison, of course, but it also has homeopathic uses: Digitalis can be a lifesaver, and it also can be deadly. That is true of many things, of course. The dosage is what makes the difference, and the way it's administered."

"What about mushrooms?"

"What comes to mind first is the death's cap mushroom. I've seen it in Raven's Wood quite often. There is no real homeopathic use for the death's cap. Best not to go near it."

"I wasn't planning to." Max looked at his watch. The time change was still playing havoc with him.

"Lucie is coming over in a minute," he told Awena. "She wanted to talk about something. She seemed a bit upset."

"That's not like Lucie. Ironic and detached, yes. Upset, no." Awena paused. "I missed you, Max. Maybe you could come over tomorrow evening? I'll have some groceries in and I'll have caught up on the laundry and things by then. We can have a quiet evening in, with all the time in the world."

He kissed her. "All the time in the world sounds wonderful."

They left it that he would be at her house by eight the next evening. They stood apart at the vicarage door, saying their goodbyes and husbanding their body language on the chance they were being observed—a very good chance in a village as tightly woven as Nether Monkslip. Max leaned casually against the doorpost with arms crossed, watching her. Nothing could hide the contentment on his face from the most casual observer.

Awena left, and he went inside to keep watch as she passed by the vicarage window. He felt his heart expand at the sight of her, although she'd just left his side, stepping smartly out with her basket swinging from her arm.

CHAPTER 20
All That Glitters

A few minutes later Max again picked up his thriller, and once again put it down. Halfway through the telling, the author began to describe the torture and killing of innocents, and Max realized he'd never get through this particular book. He had, after all, had to live among maniacs, and had come to understand the twisted rationalizations that guided their choices. That reality had been enough for several lifetimes.

Beyond that, he suspected he'd have trouble focusing on any sort of story right now, being in the midst of his own. Nether Monkslip seemed to be being tested at every turn lately. Why here? wondered Max. Of all the blameless, innocuous places on the planet, why Nether Monkslip?

Mrs. Hooser knocked, opened the study door, and shouted through that Lucie Cuthbert was here to see him.

And Lucie came in carrying a dripping umbrella. This could only mean Mrs. Hooser had again repurposed the stand by the door. Sometimes she used it as a vase, sometimes to hold her mop and broom as she worked in the kitchen. Max, taking the umbrella from Lucie to set it near the hearth, looked out the window and saw it had started to rain. Umbrellas in bright primary colors bobbed everywhere he looked.

"Have a seat, please, Lucie," he said, waving to one of the leather chairs flanking the skirted sofa by the fireplace. "And tell me what this is about."

For a visit from Lucie Cuthbert was unprecedented. Lucie kept her own counsel and made her own decisions, as a rule. And as a rule, they were wise decisions.

"Something happened. I don't know what to do. I thought maybe you . . ."

"Go on," said Max. It must be important, for her to bring him into it. Just not important enough to go to DCI Cotton with.

"It happened the night of the dinner party. As all of you were leaving, there was the usual fuss and confusion in the hallway over coats and umbrellas and things. So I almost didn't notice, and the chances were against my noticing. And I think he knew that *very* well, the sneak."

Max waited. Lucie would tell the story in her own way. He didn't need to ask who "he" was, either, although he supposed it might have been Dr. Bruce Winship who had aroused this little fit of passion.

"It was Thaddeus, you see. Quick as a flash, he reached out his hand; all our backs were turned, and, well I'm almost certain, you see . . ."

"Yes?"

"He stole it."

An encouraging nod here.

"He stole a vase."

"A vase?"

"Yes, a little vase, big enough only for one bud. It is not a valuable vase, but it has sentimental value for me, as it belonged to my mother. I keep it—kept it—on top of the little table in the hallway. You may have noticed it there when you came in?"

He hadn't particularly noticed it. The little table she mentioned contained a hazardous collection of little breakables, most of them crystal or porcelain. His only reason for looking at it had been to avoid accidentally knocking into it.

"You're certain it was he?"

She nodded, allowing herself a single dramatic gesture, waving her arms about to demonstrate her outrage. "But of course! As certain as I can be. He was the only one near enough. It couldn't have been anyone else."

He considered what she had told him, and the word *kleptomania* emerged. Thaddeus was a kleptomaniac? Max turned the idea over in his mind. From what little he knew about the disorder, kleptomaniacs stole items they didn't need or even want. Both valuable and useless things. It was an impulsive act; the *thrill* of stealing was what mattered.

Max felt there was a stray bit of precious metal in what she had said and he struggled to glean what it was.

Then he remembered Melinda's telling him her earrings had been stolen. Did that fit into what Lucie was reporting, somehow—a little puzzle piece that not only matched the color of another piece but slotted in beside it? But—would a man steal earrings from his own wife? It didn't fit any definition of kleptomania he had ever heard of, but he supposed it was possible.

"And you're wondering what to do," said Max.

Lucie nodded. "It's awkward; you do see? Melinda has just lost her husband. I can't think of a way to say that he stole something from me just before he died and 'Can I have it back now, please?' And now she's talking about moving away. I'm afraid the vase might go with her. She won't realize it's stolen. You do see . . ."

Max did. She didn't know how to ask for it back from Melinda—and clearly she wanted Max to ask for her.

But he was more taken by what she'd said about Melinda's leaving.

"Did she tell you herself she was leaving?"

"Yes," she said, nodding as she pushed back the glossy wave of hair that fell over one eye. "Well, it's all over the Cut and Dried—and I did panic a bit when I heard. It meant that asking her couldn't wait forever."

"Yes, I see," said Max. "I'm not certain I could intervene right now. But I can assure you she will officially be dissuaded by DCI Cotton from going anywhere until this matter is cleared up. I shouldn't worry too much in the meantime, if I were you. If there is any way to introduce the topic to her, I will."

Actually, knowing what he knew of Melinda's blossoming relationship with Farley, he doubted she would be too cut up by news of her husband's weakness for taking what didn't belong to him. Odd as the whole conversation was, he wasn't inclined to dismiss it out of hand. The problem was, it didn't go much further toward explaining the motive for the crime. The last thing he would expect from Lucie would be that she'd kill someone over a minor theft such as this. There were dozens of motives that could lead to murder: lust, anger, envy. Even love could be a motive. But these were strong impulses, the unhealthiest of which often were the result of a long, festering process.

Not long afterward, Lucie left the vicarage, looking more relieved and grateful than perhaps the situation warranted. A burden shared being a burden halved, thought Max. Clearly she felt the ball was now in his court.

He was turning toward his desk when Mrs. Hooser, in her abrupt, aggrieved way, announced Bernadina Steed. Max always wondered at this tone she adopted; it wasn't as if Mrs. Hooser were doing much of anything important, yet she treated each interruption as if she had just been on the verge of a major scientific breakthrough.

Bernadina strode in, hand outstretched in the exuberant sort of greeting perfected by the successful estate agent. She wore designer jeans that defeated the original practical purpose of jeans, since they carried a famous logo that priced them in the three-figure range. She also wore the top half of a bright yellow suit over her open-necked shirt, the jacket boxy in style and with black piping and an inviting nubby texture. Even Max knew it was Chanel.

"Hello, Father Max. I was just driving by and I saw Lucie leaving the vicarage. I worried . . ."

"Yes?" prompted Max. "Worried about what?"

"About something Lucie may have told you. Something she may have caught wind of. If so, I'd rather it came from me. I didn't want you to get the wrong impression."

"Lucie isn't really a gossip," said Max. It was true: Lucie was generally too busy running her shop to be caught up in the village gossip stream.

"I know. I meant . . . Lucie wouldn't see it as gossip, you realize. To her, it's just part of life. She is very, well, *French*, you know. They see these things differently. But in these circumstances . . . when there's been a murder . . ."

She sat very still, blushing but unbowed.

"It's best to come clean." This had to be about her affair with Thaddeus. Max was grappling with whether to tell her he'd already heard all this from Cotton. Or would she be aware of that? Max's involvement in anything that looked like a murder investigation in or around Nether Monkslip was getting to be common knowledge. Her coming here might all be part of an elaborate double bluff. It was precisely what an innocent person would do—as would a guilty person pretending innocence.

In the end, after a bit of hemming and hawing, she admitted to the affair in a gush of reminiscence tinged with remorse.

"It was over ages ago," she told him. "I am not particularly proud of it, I must say. Particularly since he turned out to be the most frightful little creep: It was like he was kissing a mirror the whole time. But it seemed better to be open and aboveboard with DCI Cotton when I spoke with him."

Max, for his part, was having the strongest sense of déjà vu. Both

Kayla Prince and Bernadina Steed. Who else? Thaddeus, despite his years, certainly got around.

Max hoped it would prove to be no one else he knew, someone even more unlikely than Bernadina—for it was starting to look as if Thaddeus had had quite the checkered past, with women from all walks of life.

She added, "Awena would say I was dishonoring my ancestors by my behavior. I have come to believe she is right about that."

Max almost missed the import of what she was saying.

"Awena knew about the affair?"

"Yes, I confided in her. It worried me when he came to live here, you understand. I was afraid of the awkward meeting. You know the kind of thing. I needn't have worried. He didn't care anymore and nor did I. Melinda, if she guessed, certainly didn't care."

Max was still struggling with the concept of Awena's withholding this information from him, when surely she knew it was relevant to the investigation. Bernadina seemed to sense the problem.

"It was women's business, Max. Something told to Awena in confidence. She would never break a confidence, but she *would* encourage me to tell the truth. Which she did. Which I did—just now."

Max was slightly taken aback. It was the first sense he'd had of an Awena operating on her own, out of step with him.

Bernadina left soon afterward. Max remained in his seat, staring at the trainers on his feet, and thinking. This made two women who'd been involved in some manner of affair with Thaddeus. What were the chances there were more abandoned women in his past? Whoever did the abandoning, breakups were always painful and difficult, and no one's idea of fun.

Who would be likely to know more? Max wondered. He logged on to the Internet, with its agonizingly slow vicarage connection, did a search or two, and came up with the name of Thaddeus's agent, and his phone number. A young woman, the agent's secretary, came on the line on the third ring. Max invoked Cotton's name and learned the name of the director with whom Thaddeus had most recently had dealings: one Henry Cork. No doubt DCI Cotton's people had gotten there first, but one never knew. . . . People talking to the police often left things out—either from nervousness or out of an abundance of caution.

So Max dialed the offices of Henry Cork, where he exchanged words with Cork's answering machine. The machine assured him that its human checked messages from its mobile phone regularly and would get back to him shortly.

To Max's surprise, the enormous black Bakelite phone on the study desk rang back almost instantly. He'd told the answering machine that he was arranging the services for Thaddeus Bottle and would like the director to deliver a few words. This was nothing but the truth, so far as it went.

The two men exchanged introductions.

"I'm afraid I'm in the middle of rehearsal, so I'll have to keep this short," Cork told Max, who could hear the hubbub of a stage production in the background. In Max's imagination, the man wore the costume of the auteur: the satin-lined cloak, the hat, the cigarette holder. Then: "Why is the decanter sitting on the chair cushion? And where in hell is Rufus?"

A tinny little voice answered in an apparently displeasing manner.

"Go tell him to take his hands off the prop girl and get his ass out here. He enters stage right, in case he's forgotten, or thinks we're going to drop him from the rafters like Tinker Bell."

Cork returned his attention to the phone call.

"Now, you want me to say a few nice words about the deceased, is that it? Well, this will call on all my skills of diplomacy, I hope you're aware. But I'll give it a shot. The old bast—I mean, the old man helped me keep the lights burning for a number of years, in his heyday. It's the least I can do. That one play of his about the blacksmith . . . Funny how an irredeemable shit can write such moving prose at times. But he was a sneak, always creeping about, listening at keyholes. And I think he stole my pen once—my good pen. Where is Mary Ann?"

Again, the sounds of consternation and feet thumping heavily across a wooden stage.

"Ah," said Max, almost as though it were news to him that Thaddeus was not universally beloved. "He could be difficult?"

The man laughed. "Yes, he could be all that. He could be self-involved. All of them are—actors. You won't find any shrinking violets onstage, to begin with. And the competition for dwindling parts makes all of them worse. That said, Thaddeus had a gift for getting people's backs up, for the left-handed compliment, if not the outright lie, usually delivered in a roomful of people, so that to respond would make the target of the moment only look foolish or ungrateful. It was subtly done, but the malice behind it was real enough. And that was only when he was feeling charitable. God help you if you really got on his nerves."

"I see," said Max quietly. Delicately, he cleared his throat before saying, "I also was rather given to understand he had a roving eye?"

"Got it in one, Vicar. That he did. He coveted his neighbor's wife, and he coveted his neighbor's goods, and he coveted his neighbor's success. How I am expected to turn all that into a comforting eulogy for the grieving widow, I don't know. Although, something tells me she won't be grieving long. What was her name—Melissa?"

"Melinda."

"Right. I don't imagine that hookup worked out as she'd planned. Somehow, she'd gotten the idea Thaddeus was awfully famous and just rolling in it when they met—at least that was my impression. That was certainly my first impression," he added, underlining the point. Then once again, he broke off, shouting, "Stage left! Stage left! What do you mean, you can't? You can walk, even if you can't act—but do quit shuffling about

like someone's stuffed a goose in your knickers. Well, move the god-
damn coffee table, then. Where in fuck has Props got to?"

There was a mumbled response, as from a man underwater.

"Well, go and tell her we do not pay her to talk on her mobile all day
with her boyfriend. Get her in here. *Stat!*"

Into the receiver, he said, "Was that all, Vicar?" Max could almost
hear him removing the snarl from his face as spoke in (what was for him,
anyway) a more modulated and reasonable tone, like a conductor shouting a train arrival.

"I think so," said Max. "I'll have someone let you know the date for
the service."

The phone rang as soon as Max put the receiver back in its cradle.
It was Cotton, calling to tell him the coroner, following up on his wild
idea for what had been the actual cause of Thaddeus's death, had hit the
jackpot.

Several minutes later, when Max rang off, he was more puzzled than
before.

He opened the leather-bound copy of the King James Bible that always sat on his desk; it had been a gift from his mother on his ordination. He turned the pages to the Book of Job, looking for the quote he
knew was somewhere in there—the quote printed out in the first letter
he had received through the mail slot. There it was, in Job, chapter 20.
The quote about the poison was sandwiched in between verses fifteen and
seventeen:

He hath swallowed down riches, and he shall vomit them up
again: God shall cast them out of his belly.

He shall suck the poison of asps: the viper's tongue shall
slay him.

He shall not see the rivers, the floods, the brooks of honey
and butter.

In their focus on poison, had he and Cotton missed other clues, clues as to motive? Max read on. Lines eighteen and nineteen read:

That which he laboured for shall he restore, and shall not swallow it down: according to his substance shall the restitution be, and he shall not rejoice therein.

Because he hath oppressed and hath forsaken the poor; because he hath violently taken away an house which he builded not . . .

Well, that made no sense at all. So far as he knew, Thaddeus and Melinda had bought their hideous big house in the normal way. With a sigh, Max closed the book, leaving a bookmark at the passage. Something might occur to him later.

He heaved himself up out of the chair, throwing his arms wide with a stretch.

Then the idea struck him, stopping him, arms still flung wide. A tantalizing hint tugged at his mind. He thought it might be related to the conversation at Lucie's dinner party.

Max decided to take Thea for a walk by the river. A spot of fresh air might help him think things through.

CHAPTER 21
Matters of the Heart II

Several girls from the local soccer team walked by Max and Thea. They wore neon lime green socks, and were apparently on their way to or from practice. Several sneaked a peek at Max from under thick mascaraed lashes, and one of them managed a shy, whispered "Hello." Max distractedly returned the smile.

The river this morning wore gray on gray, shimmying its way to the sea like a fashion model down a runway. A mist that carried the smell of metallic rain washed his face. He stopped and closed his eyes a moment, breathing deeply of the reviving scent.

When he opened his eyes, it was to see Dr. Winship headed his way. He'd come out the back gate of the garden of his house and office, which led into River Lane.

"I was just on my way to see you," began Max, but the approach of a good-humored, if pompous-looking, man from the direction of Vicarage Road stopped his thoughts. Marching to the sounds of a military band only he could hear, the Major beamed at both men in turn, then said, "No need to ask what you're talking about. The village is on fire with it, what? The scuttlebutt around the canteen says Thaddeus Bottle was *poi*soned."

How the devil, thought Max, had word of that got around so quickly? Had someone overheard his conversation with Cotton, or one of Cotton's conversations with his team? Actually, Max realized, there were a dozen other ways Miss Pitchford or one of the trained assistants she kept on a string could have sniffed out the story. He'd have to warn Cotton.

"And by a poisoned arrow, no less," added the Major. "Fiendishly clever. I knew a fellow once who'd been in North Africa with Monty. Now *there* was a chap who had seen it all and lived to tell about it. . . ." And the Major launched into another of the thundering war stories he so loved, stories that managed to imply he had been engaged in constant hand-to-hand combat on the front lines, when, in fact, great effort had been expended to keep him behind a desk, where he could do as little harm as possible.

Max was torn. Was there any point in trying to squelch the wildest versions of the stories? Did it matter? They'd have poor Thaddeus being eaten alive by crocodiles before too long.

He decided on a more subtle tack—an appeal to the Major's tendency to follow anything that could be couched as an order.

"Major," Max said, interrupting the fusillade of memories, "that is, as you know, highly confidential information. I cannot impress on you enough the importance of keeping all this sub rosa, as it were. Eyes only—you know the sort of thing. However you came to hear of it, you must tell the person responsible that DCI Cotton will deal most severely with anyone passing along these reports."

"Shot at dawn?" said the Major, delighted. He actually tapped the side of his nose, winked, and said, "Leave it with me, Padre. Loose lips sink ships, what? I'll soon put a spoke in the rumor mill."

Max doubted that very much, but it was a start. The fewer

embroidered stories going around the village, the better the chances the truth might emerge.

On occasion, the Major had been known to say something useful, without meaning to. This, apparently, was not going to be one of those times.

"I assume Interpol has been notified?" he asked, lowering his voice, and meeting the eyes of the other two in man-to-man fashion. He breathed the name Interpol with the sort of awe reserved by low-level functionaries for that holy of holies in the bureaucratic temple.

Max, who was dying to ask "Why would Interpol be interested?" said instead, "They're on it. Lyon is standing by for further instruction."

"Ah, good," said the Major. "That's well in hand, then. They always get their man."

"That's the Mounties, isn't it?" asked Bruce. Max gave him a furious nudge, but it was too late.

"Yes, you're quite right," said the Major. "Do you know, that reminds me of a chap I met once, a captain in the Mounties. Sterling chap. Terrible lisp, though. His horse was a direct descendant of Seabiscuit. . . ."

Max made ready to make his escape, leaving Bruce, who had stirred that particular pot, to deal with it alone. Thea, having sat patiently at Max's side for *hours,* was starting to look exasperated: This was not much of a walk.

"Of course, it's the Frenchies who saved his bacon during the war," said the Major. "The resistors."

"The French Resistance, yes," said Max.

"Brave people. Barking mad, of course, to have taken the chances they took."

"We need more barking mad people, then," said Max.

"It all puts me in my mind of the Peloponnesian War." He was on to his favorite topic, wartime strategy. Max's heart sank, all hope lost.

Just then, Lily Iverson came into view. She was leading a lamb by a rope around its neck. Max knew no lamb of Lily's would ever be headed for the slaughter, but what she might be doing other than exercising the animal it was difficult to say. It might be a show-and-tell offering for the knitting circle.

Also knowing the Major's tender spot for Lily, Max unabashedly made use of it now.

"Look," cried Max. "It's Lily. She was telling me she'd like a word with you, Major."

Lily actually had said something like that months ago, Max reasoned.

"Did she now?" The Major, already standing at full attention, drew himself a little taller, tugged his jacket firmly over his wide belly, and very quickly indeed walked away, without another word.

"Whew," said Bruce. "That was close. If I had to listen to one of his Falklands tales again, I think I'd scream."

"Actually," said Max, "I wanted some medical advice from you."

"It's that ankle again, isn't it? I told you so. I'll have Suzanna make an appointment for you in Monkslip-super-Mare. You're going to need X-rays."

Max nearly said, "What ankle?"—so thoroughly had Awena healed whatever had been wrong with it. The swelling and redness were completely gone.

"No," he said, "it's not that. I was talking with DCI Cotton earlier. As the entire village seems to have heard by now, he had mentioned strophanthin as a likely culprit."

"In connection with Thaddeus's death, of course."

"Yes. This was meant to be in confidence, you understand. At least until he's called his own press conference to supersede Miss Pitchford's. And even then I don't think he'd want all the details out there. It's just been confirmed by the coroner."

Bruce Winship's face was alight. "Ah," he said. "Now, that's interesting."

"How so?"

"Well, I must say, the Major wasn't entirely on the wrong track. First of all, strophanthin is made from *Strophanthus* seeds. It's a plant, you see—a climbing plant. And it's one of these things that occur in nature that appear to be little short of miraculous. You'd appreciate miraculous, wouldn't you, Max? God's divine plan, and all of that. Awena would certainly agree, and she would know all about *Strophanthus*. Anyway, when it first came to notice in the UK, physicians were very excited by it because it seemed to improve the body's circulation. Well, it *did* improve the circulation. The *Strophanthus* genus of plants was one of the wonder drugs of its time. Rather like digitalis, which, of course, is also found in nature, and is also a cure and a curse.

"The Scottish physician Fraser was a big promoter of *Strophanthus*. The isolation of purified strophanthin—yes, it all caused quite a stir. This was a hundred years ago or more—late nineteenth century. The explorer David Livingstone knew of it, too. However, the dosage had to be just so, and the method of delivery just so, and there were different varieties, and because it is fast-acting, one had to be extremely careful, you know."

"And why is that?"

Bruce regarded him over the top of his glasses. "Obviously because it's deadly poisonous, my good man. Deadly! A bitter and highly toxic glycoside. Nothing to lark about with if you don't know what you're doing. Ghanaian healers knew what to do, even if the colonials didn't, and the healers guarded their secrets carefully. What you do is mash the stems and boil them, steeping them into a sort of fermented alcoholic tonic. But the dosage had to be just right, or you'd kill the patient. Heart failure."

"What if you *wanted* to kill the patient?" asked Max.

"You'd inject him with it. And for choice, you'd use an arrow. Grind up the seed, you see. That's where you get to the heart of the matter, so to speak—in the seed."

"Poisoned arrows," said Max, barely able to contain his skepticism.

He had dismissed the idea because it came from the Major, who was living proof that even a broken clock is right two times a day.

"Poisoned arrows aren't a myth, Max. They're absolute fact. Knock your enemies flat out with a bit smeared on the tip of your arrow, you would. Once it entered the bloodstream, your enemy wasn't going to cause you any more trouble."

"But is it still in use today?"

"Of course it is. Once something like that is discovered, it can't be *un*discovered, if you know what I mean. And it has its legitimate uses, as I've said." The doctor cleared his throat, always a sign with Bruce, as with the Major, that one was going to receive possibly more detail than one wanted.

"It all puts me in mind of a notorious murder case from the late 1940s, in Australia," Bruce began. "You'll like this, Max—it's a spy thriller, really. A man was found on a beach, nearly unconscious, but able to move about slightly. People thought he was drunk and they left him alone. He was dressed in a suit—flawlessly dressed, in fact. When at last people realized he was dead—the next day—it was too late, not that much could have been done to save the poor beggar anyway. There was an autopsy, which concluded he'd probably died of poisoning. Digitalis and strophanthin were the leading candidates, but all they had to go on then was the condition of the body, you see. His eyes, spleen, and liver all showed abnormalities. Repeated testing showed no trace of poison, however. Too much time had passed, and strophanthin back then was as close to being an undetectable poison as you can get."

"Why do you say it's a spy thriller?"

"They never did figure out who he was, or exactly how he was killed," Light from the river glinted off Bruce's glasses, and the eyes behind sparked with intense interest. Max sometimes wondered whether Bruce's fascination with crime was entirely healthy. "No one ever came forward to claim him," Bruce Winship went on. "Sad, that. Someone had removed all traces of anything that might help identify him. At the main railway station, they found a piece of abandoned luggage that, for various reasons, seemed to have been his, but anything identifiable had been removed. They couldn't even say for certain if it was a case of murder or suicide.

"Finally, John Cleland, an expert at the University of Adelaide, was brought into the examination. And he found a concealed pocket in the dead man's trousers that other investigators had missed. Inside was a scrap of paper torn from the *Rubáiyát;* translated from the Persian, the words meant 'It is ended.'"

"I am remembering this story now," said Max slowly. "Months later, the rare book from which the words had been torn was found. There was a code written inside."

"A code that could only be seen under ultraviolet light. No one could ever break the code, neither experts nor amateurs. They couldn't trace that particular edition of the book, either. One possibility was that it was a ginned-up copy and the code was some kind of key. There also were potential witnesses who refused to cooperate. It's a mystery, Max, but almost certainly he was a spy."

Max was thinking that was how spies too often ended up: murdered.

"Did you notice," Max asked Bruce at last, "that Gabby had a strange reaction to that painting on the wall, that night we had dinner at Lucie and Frank's house?

Bruce shrugged. "Maybe it was the wallpaper," he said. "I thought it was ghastly, but Suzanna tells me I have no fashion sense. Do you know, Suzanna said something rather interesting to me just now, about the case. She said, 'Why didn't the dog bark?'"

Max looked at him. "Did she mean the Bottles' dog?"

"Yes. She said it put her in mind of that Sherlock Holmes story."

"The Hound of the Baskervilles."

"The very one. You see, Suzanna suffers from insomnia, and the seasonal time changes make it worse. I've prescribed long walks before bedtime, especially now, when it's not too cold outside. She says she walked past the train station the night of the murder and just after she passed the lane to the Bottles' house, she heard something that made her turn around. It was the sound of a footfall, or of leaves rustling, or something. She thought perhaps it was a rabbit. Anyway, when she turned, she saw the back of someone—someone wearing a hooded coat against the light drizzle. And the someone appeared to have emerged from the path to the Bottles' place. But it was quiet otherwise, and that was what was wrong—she realized much later that the dog would have barked at an intruder. But it was dead silent. As the dog wasn't harmed to keep it silent—she asked around about that later—she wondered . . ."

This, thought Max, explained her new detective role. "Why didn't she say something right away?"

"As I say, it took her a while to put things together. And just as she realized this might be important, Elka gave her a hard time about her habit of speaking before thinking things through. Besides, she couldn't tell for certain where the person came from—the Bottles' or just from the woods near their place. So Suzanna asked me just now what I thought she should do. I said she should say something to Cotton immediately, even though it may not mean much. Maybe the dog was asleep, after all."

"Or if it was the killer," said Max, "it was someone the dog knew well."

Max parted from Bruce some time later, lost in thought. One nagging idea kept at him, and it seemed to center around something that had happened at the dinner party at the Cuthberts' home. He remembered Bruce talking once again on his favorite topic, which could best be summed up as "The Killer Amongst Us."

Max walked back to the vicarage, released Thea from her leash, and wandered aimlessly around the study, unable to settle, taking books off the shelves at random and putting them back. He shuddered as he put back on its shelf a modern-day edition of *Foxe's Book of Martyrs*, with its woodcuts of people being burned at the stake. Somewhere he had read that kindly executioners, taking pity on the victims, would make sure the wood smoked as much as possible, so they might die (somewhat) less painfully of smoke inhalation before the flames could consume them.

Suddenly, he took a decision. It was a long shot, but anything odd that had happened in recent days needed to be investigated. And Gabby's reaction to that painting surely counted as odd.

Grabbing his coat, he shouted upstairs to Mrs. Hooser that he'd be back soon.

Minutes later, he was tapping at the brass knocker on Lucie's door, a knocker molded in the shape of a fleur-de-lis.

Max explained his mission.

Lucie hesitated.

"Father, I need to be at the shop in ten minutes," she told him, pointedly bending an elbow to look at her wristwatch.

"I know, and I'm so sorry. I won't be a minute," he told her. "I just want to look at that seascape of yours again."

"The Coombebridge?" she said. Well, it *was* Father Max; even Lucie had trouble saying no to Father Max. "All right, go ahead. Just close the door behind you when you leave. It locks automatically."

He thanked her and moved toward the dining room.

There it was. A painting of the sea, hanging against the black-and-white-striped wallpaper. A painting of exquisite colors—every shade of blue was represented—and pearlescent lighting, and magnificent proportions that drew the viewer inside, forcing the inevitable thoughts of the eternal sea, and the tides that unceasingly came and went—depositing debris, and dragging back the sand.

But that was all it was. A splendid painting. There were no human figures, no recognizable features to the landscape, no houses or buildings—nothing.

He stood there, remembering. Remembering how Gabby had ignored Lucie's instructions on where to sit, as if Gabby couldn't hear. Max had concluded that perhaps her hearing wasn't good—he had had to repeat a question he had put to her during dinner. Now he considered that maybe she'd had her own reasons for avoiding sitting in that chair. She had wanted her back to the painting.

How had they been seated that night? Lucie and Frank each at one end of the table. Gabby next to him—Max—and Bruce Winship next to her. Melinda Bottle across from Bruce, Thaddeus Bottle at her side, and Bernadina Steed next to Thaddeus. Max looked in vain for a hidden connection, something that might have been sparked by proximity to Thaddeus.

Shrugging, Max left the room, and left the house, pulling the door closed shut behind him.

The bells of St. Edwold's rang out the hour as he left.

Subject: Bernadina

From: Gabrielle Crew (gabby@TresRapidePoste.fr)

To: Claude Chaux (Claude43@TresRapidePoste.fr)

Date: Wednesday, March 28, 2012 3:48 P.M.

Well, well, well. Bernadina Steed, you will not be surprised to know, is also having an affair with "Melinda's" Farley. I saw them talking together, and I'm afraid there's no question of what is going on. Body language is such a giveaway.

Poor Melinda really knows how to pick them! I am debating whether to tell her. What a ruckus that would stir up, though, and what would be the point?

I've been so preoccupied by all of this. So nervy! I actually let the scissors slip today, and dropped a bowl of hair color. I must get a grip.

You see, I've remembered one other thing. Not long after I saw Melinda gathering mushrooms, her husband fell ill. She told me herself he had "a tummy." I didn't, to be honest, connect the two incidents right away. The flu was making the rounds of the village about that time.

But that's how I was so sure what she was thinking, what she was planning—what she was up to. She must have gone back to pick more mushrooms on her own, more of the death cap. Well, what is done is done. Melinda's wanting to kill Thaddeus is certainly understandable—practically justifiable homicide. Talk about "sounding brass, or a tinkling cymbal." The man was pure bombast.

Anyway, I plan to invite her over for tea, to try to get a sense of which way the investigation is going. The police seem to talk with her more often than anyone else in the case. I suspect she's in their crosshairs but doesn't know it.

Maybe I should invite them both over—Melinda and Farley? Reassure them their secrets are safe with me. What do you think of that idea?

I send all my love, your Gabby

CHAPTER 22
Coombebridge

Max walked slowly back to the vicarage from Lucie's house, his thoughts chasing one another in circles. What was it that was nagging at him? What *was* it?

The case, it occurred to him, was like an Impressionist painting: If you stood very close, you saw a blur of colors and dots. From far back, it was like viewing a completely different painting, where it all came together.

Back in his study, he pulled out his notebook and pen and flipped through the pages until he found a sheet that didn't contain notes for a potential sermon. He hesitated, then wrote boldly at the top, with a surge of hope, "MOTIVES." This was followed by several bulleted points:

- Revenge
- Money?
- Anger?
- Loss?
- Blackmail

Max paused, then added:

- Love

Since the subject was Thaddeus, revenge seemed the most likely motive. Anger suggested a spur-of-the-moment crime, and this didn't bear that hallmark. Who, after all, in his right mind would carry about with him a knife or dart dipped in poison, just on the off chance he might need to use it? No, this was clearly a planned crime, although the question of a "right mind" loomed large. The grim Scripture quotes slipped through his door indicated a slippery grasp on the situation. Someone in complete control would have maintained silence.

Max put down his pen and wandered over to the one wall of the vicarage study that contained personal treasures: his own collection of small seascape paintings. The works of artist Coombebridge, who lived in nearby Monkslip Curry, featured largely in the collection. Max had purchased most of the paintings unframed, and the owner of Noah's Ark Antiques had found antique gold-leaf frames to fit. The frames, which Noah had to all intents gifted to Max, still cost more than Max had paid for the paintings themselves. This situation rapidly had reversed itself: The formerly obscure Coombebridge had caught on in a major way, partly because his chaotic private life was a bit of a scandal. Max didn't know the current value of the works; he had bought them only because he liked them and had thought the artist had great talent that should be encouraged.

Max sat in one of the leather chairs before the now-extinguished embers in the fireplace and stared at the paintings, thinking back to the dinner party. He remembered Lucie being animated, anxious that her guests enjoy their meal, and her husband, Frank, being uncharacteristically reserved. And he thought of the strange anomaly of Thaddeus stealing from his hostess at the end of that splendid evening. He never doubted Lucie was telling the truth about that—for one thing, he felt he knew Lucie's rock-solid nature well, and it was too wild a story for her to make up.

He remembered Gabby changing her assigned place at the table. *Was* it not because she'd wanted to sit next to him, as he had flattered himself at the time, but because she'd wanted not to sit next to someone else? Or had wanted *to* sit nearer to someone?

He struggled to remember where the card had been before she'd moved it, for their hostess, Lucie, had avoided the boy/girl assignments usual to these affairs.

It seemed to him now that in moving the card, Gabby had avoided sitting next to Bernadina Steed. Could that have been it? Some sort of grudge match with Bernadina? That was rather typical of the village, these sudden spring storms that came up in friendships, storms that soon evaporated, leaving behind only minor damage. The church flower rota; a perceived or actual snub during the organizing of the Harvest Fayre; a squabble over the choice of reading for the Nether Monkslip book club. He often had been forced to play the peacemaker in these situations, for some of the skirmishes had approached a near-deadly standoff before cooler heads prevailed.

However, he'd been under no impression that Gabby and Bernadina had had any sort of previous relationship, or even that they'd met each other before the dinner party. In fact, he'd formed the distinct impression they'd not met before that evening.

It was Bernadina and Thaddeus who had had a prior relationship.

And so, clearly, had the Cuthberts with the Bottles, as evidenced by the photograph taken of the two couples together at the White Bean.

Suddenly struck by an idea, Max jumped up from his chair. Tom Hooser, who, as Max pondered, had wandered quietly into the study, and whom nothing startled, gazed up helpfully from his coloring book, as if wondering if Max's hair had caught fire and he needed some water.

Max took Tom by the hand and left him in the care of his sister in the kitchen. After shouting a farewell up the stairs to Mrs. Hooser, Max grabbed his coat and jumped in the Rover to drive to Monkslip Curry.

As he drove off, he saw Awena talking outside the Cavalier with Gabby and Melinda. He pulled over to say hello.

"We're going for tea," Awena told him. "And later I'm getting some fresh eggs from the Stauntons. I thought maybe a mushroom omelette for tonight?"

"Sounds good," said Max neutrally, on the off chance the other women didn't know these food preparations were intended for him. "I'm going to . . ." he began, and realized it was too difficult to explain. He was going to what? Even he didn't know.

"I've an errand to run," he amended. "See you soon."

"I'm interested in what lies beneath," Coombebridge was saying. He stood next to Max, staring with admiration at one of his own paintings, which rested in a half-finished condition on an easel in his artist's studio.

So am I, thought Max.

The locals called him Painter Coombebridge, but Max knew his Christian name was Lucas. He knew this because any book purporting to provide a comprehensive retrospective of painters at work along the South West coast of England always devoted several illustrated pages to Coombebridge's work. He was a legend as much for the quality of his painting as for the scandalous, wanton nature of his all-too-public private life, and was probably now at the stage of fame where neither element could be separated from the other. His talent had made him famous, it seemed to Max, but his notoriety had made him rich.

Max had amassed his small collection of Coombebridge's seascapes before he knew much about the man, captivated by the artist's mastery of light playing on a darkened sea. A dealer in Monkslip-super-Mare (as it happened, a former lover of the artist) had been granted exclusive rights to display and sell the works. The seascapes, so whimsically acquired from her gallery, were often a source of solace at the end of Max's long working day.

The artist himself was short and muscular, with pale eyebrows that sprouted like sea grass over his—yes—sea green eyes. Max knew he was approaching his eightieth year, which was impossible to believe, for he had the vigor and the sturdy build of a man half his age. His gaze and his hands were steady, and he looked set to create for easily another twenty years. Dried paint was in his hair and all over his clothing; the walls and floor of the studio were blotchy with paint and clearly had been used as a palette, a place to mix his colors before applying them. Brushes sprouted everywhere from assorted containers, like dried-flower arrangements. Randomly pinned to the walls or lying about were images torn from newspapers and magazines. Max could discern no unifying theme: There were buildings of stone and salt-and-pepper shakers and sunsets and blocks of color and dogs and, generally off in the distance, humans. Oddly, there was a magazine photo of the infamous, handsome Lord Lucan, the focus of a long-ago murder investigation, missing and presumed by many to be dead. Max remembered that the working theory was that his friends in high places had helped the man escape justice.

The painter caught Max's eye and said, "I remember that case like it was yesterday. The nobs—they always stick together, don't they?"

An American country-western song played softly in background, coming from speakers mounted near the ceiling of the studio. It was one of those songs of longing and loss: losing your girl, losing your horse, drinking too much and falling off your horse—the lyrics were easy to anticipate, and seemingly interchangeable from one song to the next.

Coombebridge's studio was just outside Monkslip Curry—a village so obscure as to make Nether Monkslip seem by comparison a metropolitan hub. It had taken Max half an hour to drive there over narrow roads, and a further quarter hour to find the cottage down one particularly rutted track.

It was a place bohemian and rifely picturesque, perched as it was on a remote, spindly outcropping overlooking the sea—the sea which was the artist's constant if ever-changing subject. From this vantage, Coombebridge had a gull's view over the water, to the east, south, and west. He had painted a famous series of fifty-two paintings in a fevered rush—one painting a week throughout the seasons. Each was of the same scene outside the cottage, and each was as different in color and composition as if painted in different countries.

"Look at the turquoise and purple in this picture," Coombebridge was saying. "The blue of the turquoise sea and the deep amethyst of the sky and the streak of goldenrod at the horizon. I don't make this up. God makes this up, and you can see evidence for Him—for Her—everywhere you look."

Looking at the seascape, Max felt that if he put out a hand to touch the water shining in the sunset, his hand would sink into the canvas like a hand sinking in bathwater. The illusion was so powerful, he felt the nerve endings of his hand tremble, stinging with the desire to touch and see if the illusion were real.

Struck by the man's unexpected religious leanings, Max smiled. He said, "I keep your paintings in my study at the vicarage. They inspire me as I write my sermons. Perhaps that is why."

"I draw no conclusions," said Coombebridge. "I can only paint what I see. I leave it to everyone else to interpret what *they* see on the canvas—as they see fit, so to speak. It's amazing to me, some of the stuff people come up with. The 'deep meaning' behind my 'intent.' When I paint, I'm on autopilot, and nothing else exists. I see, hear, think nothing. Once, I nearly burned the cottage down when I let the kettle boil itself to a melted mass. But the amazing moment comes when I step back from the canvas, to discover I've put down brushstrokes there. It's almost as if someone else came in, knocked me out, and did the painting for me while waiting for me to come around. It's 'in the blood,' I suppose. My father was an artist, too. During the war, he went over to France and used his painting as a cover so he could roam about the countryside, recruiting people to the Resistance efforts. It helped that his French was flawless. And that he could charm the paint off furniture."

Apparently, the apple had not fallen far from the tree: If his father had been able to persuade people to risk their lives participating in the Resistance, he'd been persuasive indeed. As Coombebridge turned toward him, Max felt the blast of his personality warming the air around them like a furnace.

"Now, I'm sure you didn't come here to swap theories of creativity with me, nor to seek out my views on the Creator."

Max smiled.

"It's a bit hard to explain. You've heard we've had a murder in Nether Monkslip?"

Coombebridge shook his head. "I don't read the newspapers until they aren't news anymore. I don't really care, you see." Coombebridge picked up a brush and turning slightly away, made a well-considered dab at the canvas.

"Ah," said Max, as there seemed to be no answer to that. Most people would at least ask a token question about who had been murdered, how, and why.

"Does the name Bottle mean anything to you?"

Coombebridge shook his head in the negative.

"How about the name Crew? This would be from some years back."

Again, no reaction.

"Do you remember selling a painting to anyone named Cuthbert?"

"I'm not a car salesman. I let other people handle the selling for me." Coombebridge stepped back to eye the painting from several feet away. Then resuming his stance, he made several more dabs at the canvas.

"It's just that—I'm not sure what is going on yet, but perhaps you should take extra care," said Max. "My concern may have nothing to do with your paintings, but one of them sparked a very strange reaction in one of the villagers of Nether Monkslip. I can't help but think it's tied to the murder, which occurred the next night. The police are keeping an eye out for any peculiar activity in the area, but you're so isolated here, and the police are so few. So it will be up to you, you see, to take care of yourself. Certainly any strangers out here would be noticed."

"Strangers like yourself?" asked Coombebridge, smiling. "You needn't have worried. I always look out for myself."

If the rumors he'd heard were halfway to being true, Max knew that was the case. Even at Coombebridge's age, the stories of simultaneous affairs and discarded friends and mistresses swirled. Taking care of Coombebridge would always be his number-one priority.

"Which painting of mine was it?" This was Coombebridge's only concern.

Max told him, although he soon realized that describing a seascape in words made it sound awfully like another seascape.

Coombebridge made a stab at remembrance, casting those unusually colored eyes to the ceiling, as if making a mental survey of his creations, before shaking his head. A local reporter had had a try at explaining the artist's personal appeal, which Max was experiencing for himself, despite the fact Coombebridge did have a gift for turning a blind eye to anything and anyone who wasn't directly concerned with his art. The reporter had interviewed various people who had known the artist in his youth, and the fewer who knew him now, since in some ways he was a reclusive man. Most of them were former lovers, so any chance of a balanced assessment, one would have thought, was slight. Still, most people, even though they had been suddenly left in the dust by the painter, were generous—thrilled, even, at having had the chance to bask in the man's greatness. Such was the power of charm, Max reflected. "He was selfish," said one, a young woman more than half Coombebridge's age at the time. "But he was up front about it, he made no apology for it, and he was absolutely no hypocrite about taking what he wanted. The art was what mattered to him. You had to respect his genius, and his single-minded devotion to his art—which was, as he was first to say, far more important to him than people."

Without stopping his work, Coombebridge said, "I don't suppose you approve of me, Padre. It's true, I've left some broken hearts behind, and more than a few children born on the wrong side of the blanket."

Max paused, as if considering. "I don't suppose it would be worth my while to try to change you."

This was greeted with a bark of laughter. "That hasn't prevented many people, mostly women, from trying." Coombebridge returned his attention to the sworls of colors on his painter's palette. A bit of paint splashed onto the floor. Max resisted the urge to inspect the soles of his shoes—too late now; he'd already stepped into whatever wet paint there was to step in. Pictures of incalculable value were stacked everywhere, against walls, waiting to be tripped over. Max supposed the preferred word was *paintings*. He thought of the Picts of Scotland, so-called by the Romans, from the Latin word for "painted" or "tattooed," a train of thought perhaps inspired by being around all these canvases with their infinite shades of blue. The warriors had used some sort of a plant dye mixed with animal fat for their blue body paint.

Coombebridge suddenly astonished Max by turning, running his eyes over him as if measuring him for a suit, and asking Max if he would pose for him.

"Me? I thought you did only land- and seascapes?"

"I *sell* only land- and seascapes. Portraits go into my private collection.

They are mine; they are never for sale. They are seldom for public viewing, either." He scrabbled around in a stack of paintings and turned to Max's gaze one of a slender young man standing at the water's edge. Gold gleamed from the sea and on the golden curls at the boy's neck, and on an earring created by a single stroke of white paint. The boy's pensive expression was caught in profile, his face half-turned to look at the painter. Max wondered if the boy might be one of Coombebridge's sons.

Max remembered now that someone at the dinner party—Lucie— had said this was true, that the artist kept the portraits to himself. Something about the possessiveness in Coombebridge's voice and words made Max hesitate. There was something off-putting about being part of anyone's private collection.

"That is too bad," Max said. "That you won't sell the portraits. There is a friend of mine I would love to have a portrait of."

"Depends who it is. I don't take commissions. I paint who and what I like."

"You would like her."

Coombebridge, who was nothing if not perceptive, gave Max a sharp glance. And then he smiled.

"Depends," he repeated. "Maybe I could make an exception in your case, Father Max."

It was some time later, and Max was making moves as if to leave. Coombebridge invited him to help himself to instant coffee if he wanted it. Max declined.

"I never," said Coombebridge, "was able to drink coffee in the afternoon. It doesn't pick me up; it makes me irritable." Max wondered briefly how he could tell the difference. Coombebridge added that he thought the whole afternoon coffee routine was a plot by French invaders from across the English Channel. "However, I guess we won that particular war; otherwise, we would have to call it the French Channel."

"That probably is what they call it, among themselves, as they sip wine or coffee in their cafés, not la Manche."

Suddenly, he was struck by Coombebridge's words: "French invaders." Now, what did that remind him of? He recalled Thaddeus saying something to Lucie Cuthbert, something about the proof of a craftsman being in the work he produced—something pompous and self-referential like that. Later, Max had heard them murmuring together in French, and Lucie laughing at Thaddeus's joke, a joke that seemed to involve just the two of them. Max's French was just good enough for him to have understood what was said. Gabby must have understood, as well, if she'd overheard, although she had left the nuns in France behind long ago. A language learned as a child tended to stayed with one.

Melinda had said and Cotton had confirmed that Thaddeus was adopted. Had he possibly been adopted by a French family? Or had he been born into one?

And why did he, Max, think it mattered?

Melinda had said Thaddeus's accent *stayed*. He could hear her high, childish voice now, saying that Thaddeus's French accent had stayed in such good form. Because of his first wife, the suicide.

There was some old wallpaper, peeling and splattered with paint, covering one wall of Coombebridge's studio. It had once been white, with red roses and blue geraniums; now the design was almost indistinguishable from the bright splashes of paint, the white background nearly obliterated. Coombebridge had hung several paintings against this wall—not the best background for display, but the strength of the work, the strong lines, overrode these aesthetic considerations. Still, there was no avoiding the fact that the Coombebridge that hung in Lucie and Frank Cuthbert's dining room had looked much more striking against their black-and-white-striped wallpaper.

Somewhere behind Max's eyes, a sensation grew—a queasiness of mind, as it seemed to him. He watched the paintbrush as Coomebridge dabbed it against the canvas, filling in the blank white spaces with color. The blue water stood out against the striated cliffs, carved into shadows of black and white, and the white clouds. Black and white.

Max quickly turned away. "What I just said—you can forget all that."

"Which part?"

Max was already headed for the door. "The part about taking care. It's nothing to do with your paintings. You're quite safe. Safe as houses."

"Of course I am."

And Max flung himself out the door, to be met by a heavy shower of rain. He jumped into the Land Rover, starting the engine before the door was quite closed.

Coombebridge stood at the door of his cottage, mystified.

"Well, adios, Padre," he said to the rapidly retreating, blurred vision of the Rover's back window.

A theory was forming in Max's mind—hazy and disconnected. But through the mist he could glimpse a shape—then hundreds of shapes, thousands, multiplied and floating eternally above the earth. They served as a caution or a warning, perhaps—or did they come seeking retribution?

Max had left his mobile in the Land Rover. He used it now to call Awena's mobile.

She answered on the first ring.

"I'm glad you called, Max. Melinda's been taken ill."

"Melinda?" said Max. "But . . . how are *you*? Where are you?"

"I'm fine, Max. I'm at Melinda's house—she started feeling unwell while we were having tea at Gabby's place. Some sort of stomach bug. Or the mushroom quiche disagreed with her. We brought her home, and when she seemed to be getting worse, Gabby called for an ambulance. But Gabby isn't well, either. She's just leaving to go back home."

Oh God. It's moving faster than I thought. Everything was slipping out of control—his control, and the killer's. In which case it was hard to know how to prevent the worst, except—"*You must get out of there*," he said in an intense, quiet voice, so as not to be overheard. "Wait until Gabby leaves; then *you* leave." He was now frantic with fear, willing himself at Awena's side, and unsure of how best to protect her apart from keeping her isolated. "Wait for the ambulance outside," he said. "You feel all right, don't you?"

"Yes, I'm fine; I only drank a little tea. But I can't leave her. She's—"

"*Don't* talk," Max said. "Don't say another word. Just say good-bye to me, like nothing's wrong, and ring off. If Gabby doesn't leave, *you* leave right away. Say you've gone to look for the ambulance. Call 999 once you're safely outside and once you can't be overheard. Make sure everyone understands poison is involved."

"Poison!"

But Max had already rung off. Putting the vehicle in gear, he tore off as fast as the narrow, winding roads would allow.

Awena, at the other end of the satellite beam, was left staring at the mobile screen.

The mist in Max's mind cleared some more. He searched his memory, and the many odd things he had noted began to make more sense. He felt certain he was right, but . . . Suddenly, he pulled off the road, raising a spray of mud.

He woke his mobile from sleep and put in a direct call to DCI Cotton. He got him on the first ring.

He filled him in, adding, "So there's something you need to check on."

Cotton listened, then said, "On it."

"But first make sure Awena's okay. Make sure they're all okay."

He turned on the engine and gunned it, only to find the left side of the Rover was sunk in mud up to its hubcaps. It was the kind of stuck that meant the only hope was finding a piece of wood—a tree branch, or something to create traction for the wheel. Even the four-wheel drive was going to be useless in this situation, although he did try, rocking the

Rover back and forth, and quickly reaching the point of making things worse.

Meanwhile, water from the heavens continued to pour down. Max uttered a rare curse—quite a loud curse—and, pulling his jacket tightly about him, ran back to Coombebridge's cottage.

CHAPTER 23
French Connection

Max and a surprisingly helpful Coombebridge got the Land Rover unstuck after about twenty minutes of trial and error and a great deal of grunting and swearing, wedging firewood and the floor mats under the front wheels for traction. Max had driven off at last at a more cautious pace, arriving in Nether Monkslip within the hour and heading first to King's Rest—the Bottles' house.

Where he found both Awena and Melinda gone, the house locked. He headed toward the flat over La Maison Bleue. But inside the shop, Lucie told him Gabby had left, saying she was going to Hawk Crest.

"I saw the ambulance go by," she told him. "Gabby said Melinda had been taken ill, but Gabby was sure she'd be fine. Awena went with Melinda in the ambulance."

"Where on the Crest?" demanded Max.

"Gabby? She is probably in Nunswood," Lucie told him. "She likes it there, by the spring. She says it's a sacred place, and she goes there to pray for her mother." Lucie paused. "I didn't like the way she looked, Father Max. But she made it clear she wanted to be alone."

But Max was already headed out the door. Over his shoulder he said, "Her mother—she is ill perhaps?"

There was such a weighted silence, he turned to see Lucie looking at him, a puzzled expression on her face. "Her mother is long dead," she said flatly. "She died in the war."

He found Gabby sitting quietly by the spring, on one of the stones that had once been part of the ancient ring of menhirs, most of them now tumbled over in disarray. He had the idea she had indeed been praying, an idea confirmed by the desolate, unfocused look in her eyes as she turned to him. It was almost as if she were willing herself back into the present. Otherwise, she looked much the same as ever: the excellent proud posture, the immaculate white hair.

She sighed, making an evident effort to focus her attention.

"'I have no pleasure in the death of the wicked,'" she quoted. It was of course a phrase from the Bible. "No pleasure left at all, in fact. Will you hear my confession, Father?"

"Of course I will." It was a request no priest could refuse. The Rite of Reconciliation, the new name for what was commonly called Confession, was a healing ritual that was intended to return the penitent to a merciful God. To reconcile anyone who had strayed. He had been asked only a few times in his ministry to perform the rite, but on each occasion the person confessing had spoken afterward of being overcome by a sense of healing, of renewal. "Reassembled," as one man had put it.

"Of course," Max repeated, and he sat near her on another of the fallen stones, waiting quietly for her to begin to speak. She opened her palm and he saw that the medallion she always wore around her neck had been clutched tightly in her hand. Her flesh was red and torn where the nails had dug in. He was not surprised to see she was wearing the same earrings he'd seen in the photo of the restaurant, the earrings that had been worn by Melinda.

"Your first question, Father Max, will be: How did I come to find him?"

Max nodded. That wasn't, in fact, his first question—as always, he wanted first to confirm his suspicions as to the "why." But he let her tell the story in her own way.

"But perhaps you have guessed that already," she went on. "How this all came to be. For that is the wonderful, the miraculous part of my story. Full of wonder. Now, those are words someone of your profession should understand. I found him via a pair of earrings. Earrings I'd seen in a magazine photo." And she reached up to touch the jewelry at her ears. The jewelry that had so recently adorned Melinda.

"I was leafing through a magazine at the place where I was working, in Bradford. I had gone there with my husband, planning one last stop before we retired for good, or so I thought. We had so many plans. We would travel. Most of all, we would travel. Maybe I would write a book, perhaps about my life as a child growing up in a convent. He would paint. Harold always looked forward to having that sort of time to explore.

"And then within a few months, he was gone. The heart and soul of me was just *gone* one day. In the mornings as I sat reading the paper, try-ing to read, I would turn to say something to him—I would forget, you see. That was how we always started the day: I would read, and he would do the crossword puzzle. Sometimes I would read aloud to him some bit of outrage from the news.

"But then I would remember he was gone now. I had no illusion he was hovering about the room somehow, like a ghost. He just wasn't there. It was unbearable, Father. I'm not making excuses, but pain like that, a loss like that, after a lifetime together . . . my friend and soul mate . . ."

Max nodded, remembering how he had missed Awena in much the same way during her very brief absence. The thought of its being more than a temporary separation was unbearable to him.

She swiped at a tear that trembled at the corner of her eye. "I didn't know what else to do with myself, so I kept working. And one day, I saw the magazine. It was one of those 'lifestyle' publications that flourish in good times and bad—magazines that permit one at least to dream during the bad times. I came to a page with a photo showing a crowded dining room at a new restaurant in Nether Monkslip. The White Bean, of course; you know it. Several of the people in the forefront of this photo were shown from behind or in somewhat blurry profile. Then there were many more people sitting in the far distance, their features indistinguishable. In these days, when everyone worries so about invasion of their privacy, their precious privacy—surely a modern construct—no photographer would dare publish a photo too exact of such a crowd. It looked, in fact, as if the photographer had deliberately blurred certain areas of the photo. What, after all, if a man were there, sitting on a banquette with a woman not his wife?

"So all that could be seen of the woman closest to the camera was the back of her head; she had her face turned away from the camera, presumably in conversation with the man beside her.

"But what caught the eye—what caught *my* eyes anyway, and instantly—was the earring, which could be seen, quite clearly, dangling from the woman's right ear.

"There could be no doubt, so large and distinctive was that earring. The photographer had artfully captured its golden glimmer in the candle-light, so that it stood out like a sign. A sign to me.

"As I say, distinctive they were, those earrings—one of a kind. Literally, one of a kind. I recognized the design immediately. For I had seen them before, in another photograph.

"And who would wear one earring? It had to be one of the set.

"Where had she gotten them, this woman? How had she come by them? I had to come to Nether Monkslip to find out. Of course I knew of the place already because of Lucie—another sign it was, that she was also in this photo. An unmistakable sign. I hadn't seen her in years, but still I could tell it was Lucie sitting at that table, and even though his face was blurry, it had to be Frank beside her.

"I had to get here, and see for myself, and find out where the other woman in the photo, their dinner companion, had gotten those earrings.

"For they had been my mother's, those earrings.

"And they had been intended for me.

"I had to see them up close. I had to investigate. I had to *know* what happened.

"It took only moments of online detective work to find out he'd moved here, that he actually lived here, and hadn't just been visiting on the night the photo was taken. He kept making announcements to the media about what he was going to do, that he was going to retire, so learning more about his life was easy.

"And once I knew where to find him . . . well. I put my plan in motion. I called Lucie, who offered me a place to stay. I encountered no difficulty in finding work in Nether Monkslip, especially with Lucie to vouch for me with Annette. All my qualifications were in order.

"I am, of course, not really Lucie's aunt. Lucie's mother was an orphan, raised in the same orphanage as I was. When you have no people of your own, you adopt others quickly into your life. You call them 'cousin' or 'sister' or anything that makes you feel you are a little bit a part of this world. Anything that makes you feel less alone.

"So, her mother and I were raised together by the Sisters of St. Ardelle. You could say we all raised one another. There were so many of us girls without a real home or family."

She was silent so long, Max wasn't sure she would speak again. Finally, he returned her to the present tale. "The earrings?" he asked.

With a visible effort, she said, "Yes, of course. The earrings.

"The thing you need to understand is this: There was no way anyone had come by them honestly. They were mine. They were intended for me alone. My first step became to find out exactly how Melinda—for it was

Melinda in the photo, of course, as I readily learned from Lucie—how she'd come to possess them.

"Once I had packed up and moved and settled myself in Nether Monkslip, I set about learning all I could about the Bottles. With one salon in the village, it was perhaps only a matter of time before Melinda became my client, but I was, of course, more "proactive," as they say, than that. I cultivated her; I earned her trust, which was not difficult— Melinda desperately needed someone to talk to.

"Even as I began gaining her confidence, I told myself I had come to grips with the past and that I was just satisfying my curiosity. That I had put aside all thoughts of revenge. But once I had confirmed to whom Melinda was married, and of course when I actually met the egomaniac, all of that vanished. On the instant, it vanished.

"A pompous little boy had grown to be a pompous, self-important, and petty little man who belittled and mistreated almost everyone who crossed his path.

"Do you believe we change, Father? Of course you do—you must believe, in your line of work. But you'd be wrong about that. We don't. People don't.

"Anyway, there he was. I wanted to make sure he hadn't, by some miracle, changed—I was trying to play fair; isn't that a joke?—but of course he was just what you'd expect of a snitch. A cowardly, pompous braggart, bullying his sad little wife. I did feel sorry for Melinda: so much younger than he, filling her days with shopping and an affair— someone to pass the lonely hours with. A bit of intrigue in an empty life of playing handmaiden to the Great Thespian.

"How do I know all this? She told me. I cultivated her; you see how I cultivated her: I needed to know her and him and their habits as a married couple.

"I learned from Melissa how Thaddeus had come to be in England: He was adopted out of France by the Bottles, when his own parents were killed in a car accident just as the war ended. Later, Thaddeus—or 'Thaddee,' as he was originally known—left the village and the Bottles behind for a career in London. I gather the Bottles had by this time come to realize they had taken a viper into their nest. Just as in the Aesop's fable about the snake that was saved from freezing but bit the farmer who had saved him.

"Anyway, the rest, as Thaddeus would be the first to say, is theatrical history. Of course, most traces of accent had been sanded away with the years and the stage training, but he spoke the sort of excellent French you learn at your mother's knee—I heard him as we all did, speaking with Lucie. Even the little dog Jean, so Melinda told me, was named for Jean Cocteau.

"Of course it was little Jean Cocteau that allowed me to go to and from the house with ease: The Bottles' dog didn't bark because it knew me. I went there all the time and I would slip the dog a little treat, so it got used to me."

"Why were you there so much?" Max asked. "Surely Melinda went to your shop to have her hair done."

She held up a forestalling hand. "I will tell you why, Father. I will tell you. I will tell you all of it.

"You could not have failed to have noticed how vain Thaddeus was about his appearance. He'd had at least two face-lifts—a hairdresser can always tell. And he dyed his hair. Of course he dyed his hair.

"Do you remember that old advertising slogan—'Only your hairdresser knows for sure'? I was sworn to secrecy. He was so vain! He would stop by the shop for a haircut, but he'd pay me extra to go to the house on evenings when Melinda wasn't there. It's not unusual for people who can afford it to have these sessions in their homes, and of course Thaddeus was used to having this sort of personal treatment. So I'd go over there to the house once a month, like clockwork, to do his hair in private. If I do say it myself, I'm very good at what I do. No one could tell.

"And while I was there, of course I took the opportunity one evening to take back the earrings he had stolen. They were in Melinda's jewelry box, in the bedroom—I would do his hair in the master bathroom. I was careful never to wear them around her—anyway, I wasn't interested so much in wearing them as taking back possession of what was *mine*. What had been left for *me*.

"So on the night he was killed, he had invited me to the house for our regular monthly top secret appointment. Melinda was not at home on these occasions, and she was of course only too happy to oblige. I honestly think it never occurred to Thaddeus that she might be cheating on him. That blinding ego at work again.

"This particular night, the night I killed him, Father . . . This particular night I dyed and washed and blow-dried his hair as I always did, and when I had finished, I took the brush I'd used to apply the hair dye, pretending to do a little touch-up on his roots at the back of his neck, where I'd missed a spot, and I dipped the brush in poison. I painted the strophanthin, which is brown in color, like the hair dye, into the little nick I'd 'accidentally' made in his neck a few days previously, while I was cutting his hair.

"That was all it took. The merest dab. Of course it stung. It was meant to. He complained loudly, so I pretended to wipe the residue away. But he didn't complain for long. It's an extremely fast-acting poison.

"It is not a painless death, and given the small amount I'd used, it wasn't fast, either. It wasn't meant to be fast. I waited and watched to make sure the poison worked. To make sure he died, Father.

"I had already given him a sedative—I put it in the whiskey he always drank while I worked on him. I'd borrowed the sedative from the medicine cabinet on a previous visit, and I used it now so he wouldn't have time or strength to fight me or call for help. It wasn't as if I'd had a lot of experience with this, and I had to be sure nothing went wrong.

"I needn't have bothered, really. The poison rendered him helpless almost immediately. You would think the sight of this helpless old man would have softened my heart. I will not pretend and tell you that it did.

"I had wanted him to know it was me who had done this to him, and why, but then I realized it would be like explaining algebra to a zebra: He couldn't begin to understand that what he had done was wrong, nor could he be made to care. Thaddeus, even as a child, suffered from an extreme arrogance that made him think he was above the rest.

"I want to tell you everything now, Father Max. I think I wanted to tell you all along."

"The Bible verses through the letter slot . . ."

She nodded. "Writing those was like a safety valve. And I think in a way I was hoping you'd guess it was me. But then . . ."

"But then it all became too big a secret to keep. Difficult for you, impossible for Melinda."

She nodded. "Well, there you have it, Father, or most of it. I had only to get him out of the chair and into bed. Not too difficult for someone like me. I have kept myself strong. I am strong, and he was old now. It was a reversal of our conditions when he betrayed me. I was a helpless baby then. Now he was helpless. Don't you think it fitting?

"I waited calmly to make sure he was dead. I surprised myself. I was not bothered at all by what I had done, at least not then."

"But you do regret it now, don't you, Gabby?" Max asked quietly. It was not curiosity that made him ask. It was a condition of the Rite of Reconciliation that she regret what she had done.

She looked at him a long time, understanding his meaning. At last, she nodded her head ever so slightly. But she would not meet his eyes.

"Let me tell you," she said. "Let me tell you all of it. Then you'll see. I think you'll see. It's Melinda—it's what happened with Melinda that changed everything.

"I think all would have been well if not for Melinda.

"I was just getting ready to place the body on the bed—it was meant to look like a heart attack, like he'd simply collapsed—when Melinda came home early. She'd already set her watch ahead for the time change, you see, but I had not done so. It was ten P.M. by her watch, but nine P.M. by mine.

"She'd been with Farley, of course. She'd briefly joined the Writers' Square back when it met on Saturdays, to establish an alibi so she could be with Farley. When the group stopped meeting on Saturdays and switched to Thursdays—at first she wasn't aware of the change, but then she realized Thaddeus didn't pay a lot of attention anyway to what she got up to. Other times, Melinda would tell him she was at the movies in Staincross Minster with a girlfriend—something like that. Either he trusted her or he didn't care.

"She did tell me at one point that Thaddeus had become suspicious and for a while her life was even more difficult than before. That is why—well, somehow, things kept arranging themselves so that it was easier for her to see the value in ridding the world of him. By this point, I had become her complete confidante, you see. Her accomplice.

"I knew all about Farley, and I used to help Melinda by changing the bedroom clock before I left Thaddeus, so he would not be aware of how late it was getting. His memory was not what it had been, which helped with that particular deception.

"Melinda would change the clock back on her arrival home or even the next morning. This would buy her an extra hour. But the time change threw a spanner into the works.

"Anyway, she came home and found me arranging the body in what I hoped would be an artful, believable pose. At first I was afraid she would raise the alarm, but of course she did not. I had seen her collecting poison mushrooms in Raven's Wood; I knew already what she was thinking, what she most wished for. She just took in the scene, hesitated a fraction of a second, and then walked over and helped me position him half on and half off the bed.

"I had done her a favor, and she knew that. I'd done the whole world a favor. She didn't even ask why, not until later. I simply told her that decades before he had betrayed me and my family. She accepted this unblinkingly. She knew perfectly well what kind of monster she was married to, you see.

"So even though she didn't know at first *why* I'd done it, she felt only relief that I had. I'd done what she'd not yet worked up the courage to do.

"She helped me pack up my gear—the towels and hair dryer and so on. When I got home, I burned the brush I'd used to apply the poison in the fireplace, and the gloves. Of course I wore gloves—I always do when dealing with chemicals, but especially this time. For that is a poison not to fool about with, especially if you have even a tiny cut on your hands, as people in my line of work often do.

"We left him there in the bedroom and went to the kitchen. Over a drink, we put our heads together and came up with a cover story. Melinda would pretend to have fallen asleep downstairs watching the telly and to have gone up to bed very early the next morning to find him. This wasn't an uncommon occurrence in that household. Thaddeus was fussy about his 'beauty sleep,' as he called it, and would go to bed early. He had his little routine. And of course Melinda had hers.

She and I turned on the telly so that, if asked, Melinda could say what shows had been on before she fell asleep. My alibi was the same— that I had been watching the telly in my flat over the shop. It wasn't perfect, but who would ever suspect me? And if it came to that, and she was officially accused, the plan was for me to alibi Melinda—I would suddenly 'remember' that she'd dropped by to return something and we'd watched a show together. But for the present, we decided to keep it simple. The truth, that she had been with Farley much of the evening, might also suffice. Better an adulteress than an accessory to murder."

At last Gabby looked straight at him.

"Strophanthin," said Max. "Of all things. You must have brought it back from Africa."

"That's right. My husband and I, as I told you, were missionaries for many years. The poison wasn't difficult to come by in tropical Africa, and I held on to it when we left."

"Why did you? Why did you keep it?"

"Think about it, Father. It's not the kind of thing you can just toss out anywhere, is it? The smallest drop will kill quickly, which is of course why it was so useful in warfare. The poison-tipped arrow is not the stuff of fiction, but of fact.

"And maybe . . . since this is my confession, I will confess: Maybe in my heart I always hoped I'd be able to use it on someone as deserving as Thaddeus Bottle. It was the purest luck I came across the actual criminal, the one who mattered most to me. There were so many betrayers from those days, some still at large, and never brought to justice."

Max had surmised that since she had been a baby at the time of Thaddeus's betrayal, "those days" could only be the days of World War II. And she was right: So few had been brought to justice.

"So I had the means," Gabby said, "but I puzzled long and hard over the delivery. How to make sure Thaddeus suffered a cut, so I could then somehow insert the poison into his bloodstream? I work with scissors all day, and I thought of trying to entice him into my chair. A little slip of the blade, a little poison on the blade, and . . . done. But that would be a dead giveaway, wouldn't it—if you will please excuse the pun? To have him die literally at my hands? So I thought, and I thought some more. How I could pierce his skin, so he wouldn't even realize. I could have him cut himself on something coated with the poison. I thought of a lightbulb shattering in his hand, something like that.

"And then I realized the two events didn't have to occur together. I could wound him slightly with my scissors. Then I could put poison into the wound, even a day or two later. The beauty of that was that one event need not be connected with the other. No one need suspect there was poisoning involved at all. No one except you, Father Max.

"Of course, what is truly unforgivable is what I did to Melinda. She was unstable at the best of times, and she did have that tendency to prattle on, letting the cat out of the bag. Melinda wasn't the type to stay silent forever with what she knew or suspected; she was anyone's last choice for a partner in crime. And when all was said and done, I did want to get away with it—at least, at first. I wanted to live.

"I'd saved the mushrooms I'd caught her collecting that day, and dried them in the oven. I guess I thought of it as my backup plan for killing Thaddeus. Whatever it took, I would succeed in killing him.

"I made individual small pies and gave Melinda the one I knew was poisoned. It took effect surprisingly fast—drying the mushrooms must have concentrated their potency." She added quickly, "Awena was never in danger, Father Max. Please believe that. But my attempt to kill Melinda, even though immediately regretted, was wrong. And for that, I truly am sorry.

"I wouldn't have called the ambulance right away if I'd really wanted Melinda to die—now would I?"

"The worst of it is, the confusing thing is: I didn't count on caring so much that an innocent person might become a suspect. That innocent people would be caught up in this. I didn't think beyond ridding the world of Thaddeus. But I think that's partly what tripped me up. Good old-fashioned Catholic guilt: the nuns' specialty."

"Caring about the innocent—that will be your saving grace in this," said Max. "You do see that, don't you?"

But again she might not have heard. "I kept some of the arrow poison back, not using all of it. Just in case, you see. If I were found out, I would end it. I had already made up my mind about that. I would see Thaddeus Bottle in hell, then."

"Gabby," Max said sharply. "If that still is your intention, then it—"

Quickly she shook her head. "Don't worry, Father. It was, as I say, 'just in case.' I don't think I have the nerve.

"I don't think any one of us is ever completely prepared to die."

CHAPTER 24
With Sleep Come Nightmares

"You haven't told me the why," said Max, watching her closely. "It was to do with the war, wasn't it? The Occupation. You said Thaddeus had betrayed you."

She nodded. When she spoke, her tone had subtly shifted. She spoke now in a harsh whisper. Max shifted his weight, leaning in closer to hear.

"It was everything to do with the waking nightmare that was the war," she began. "With what happened to my family. With the loss of my family, of my home, belongings—of my *self*. Of all that might have been, the life I might have had, if not for the man who grew up to be known as the 'famous' English actor, Thaddeus Bottle.

"I had to learn most of what I am about to tell you at secondhand, from a woman who knew my mother, Claude. A woman who was one of the survivors of that time. For of course my mother didn't survive to tell me her story.

"I'll start with the earrings.

"With my father, who gave my mother the earrings.

"My father was a British airman whose plane had flown off course due to equipment failure. He'd finally had to ditch, to bail out. My mother found him washed ashore, only half alive. This was in Bordeaux. There were the bodies of other crewmen, and they all appeared to be dead, but then she saw one body move.

"Other people had begun to gather. She bent over this man, gripped his hand as if taking his pulse, and whispered that he should be still, that he should play dead—*faire le mort*. He knew enough French to understand. And the urgency of her voice conveyed the danger he still was in. She saved his life.

"My mother already was a *passeur*—one who smuggled people to safety. Many RAF airmen had to bail out of their planes during WW Two. I hardly need to tell you how dangerous this was for her to help them.

"But this man she protected and sheltered and fell in love with, and I was the result. *Quel scandale* for those days. But it was wartime, with never a sense of what might happen hour to hour. Who was there to care?

"I never learned exactly what happened to my father. My mother took him home, to where she lived with my widowed grandmother. When he was well enough to travel, they altered his appearance, as they did for many others, and gave him fake ID papers. The plan was for him to be passed along by helpers who would show him the way through the Pyrenees into northern Spain. Sometimes he would pretend to be a deaf-mute, to explain why he, a young man, wasn't helping the war effort. He never knew of my existence, of my birth.

"He would manage to get a letter passed to my mother now and then, but more and more it was like a fading transmission, a radio broadcast broken up by static. And then even the letters stopped.

"Because, you see, what happened was this: To speed up progress to the border, he and his guide finally hopped aboard a train, which was risky. Too risky. They were spotted by a Gestapo agent. Perhaps he noticed my father could hear what he should not have been able to hear.

They both were taken to the camps, undoubtedly to die there. My mother never was able to learn more of his fate than that."

"Your parents must both have been brave people, Gabby."

She nodded. "And my grandparents. I would give anything I own to have met them, even for a little hour."

"How did she become involved in the Resistance, your mother? You say she was a *passeur.* . . ."

"Again, all I know came from a friend of my mother's, a woman she would talk to, a woman who managed to survive it all. My mother helped write and distribute Resistance pamphlets against the occupiers, also using the beauty salon she ran with my grandmother as a cover for all manner of dangerous activities, including the manufacture of fake IDs and passes. She and my grandmother became part of a chain, hiding people and moving them across the demarcation line to the free zone. Beauty salons were perfect places for doing what they now call the 'make-over.' Dyeing or straightening or cutting hair, applying makeup, then having the photo taken for the fake ID, using a setup in the back of the shop, and the services of a photographer working for the Resistance. Salons also were good places to hide chemicals and powders. They figured, In for a penny, in for a pound. Even having the pamphlets in one's possession was potentially fatal—what did all the steps that came after that matter?

"A hair salon is where women gather and exchange information anyway. Nether Monkslip provides the perfect example. So how natural that an escape network should operate under the noses of the authorities, who probably regarded whatever went on in a salon as women's foolishness and beneath their notice. What went on was quite a lot that would have fascinated them, including the forgery of identification papers, the creation of false certificates of baptism, and the distribution of tracts against the occupiers.

"Mother's clients would arrive with packages they would 'forget' to take with them. Then others would come and take the packages away. She didn't always know what was in them. Guns or tracts, weapons or words—whatever might help put a stop to the hell that had sprung up around her.

"Weapons for the resistors were often hidden under the vegetables in shopping baskets. And on at least one occasion, a tiny child, nearly newborn, was hidden that way, as well."

"And that child was you," said Max softly.

She nodded. "She left me with the nuns, at the orphanage. It was the only way she knew to save me, in case she was caught, in case the worst happened to her."

Her voice caught on the last phrase. After a long pause, Gabby went on. "She was right to be worried. False birth certificates, marriage licenses, permits, ration books—how clever they were! All of this forgery, with the equipment kept hidden behind a door in a closet that led to a secret room. Even owning a typewriter in those days could make you a suspect, because the sort of person who owned a typewriter was often the sort of person to be found writing propaganda.

"Did my mother really understand the danger to herself? It is difficult to say. She was so young, and passionate, and certain in her knowledge that what was happening in her country was wrong. *Liberté, égalité, fraternité*—these ideas had gone out the window. Maybe she saw it as some sort of game of wits with the enemy—only this, of course, was such a serious game, with deadly consequences. But my grandfather, her father, had already been taken into custody and executed during one of the mass reprisals. She knew the risks."

"And Thaddeus? He was there somehow. He noticed what was going on, didn't he?"

Again she nodded. "He lived right next door. My family had always given a wide berth to those neighbors and had been careful to give them no hint of their feelings toward the Occupiers, never to complain, not even when my grandfather disappeared—especially not then. The neighbors seemed to buy their act, which included listening with apparent interest to their mindless bigotry. The mother of that house—Thaddeus's mother—was a customer at the beauty shop. But her little boy, nearly always at her side—a mother's boy—he was sharper than both his parents; he noticed too much. He would snoop; he would eavesdrop. No doubt he overheard the whispered talk—talk about my mother's growing belly, just for one thing. And he was already an actor—a better actor at the time than he later became. Maybe the women didn't guard what they said around him. He was only a boy, after all.

"A monster of a little boy.

"My mother knew that a pregnant woman, engaged in the type of activity she was engaged in, was at particular risk. Far from being a protected species, she, if caught, would be on the Nazi's list of the expendables, along with the Romanies, the mentally ill, and the halt and the lame. In the camps, a pregnant woman or one with young children was considered a burden, unfit to work, and that was all that mattered in a world gone mad—the workforce.

"So my mother hid her pregnancy as best she could and when the time came gave birth with my grandmother at her side. But they both knew there would come a day when my mother would have to make a choice. And her choice was that her infant would be given the best chance of safety, given every chance to survive. People all around her were being rounded up and tortured for information, and even the best and bravest of them could be broken. So when I was just a few weeks old, she wrapped me in blankets and, in classic fashion, left me to be found by the nuns at the convent near her home. The Mother Superior was her mother's—my grandmother's—friend.

"My mother left me with a letter that said that my name was Gabrielle Chaux. She also left with me a small toy, a stuffed animal that long ago went missing. Into the blanket she tied an earring—one of the unique pair of earrings given her by my father.

"In the letter, she explained that she was leaving the mate to that earring in safekeeping with a friend. It was to be a sign to that friend, whenever the war was over, whenever I was old enough to come looking for my mother. A sign confirming who I was—that I was the daughter of Claude Chaux.

"My mother may have gotten the idea of splitting up a pair of earrings from the tickets torn in half that members of the Resistance used to identify one another.

"Into the hem of the blanket she also had sewn a photo of herself wearing those earrings. It was second nature to her by then, I suppose. The fail-safe. That photo and that blanket were the only things, apart from some books and some little awards for languages, that I took with me years later when I left the convent.

"She put a drop of wine in my milk, just enough that I would sleep: It was vital that I not make a sound. Giving a child a sip of alcohol was common procedure back then. Of course now you'd have Child Protection all over you, but on this day—it was necessary.

"These plans for my safety were meant to be a secret, of course, but they were overheard. They were overheard by a horrid little boy of ten—Thaddee, as he was then called. He was hanging around the salon with his mother, as usual, where no one paid him any mind. He was quiet and well behaved in those days, or he knew how to pretend to be.

"Do you ever think, Father Max, how much the smallest chance plays a part in the biggest events? If the boy had not been out of school, kept out because of a little cold, but taken to the salon, presumably because his mother didn't care if he infected everyone there? If he had not overheard my mother and grandmother talking and planning with others at the salon?

"The earring with its distinctive design was meant to be my

passport—to identify me to whoever held the mate. That also would be the person the nuns should release me to.

"But that person never turned up because Thaddeus stole the earrings—first the one, then its mate—along with the message my mother had written to the nuns. And shortly afterward, the roundups began.

"Thaddeus overheard my mother talking to her friend at the salon, confiding in her, as she gave her the matching earring and all the details of her plan. As my mother was to learn later, she had been followed by Thaddeus as she carried me, hidden in a basket, to the convent. He crept in right after she left and stole the single earring, and the letter. He left the photograph behind—it was sewn into the blanket, remember—and the toy animal. So of course the nuns never realized . . . Later at the salon, he stole the second earring from the pocketbook of my mother's trusted friend. Then he told his parents everything he knew. Who, being the kind of people they were, told the authorities. The woman, the friend—I never learned her name—she was quietly rounded up.

"Quietly, so the others could fall one by one, and lead others into a trap.

"My mother's friend was taken to the same prison where they later sent my mother. It was a sort of holding place on the way to the camp. From her and from others, my mother learned of Thaddeus's betrayal. For Thaddeus, far from being ashamed, talked openly and proudly of the part he had played in sending my mother to her death."

She was silent. Gabby struck him as the type of woman who prided herself on never crying. And yet she wiped away a flood of tears now, using a tissue that had long since fallen to shreds. Max handed her his handkerchief and waited, listening with eyes half-closed, to the slight rustle of the leaves in the nearby trees and the murmur of the spring. At last, she drew a deep breath and looked at him, her eyes rimmed in red.

"I am sorry," she said. "I thought I could get through this."

Max shook his head at the apology. "You say your mother was led into a trap. . . ."

Gabby nodded. "One day she returned home as usual. The dog didn't bark his friendly bark, which might have told her to turn and run—the dog knew her footsteps, you see. He was a little terrier, not much bigger than a cat, and in his soul he believed he was sent to earth to guard her. He would become hysterical when a stranger came to the door, but he knew when it was my mother or grandmother.

"They'd shot him, of course, when they took my grandmother. And when my mother went inside, they were waiting for her.

"But Thaddeus—he didn't tell them about you?" Max asked, picturing the helpless child she had been. "Where to look for you?"

"Apparently not. And I will never know why. It wasn't out of some sudden sense of decency, of that I can assure you. Maybe he did tell but no one could be bothered to come for me. Why would they bother? Perhaps he was afraid he'd be forced to give back the earrings if he told more of the story, even to his parents. Or perhaps even he realized that the lives of these women—their certain deaths—could be laid at his door. If he feared for his life—if he feared reprisal—he would have been right to fear. He may have come to realize it was not a game. He knew that to drag all the nuns in the convent into his betrayal, which already had had results beyond his wildest dreams, might mean their deaths, as well.

"He was a child of ten. I try to make myself remember that this evil, stupid fool was only ten. My mother essentially was sent to her death over a trinket, stolen by a thieving child covering up his petty theft. I suppose these days we'd have to feel sympathy for him. We'd say he has a disease, he suffers from kleptomania, poor tyke, and we'd dose him with pills or send him for counseling. This leaves no room for the evil that you and I know, Father Max, is real.

"It was many years before I learned of my mother's fate from this woman who had been with her in the camp. Her name was Annabelle.

She was one of the few who survived, and who had been returned to France in the summer of 1945. She carried a message to the convent for me, for Gabrielle—I was still far too young to understand anything that had happened. My mother, knowing she was dying of one of the diseases rampant in the camps, had told Annabelle about the convent and had said to her, 'Tell Gabby, when she is old enough, what happened, to me and to all of us. Tell her I kiss her with all my heart.'

"Annabelle delivered to the nuns the message that my mother was dead and then she went away, to try to piece her own life back together, to find her own children.

"As I say, it was years later, but I managed to find Annabelle through a network of the survivors. She at first didn't want to see me—the memories were too painful to relive, she said. She said I must understand that. But at long last, not long after my husband died, she sent me a letter, saying she would talk with me. I flew to Paris, where she now lived. We met several times at coffee shops or cafés, and in her home. Annabelle was very ill by this time—she had never fully recovered her health from being in the prison camp, and it wasn't long after this that she died.

"Annabelle told me she had tried to take care of my mother, who was little more than a girl. Her youth should have been a shield, but somehow it was the youngest who did not make it through the camps— and the oldest, of course. But it was as if the young had had no time at all to prepare, and no real experience that such evil could exist, and how to withstand it.

"Then occurred the miracle of which I spoke earlier: Soon after my meetings with Annabelle, the contents of which had of course occupied my mind night and day, that magazine with that photo of Melinda wearing the earrings fell into my hands. The rest I have told you."

In her eyes was a plea for understanding.

"It was as if I literally couldn't bear it, you see. After losing my husband, I couldn't bear one more thing. It was like being flayed alive to hear what Annabelle told me. Perhaps . . . I have wondered if it would have been better had I not begged her to talk with me, to tell me all she remembered of my mother, and of her last days.

"The oddest things began to remind me of what my mother, Claude, and other women like her went through in the prisons, then in the camps. Small things and large. It was Annabelle who told me she had a dozen phobias from those days, things she couldn't bear to look at or be reminded of.

"It is the trivial things that surprise you the most, that shock the most—because these sorts of reminders are everywhere. They are things you would think inconsequential and so easy to tamp down in one's mind. But Annabelle told me that all those years later, she would flinch to suddenly see a striped pattern on clothing, on a package, on a wall. And when she told me why, of course I understood. I not only understood, I understood to the core of my being. The same loathing came to fill me, too. What it reminded her of, of course, was the black and white identifying stripes that the prisoners were forced to wear, to wear until they died. Many of the survivors of the camps carried this image with them forever, Annabelle had told me, and couldn't bear the reminder.

"She always wore long sleeves, Annabelle—to hide the tattoo, of course. Her prison number. She told me they all did—all the survivors.

"And somehow once she told me this, I took on the phobia or superstition or dread—whatever you want to call it. I let it exist in me, too, in a sort of sympathy with these women."

"And that," said Max, "is why you switched places at the table that night, so that you could put your back to that reminder."

"You noticed, Father Max. That night at dinner. But I don't think you guessed the reason."

"I thought it was the painting that bothered you. But it was the design on the wall against which the painting hung."

She nodded. "Things that give others pleasure only give me pain now. And how could I tell Lucie—tell anyone? Could they ever be made to understand? My mother lived on a bowl of thin soup a day, made of God knew what, while her captors gorged themselves, living surrounded by their rich furnishings and stolen artworks. Like most of the prisoners, my mother lost her teeth to malnutrition before she died. Dysentery and typhus took many of them, the conditions in the camps being indescribable. The miracle is that some of them lasted as long as they did, with every new day like a trap waiting to be sprung."

Gabby stifled a fresh flood of tears, then slowly said, "I thought I had lost the ability to cry, at funerals or sad movies or on any other occasion. Somehow I absorbed the personality of the survivor, for whom crying is an indulgence. It takes away the energy required to keep on living. To stay alive for the sake of those no longer alive to settle the score.

"But I fight sleep every night, because with sleep come the nightmares." She sighed, "I am so tired, Father."

Max said, his voice tentative and leaden with sorrow, "We think children innocent in these betrayals, but there was a mania to those years. They caught the disease, some of them, from their parents."

She said, nodding, as if still astonished, "Who ever would dream that a child could have been a denouncer? I heard Thaddeus claim he was so young during the war that he didn't remember much. Such a liar still. But his parents were enthusiastic supporters of Hitler's 'vision' for Germany. It is where the boy got his ideas, from the parents, who were fools. They thought, you see, that collaborators would be safe. Even if that were not a despicable line to take, it also was not true. The Germans took what they wanted, but they stopped returning favors once favors were no longer needed. Then everyone in France faced the shortages together, as Germany stripped the country.

"I remember, Father Max, the little chat at dinner about evil. And I remember thinking you were kind, intelligent, and even worldly-wise. You've seen evil—I can see that in your eyes. When you are in repose, your eyes can look very sad, did you know that? But you've never seen it on such a scale—when it comes to the sort of sanctioned evil that took hold, you can have little idea. May you never see it. No one who wasn't there could know, could they? No one who wasn't alive then. And that includes me, an infant up until the war ended. But in my imaginings . . . in my imaginings, yes. Asleep and awake, I can imagine it all.

"Already dying, they were made to stand in the predawn hours in freezing mud and unimaginable slime. It was an endurance test, do you see? They wanted only the strong ones to live. The ones who were finally driven to death and madness were the ones looking for a reason, for logic in the methods of the guards. A rational system of reward and punishment that they might somehow exploit. 'If I do this, then surely this will follow.' But logic was of no use in the face of the sadism that ruled the camps. The only people who were rewarded were the guards whose methods were the most effective.

"So the women who survived accepted that the world had gone mad and the only hope was to escape notice however possible. You never wanted the guards to see you stumble from exhaustion, to see the signs of disease, the pallor, the sores and the swollen legs, or to see you had lost too much flesh and muscle to be of use to them as slave labor.

"I have become nearly obsessive about health and fitness—practically a hypochondriac. Do you wonder? Only the fittest survived. You had to stand erect—to pretend to be well, to have the bloom of health about you."

Max looked at her face, which was flushed with emotion beneath that hectic makeup she always wore. Her attempt to mimic the bloom of health, to ward off the evil spirits that sought out the weak and the faltering.

"I won't dwell any more on the details of what went on. Not because you will have heard it before, but because the details are unspeakable and impossible, in any event, to summarize. Words don't begin to touch what happened. My mother survived nearly up until the end. I don't know what she had to do to survive and I don't care to know. The single photograph I have of her, I keep on the mantelpiece in my bedroom. You may eventually come to see it. She was pretty, so pretty. And she looks so determined—you can see it. I know how much she wanted to live. To come back and reclaim her child."

Max closed his eyes against what he saw in her eyes, numb with the pain of her imaginings and his own. Gabby's anger was a live thing that changed its shape, to expand and shrink, to shimmer around them. It seemed to sear the air, scorch the trees, blacken the sky. He remembered the Bible quotations she had sent him. Only someone fixated on revenge and death could dwell on those most agonizing passages.

"As the last generation of the victims die out, too many deaths will be forgotten," she said. "They're already in danger of being forgotten."

"And yet," Max said, with all the intensity he could muster, to counter her despair. "And yet in the midst of the horror, there were acts of unimaginable heroism like your mother's and your grandparents', and compassion on a grand scale. Mere specks of decency and courage on such an otherwise dark canvas, yes, but they were there and they were brilliant. They shine a light still. Almost the entire population of the region around the village of Le Chambon-sur-Lignon helped to rescue thousands from the Vichy authorities. People of almost every religion, as well as nonbelievers, banded together to oppose the Nazis, at the greatest possible risk to themselves. They provided food, clothing, fake IDs, and the chance to escape to freedom over the Swiss border. Imagine the risks they ran—especially when it only needed one person to betray thousands."

"One little Thaddeus, yes," she said. "But it is too simple to say atrocities are sent periodically to test mankind. There simply aren't enough people in the world like these lunatic Frenchmen and French-women who were willing to risk everything they had."

She looked at him. "You still have questions, Father?"

"I do," he said. "How could you be sure Thaddeus came by that earring by dishonest means? Perhaps he stole it, yes, but from someone else—perhaps someone who had stolen it in the first place."

"And then stole the other one from my mother's friend? Only someone who had read that letter would know who had the mate to the earring. Besides, he bragged about his cleverness, remember?

"And if I needed further confirmation, there was Melinda," she went on. "When I asked her how she'd come into possession of such beautiful earrings, she smiled and said her husband had given them to her. That they were family keepsakes Thaddeus had 'found' during the war. Later, she confided that she knew he had stolen them—immersed in playing the role of the genius Thaddeus, he boasted to her one time of his cleverness, even as a child. Then as quickly, he denied what he'd said. But Thaddeus had always had 'a little problem' with taking things that didn't belong to him; Melinda knew that perfectly well."

Max knew he was playing devil's advocate. He didn't doubt her story for a minute.

"I must ask you to tell Cotton everything you've told me. As a condition of your reconciliation."

"I already have," she said.

"What do you mean, Gabby?"

But she shook her head and wouldn't be drawn back into the present. "Annabelle told me the real trick was never to make your captors angry—survival was just possible if you could manage that. You were too exhausted to provoke anyone deliberately, so you were safe. But knowing that for no reason, or for any reason at all, you could be next—as you saw others, others younger and more innocent than you, being violated—that was what kept them, day to day, on the edge of madness.

"Perhaps I am mad, too, now, made mad by the events of so long ago. I only know when it comes to Thaddeus, I don't care. I can only tell you I feel completely sane, and that in my philosophy, killing him was an act of the purest sanity.

"And I am not sorry for it, Father."

"Gabby, please try to understand. You must see how it is. . . . You must make amends. There is no one who wouldn't understand what you've been through, who wouldn't understand your reasons, but . . ."

She turned from him as if overcome, as if to hide her anguished face. She turned back, but there had been something furtive in her movement that alarmed him. Then he saw her stricken look and the blood on her wrist, and he knew what she had done.

She was dying even as he caught her fall, her heart well past attempts at revival. The same poison she had used to kill Thaddeus was powerful, and she had opened a vein to ensure it went straight to the heart. Settling her on the ground near the spring, he put in an emergency call as he knelt beside her, even though there was nothing to be done, no way to rid her veins of the poison. He said a prayer and made the sign of the cross over her body. Finally, he covered her face with his jacket.

It was then he saw the large envelope behind the stone on which she had sat. It was addressed to him and DCI Cotton. He sat on one of the large stones near the spring and undid the clasp of the envelope.

The silence in the clearing now was absolute. No rustle of wildlife, no stirring of leaves; even the spring's surface was flat and still. It was the eerie quiet Max associated with abandoned monasteries, and yet he did not feel he was alone.

Inside he found a pile of lined notepaper, clipped together at the top—page after page handwritten in a beautiful cursive script no doubt taught her by the nuns. She wouldn't have had time to write this in one afternoon; he reasoned she must have been writing it for some days, as a sort of diary.

She had thought of everything. Writing out her confession, addressing it to Cotton and him, released Max from the seal of the confessional, which would have been absolute. He could never have repeated what she had told him about Thaddeus's murder otherwise, with or without her full repentance.

Beneath the stack of handwritten pages were several e-mails she had printed out, also clipped together. They seemed all to be addressed to her mother, Claude Chaux. There were no replies, of course: Claude Chaux had been killed long ago, cheated of the richest decades of life, and alive only in her child Gabby's imagination.

He began to skim Gabby's confession. It was a summary of what she had told him during the Rite of Reconciliation. So far as he could tell, she had left nothing out. At the end, she had written:

> *I write this confession so no innocent person is blamed for what I have done. That would be the only crime. There has been enough accusation and betrayal of innocents.*
>
> *I leave all of which I die possessed, especially the photo of my mother, and her earrings, to Lucie Cuthbert, for her many kindnesses.*
>
> *Pray for me.*
>
> *Gabby Chaux Crew*

After Max had read Gabby's letter, he sat quietly on that fallen menhir in Nunswood, and he thought. He thought for a very long time.

"Why do you walk through the fields in gloves?" Charles Darwin's granddaughter had written that in a poem, and Agatha Christie had quoted it in a story of hers he'd read long ago.

It was what he had often noticed about Gabby, without seeing the significance.

Gabby had always worn long sleeves, often with gloves, every single time he'd seen her, and he'd never thought to wonder about it. But it was odd, especially for one who complained about feeling the heat of the day, as she had done just recently when he'd met her on his way to the

Horseshoe. Why not at least roll the sleeves up if she was hot? It was very odd indeed that she wore long sleeves, always, regardless of the temperature. How often had he seen her tug at those sleeves, too?

The only people he knew who did that were addicts, and Gabby was no addict.

Addicts, he thought . . . or people trying to hide a tattoo—perhaps from a job interviewer.

And suddenly he understood.

She had just said it to him. Prisoners were tattooed. Listening to Annabelle describe the horrors, Gabby had come to take on the traits of the survivors. The same fears and memories, the same mannerisms. That tugging at the long sleeves, so no one could see. Annabelle must have done that, an unconscious gesture.

At Coombebridge's place, surrounded by blue paintings, Max had found himself thinking of the blue-painted Picts of Scotland. It was a word that came from *pictus*, meaning "painted" or "tattooed."

People in the camps, even small children, had been tattooed.

It was a thought too terrible to hold in his mind, and yet impossible to chase away. Finally, a wail of sirens announced the arrival of the emergency services van at the foot of the Crest. As Max watched from above, three men emerged and offloaded a rescue stretcher.

The only access to the pagan spring was on foot, up the steep, winding trail to the menhirs.

CHAPTER 25
Whys and Wherefores

Max and Awena sat together in Awena's house, snug before the fireplace in the embrace of her comfortable sofa, sipping black coffee, his laced with apple brandy. They had just finished another of Awena's sumptuous meals—organic, seasonal, locally sourced (much of it very local—from her garden), and vegetarian. Awena's carbon footprint was very small indeed.

"Have you heard about Frank's book?" she asked him.

"I'm afraid I have. Lucie says it's doing very well."

For Frank had self-published his pamphlet as an e-book, and he was having quite a little flutter of success. An editor at Marcellus Sanders, Ltd., had discovered him, and talk of Frank's book suddenly seemed to be everywhere.

Critics had been kind, heaping lavish praise on Frank's eccentric worldview, which they took to be a pastel rendering of a mythical, Tolkeinish past juxtaposed with an invisible, parallel universe much like that of the Harry Potter saga. As Suzanna had been heard to say over a pot of tea at the Cavalier, "When Frank Cuthbert is hailed as a fresh new voice in fiction, you know that we as a nation have strayed completely off the path."

"One wonders what path that is," said Max when Awena had relayed all this to him.

"Oh, I don't know. The path of common sense, I suppose. Still, good for him. Perhaps people were attracted by his pioneering work with the apostrophe. At least he's got the words all spelled correctly, and most of the grammar is right, so far as I can tell. It's as if the Internet age were invented for just such as Frank. The last I heard, he was going on a tri-county book tour."

"I own several copies already, what with one bring-and-buy sale or another. Frank is a tenacious salesman." And, thought Max, since Frank had recited every morsel of the plot to him more than once, it obviated the need actually to read the book now.

He took a sip of his coffee and said, "I'm surrounded by celebrities. Are you really going to be on the telly?"

"I'm seriously considering it, Max. It may be a way to get people to stop the madness. If I can persuade anyone that a healthier diet is doable—and may help us save our precious planet . . . This may be too good a thing to pass up."

"You could finish writing your book and go on tour with Frank."

Awena laughed. "I think I'd sooner ride a horse naked through Nether Monkslip."

"I would pay to see that."

She nudged him. "The whole point with Lady Godiva is that the men agreed not to look."

"Oh. Well, bless her heart for being one of the early tax protestors, and undoubtedly one of the most effective."

"Did you know," Awena asked, "that Bernadina and Doc Winship are seeing something of each other now?"

Max paused, considered. "He certainly seemed taken with her. It would be nice if that worked out. Everyone—the whole world—should be as happy as we are." He held up his coffee glass against the gleam of the fire, swirling the contents to watch the changing topaz light.

"I'm just so glad," he said, "that you are here with me, and safe and sound. I realized, way out there on the tip of nowhere with Coombebridge, that you might not have been headed for the Cavalier that afternoon for tea, as I'd assumed, but might be going somewhere less public with Gabby and Melinda. I wasn't yet clear on how or why, but I was clear that you might be in danger if left alone with either of them."

He had misread so many clues, he thought, a sure sign he'd lost his touch since his MI5 days. He had, for just one example, misread the meaning of the wallpaper that had so upset Gabby, once he'd figured out the wallpaper *had* held meaning for her. He had thought Gabby herself might have been a prisoner, which is one reason why he became frightened for Awena.

He dialed his thoughts back to the evening in Frank and Lucie's dining room. Of course, he knew now, the Coombebridge seascape had had nothing to do with Gabby's distress. It was Lucie's stylish vertical-striped wallpaper *behind* the picture that had upset her. The abrupt, unexpected, and unbearable reminder of her mother's suffering.

"I was never in any real danger, Max," said Awena. "We had tea at Gabby's flat over La Maison Bleue. And Gabby seemed her usual self. Composed, confident. But then Melinda took ill. . . ."

"Gabby poisoned Melinda's meal. Premeditatively. I call that being in real danger, Awena. What if she'd become confused and mixed up the pies?"

"I mean, I was never Gabby's target. But I suppose I was lucky. Knowing I was having a mushroom omelet later, I didn't want any quiche."

Thank God, thought Max, Awena had not been a part of Gabby's plan. Gabby had helped Awena see Melinda safely home, then had faked illness herself as an excuse to leave. Even then, Gabby's will seemed to have been unraveling, faltering, with remorse setting in; she could, as she had said, have killed Melinda if she'd really wanted to.

He remembered another odd moment from the dinner at Frank and Lucie's, a moment to which he felt he should have paid more attention. He remembered that Gabby had talked about her mother as if she'd known her to talk to. Lucie had fallen strangely silent, a puzzled look on her face—for Lucie, whose own mother had grown up in the same convent orphanage as Gabby, would have known that Gabby never knew her mother. The woman had never lived to give Gabby advice on fitness or any other topic.

He had summarized for Awena the contents of Gabby's letter, and the copies of the e-mails she had left behind. Cotton had told him the police had broken into the e-mail account she'd created, where she wrote letters to her mother as if she were alive, as if her mother had survived the war. The password she'd used was Claude.

"Those e-mails . . ." Awena began.

"She used them as a sort of diary that could be hidden from prying eyes, but it also was her way of keeping in her life the woman who had been taken from her with such brutal finality."

"It is strange to think how Melinda got involved in the first place. If not for the time change . . . I suppose she'll be in some trouble for this as soon as she's recovered—as an accessory."

Max nodded. "The time change was something that dogged me throughout the case—every hour on the hour, in fact, since Maurice generally forgets to 'spring forward' and 'fall back' the church bells. It was what kept reminding me of the time issue, and I began to wonder if it might come into the equation. Gabby was caught in the act because Melinda anticipated the time change on Saturday night and set her watch forward. Gabby never wore a watch, because her hands were in water and dyes and chemicals all day, and so she vaguely thought she had an extra hour to dispose of Thaddeus and all the evidence. She simply forgot; Melinda could have died because of her own efficiency—an efficiency I'd say was uncharacteristic. Melinda kept quiet about what she knew, but Gabby couldn't trust such an uneven personality to keep quiet forever."

"It took a certain amount of daring, didn't it?" Awena said. "Gabby's method of killing Thaddeus, of working her way into the confidence of both Thaddeus and Melinda. I suppose we could say she inherited from both parents a certain strain of boldness."

"And then there was this: Gabby's day-to-day work often involved mixing chemicals, measuring effective amounts of peroxide and whatnot. She was comfortable in that world. It's no stretch to think she could work out the right dose to kill Thaddeus—and the right amount of poison to kill Melinda, if she'd wanted to. Although I gather in Melinda's case she made a slight miscalculation."

"But . . . they were good friends," said Awena musingly. "Gabby and Melinda."

"They may have developed something like a real friendship, partly because Melinda was so frequently in the shop, but in the beginning Gabby was in intelligence-gathering mode—tracking down those earrings, and learning about Thaddeus's early life, his current habits, and so on. Eventually Melinda spilled nearly everything to Gabby—her unhappiness with Thaddeus, even details of her relationship with Farley. Gabby knew exactly which way Melinda's thoughts were drifting, particularly when she found her with those mushrooms. It was highly likely Melinda would botch the job; I somewhat suspect Gabby wanted to make sure the job was done right."

Awena settled against him, listening to the rumble of this chest as he spoke.

"Otherwise, she'd have let Melinda kill him," she said. "And maybe—this is a terrible thought, but maybe she wanted to keep that pleasure to herself."

Max said, "I think you may be right. Anyway, the clues at times were nebulous. When someone—especially someone like Thaddeus—does or says something that makes no sense at all, I look for the reason. There is *always* a reason. Sometimes it's just that they're embarrassed to say what the small matter is." He set his lips grimly together. "And sometimes there's a darker reason."

Awena lifted her head to look at him. "I know what you mean. Sometimes they are masking something that would really be no big deal, if they'd just come out with it. But the small lie grows to look like a big one."

"In this case, I remember that Thaddeus claimed not to remember the war. But he was ten. How credible is it he would be too young at ten to remember anything? The world—his and everyone else's—was turned upside down."

"It's not really possible he just didn't want to remember, is it? Even though the mind plays tricks . . ." Awena added wonderingly, nearly echoing Gabby's words, "That a ten-year-old was capable of this . . ."

"I'm not sure he saw it as anything more than a bit of mischief. Still, by that age he should have been able to realize the consequences could be fatal. His kleptomania seems to have blinded him to anything beyond his immediate wants. I would imagine that particular form of illness is worse before the impulse control most adults share has fully set in."

Max added, "There were other inconsistencies, small ones. I was nearly certain Thaddeus was not native to this country, but I tied no significance to that at first. He talked about someone attending '*the* New College in Oxford'—no British person would say that. It's logical but wrong to add that 'the' before 'New College.' It was an oddity, just something I noticed at the time, nothing more."

There was a long pause as they sat listening to the crackle of the fire. Raindrops pelted softly against the windows. Awena said, "What do you think happened with Gabby? Was she adopting her mother's personality? Trying to *become* her? The e-mails . . ."

"You are thinking of something like multiple-personality disorder? No, I don't think that is the case, not at all. Gabby knew full well who she was, and who her mother was, and that they were two separate people. She just became obsessed with what had happened to her mother. I think she felt that by absorbing what she knew of her mother's life and personality and experiences into her own, she could become closer to her somehow, feel what her mother had felt, and, by putting on the mantle of this woman she never knew, fill the enormous void left in her own life, particularly after her husband passed.

"I think Gabby was trying to relive everything she imagined her mother—and all the women caught up in that hellish experience—had gone through. Trying, almost, to become *like* the person she imagined her mother might have become, had she lived. I suppose it's some form of survivor guilt—I'm not expert enough to say."

Max thought back to one of the Bible verses Gabby had left for him to find, the Psalm about the orphans. "They slay the widowe and the stranger: and murder the fatherlesse." Only now he could see how obvious a clue it was to Gabby's identity. As he and Cotton had discussed, she must have wanted to be caught. She had been orphaned so young, her mother and widowed grandmother both killed. The quote fit the wreckage of her young life, even to the fact the father she'd never known had been a stranger, a sojourner in France who had met his own death trying to escape. Gabby had been engulfed by unthinkable loss, betrayed by the malice of an evil child. Thaddeus may have suffered from his uncontrollable impulses to steal from an early age, but there was a cruelty to his actions that Max thought went beyond his mental illness. He had ruined the lives of innocents for no better reason but that he could—almost as a form of entertainment, like watching a play. Max could easily picture him bringing his secret knowledge to his parents, certain of their approval. Knowledge, then as now, was power.

"I agree. I don't think she was insane," Awena was saying.

"Not in the legal definition. She knew what she was doing. She knew her mother wasn't alive. She simply kept her alive in her own mind. And she killed Thaddeus with full knowledge that killing him was wrong.

"But I could make a long list of mitigating circumstances. Her chance to know her family in the normal way—mother, father, grandfather *and* grandmother—had been taken from her. She'd been robbed of all their lives. *And* of every personal possession, by the way—her home and belongings. We perhaps mourn more intensely over unexpected or sudden losses, or when we can only imagine the loved one, with only a photograph to gaze at, and wonder at what might have been. Losing her beloved husband, that sudden loss . . . all these injuries she suffered were at a cellular level.

"She learned the details of her mother's fate not long after her husband died. The timing of these meetings with Annabelle, so soon after his death, probably unbalanced her mind. To learn such terrible details, when she was already bereft—it could send anyone over the edge. Seeing the article about Nether Monkslip—seeing that photo of a woman wearing her mother's earrings—it all seemed like a sign from God to her, bringing her to this place.

"And there was her enemy, alive and healthy, out enjoying himself with friends, living the life others should have been around to enjoy. Tracking him down gave her a purpose, but I think it finally unhinged her, too. The thought of avenging her mother—avenging all those who had suffered so greatly—these thoughts took over her mind in a ruinous way.

"All we can say with certainty is that the atrocities occupied her mind, tipping the normally stable balance of her thinking."

Awena stood and held out her hand for his glass. On her return with a refill, Max said, "I have come to realize how Gabby sprinkled little clues of wartime experiences throughout. She talked about making do, about makeshift strategies for makeup, like using berry stains for lipstick and rouge, or red pencil lead. She could have been talking simply of wartime shortages. But she was talking of the ruses the women used to fool their captors into thinking they were healthy enough to be worth keeping alive. Otherwise, they'd have been singled out for execution. Gabby's excellent posture and her attention to her health were all part and parcel of the same, well, *fear* that she lived under. Only the strong and fit—and the very, very lucky—would survive the unspeakable conditions to which her mother had finally succumbed."

Awena said, "Gabby's mother must have been a remarkable woman in every way. I would like to have met her, too. One wonders if one would have had the courage to do what she and others like her did."

"Please God we never have the need to find out," said Max. "Gabby's story has had me rereading some of the history from those days. About the convents that were used to hide weapons and ammunition, as well as to shelter from the Gestapo the children who otherwise certainly would have died. The friend of Gabby's grandmother, the Mother Superior at the convent where Gabby was raised—she must have known the enormity of the risk, and Gabby's mother must have known in advance she would, unquestioning, accept the risk.

"The strategies used by the Resistance were so clever. Sometimes a priest would stage a funeral leaving the occupied zone, with the mourners issued a pass by the Germans. The "body" and some of the mourners would then escape.

"They didn't always avoid detection, of course, and ruses like that would work only once. Betrayals were common: It was often a way to settle old scores. One nun was denounced for calling Hitler the Antichrist, which was possibly even true—both that she said it and that he was. At any rate, it was a view many came to share. Certainly he brought hell to earth."

"And all these years later, the ripple effect . . ." Awena began.

Max nodded. "All these years later. Not long ago, a death camp suspect was located, age ninety-seven." He paused, thinking how crimes cast a long shadow, seemingly to the horizon.

"The question may be how many other people would feel the same, in Gabby's shoes," said Awena.

Max nodded. "First she lost everything dear in the world, before she was old enough to even be aware of the loss. Then one day she locates the man who had cost her her mother's life, and she tracks him here. Maybe that's all she meant to do—to track him, out of curiosity, as she claimed. But then having met him, and seen how appalling a person he was . . ."

"I can see that happening, very easily," said Awena. "The switch from thought to action."

"Well," said Max. "Three guesses what the topic of my sermon will be this Sunday."

"I thought your sermons were always the same."

"Thanks very much."

"I meant, are they not always about doing unto others? About being a force for good in the world?"

"I suppose they are. . . . But this one may be a bit different."

He stared a moment into the fire, enveloped by the peace of being in Awena's company.

"By coincidence," she said, "this year Passover intersects with Easter. It all flows together from the lunar calendar."

"Right—Holy Thursday through Easter Sunday." He set down his glass. "You'll be at the church service, won't you?"

She nodded. "The zither and banjo will make a nice change."

"Hmm," said Max neutrally. He had lost that particular debate.

"Once I've paid my respects to Ostara, the goddess of spring, at dawn," Awena continued, "I'll be there. I've already decorated my hat."

She leaned across him and turned off the lamp at the table by his side. They were left with only firelight.

"When you realize," she added softly, "how many of the old traditions were absorbed by the Church, it's remarkable the way people go out of their way to emphasize differences."

Max looked at Awena, her skin glowing like white Carrara marble, now looking up at him out of those limitless eyes. He touched her chin, almost as if making sure she was real.

"When we're married, you'll have to move over to the vicarage," he said.

There was a silence that went on a beat too long for Max's comfort.

"At least that would be the traditional thing to do," he added. "I realize you've built a life for yourself here in your cottage."

More silence.

"And it's so beautifully decorated," he went on, guessing now as to what the matter could be. "I'm sure we can find some middle ground. Obviously, I have to live in the vicarage. . . . I mean, I guess I have to. . . ." He trailed off.

She took his hand in hers, her hand small and warm, comforting. Finally, she spoke.

"Think about it, Max. Our differences are religious, which makes them as fundamental as differences get. Especially in this instance."

"I don't see it that way," said Max, surprised but calm.

She said nothing, but looked at him quietly and patiently, as if waiting for him to catch up to her. Max had never felt so vulnerable. All along, his concern had been getting his heart's desire past his bishop, past officialdom. He had never questioned whether Awena, who owned his heart, would follow.

"We never spoke of marriage," she said.

And suddenly they were starring in a reprise of *Sayonara*. Max said, "It was never not in my thoughts, Awena. This was never from the beginning anything casual or ordinary for me."

"For me either," she said quickly, assuring him. "As far as I'm concerned, in my heart I've already chosen you. I'm wedded to you. All the rest is merely . . ."

"Window dressing? Paperwork?"

She looked down, hiding from him those Awena eyes, like sea glass, clear and pale.

"No . . . Yes. Sort of."

Oh God, he thought. Somehow he'd thought—what had he thought? Not that she would officially convert to his religion, never that. Awena was too much her own person with her own beliefs to simply fall in with whatever might be convenient to the situation; she would never simply put aside her own beliefs, so passionately lived and held, even for appearance's sake. Max thought of his own faith as a flowering of mercy, an unasked-for gift, and so he well knew that beliefs arrived in their own ways and guises.

He had thought, he supposed, if it could be called thinking, that they'd cross that marriage bridge when they came to it. Certainly if he'd planned things better, he'd have fallen in love with a devout Anglican woman, her doctrines as lined up in conventional rows as the pearls about her neck. Instead, he'd fallen in love with an exuberant, stunningly attractive, magnetic woman who with her scattershot, all-embracing approach to life and religion embodied all that his own religion taught him to admire and emulate: kindness, compassion, and empathy. Her basically sweet and open nature could not be doubted. It was just that her beliefs were outside the "norm," as the Church in the person of his bishop would see it, and not that her beliefs and practices were in any way abnormal.

As often in these situations, the choice of a life partner had been beyond his control. What would be right and proper for a man in his station in life had not mattered, and he'd barely paused to consider anything beyond his soul's joy at finding its mate at last.

Right now he was too frightened of losing her, of frightening her off, to say this, or anything more.

In the uncanny way she had, Awena mirrored his thoughts.

"I suppose we'll cross that bridge when we come to it. But Max, it will become an issue one day. No one who doesn't know us well will see our partnership as anything but, well, unorthodox. And I don't have the answers, either, except that we both should pray on it."

Dueling prayers, thought Max. Or were they? Awena would hold they were all the same prayers to the same deity.

There was a longer pause this time. Another *Oh God I'm losing her* pause.

"What about children?" she said at last.

The relief rushed through him. "Yes, of course, as many as you want."

"I meant, what religion would they be raised in?"

Now there was a longer pause as he bit back the automatic, unthinking reply.

"This isn't fair," she said. "I've had a little more time than you to think about this."

He had almost missed it, but the look on her face told him there was more meaning behind her actual words. "What do you mean?" he asked.

She drew a deep breath but said nothing.

"What?" he asked. "What *is* it? You have to say."

She looked at him from those extraordinary, luminous eyes, which now blazed in the golden light thrown by the fire. "I'm pregnant, Max," she said. "I began to realize, when I was at Denman. It must have happened the night of the Winter Solstice, when we were first together. At first I couldn't believe . . . I thought it was because so much has been going on in my life. . . ."

Max's jaw literally dropped. For a full minute, he was rendered speechless.

She smiled at the look of stunned disbelief on his face. She knew it was a match for the look on her own, once she'd realized.

"The baby will arrive around mid-September, in the fall," she said.

"This changes everything, Awena." He took her hands and held them fiercely in his. "We are no longer sitting here swapping philosophical musings and theories about the origins of religion. This is—I don't know how to put it. It's a *practical* matter. This is beyond me, beyond you, even. You do see—we have to marry?"

"Why do we have to do anything, Max? If I'm honest, I don't know what to do, other than to have this baby, which has its own plans and schedule. But rushing into marriage doesn't seem like an option at any time. Not now—especially now. You do see, don't you?"

Max was staggered, and completely thrown back on himself. Every emotion went through his mind, but the overriding one was joy. Complete, undiluted joy was the base coat on top of which anxiety, excitement, astonishment, and worry were making their marks. He didn't know it then, but that would be the state of his emotions for many years to come.

No, he didn't see, but again he was afraid to push her—more afraid now than before.

"In the meantime," she added, "we don't know what may happen. None of us knows. So let's be happy while we can. Just . . . we just have to leave it alone for now. We both have to think. All right?"

And many hours later, with nothing settled in either of their minds, they made their way hand in hand up the darkling stairs, and so to bed.

AUTHOR'S NOTE

My fictional story of Gabrielle's mother and grandmother is true in its essence. The tale Gabby relates to Max is a composite of the ordeals of 230 women captured in the roundup of French resisters during World War II. As their sufferings are impossible to describe or summarize in any meaningful way, I have struggled to do justice to their lives and honor the enormity of their courage by telling you Gabby's story here.

The nonfiction book *A Train in Winter: An Extraordinary Story of Women, Friendship and Resistance in Occupied France* (2011), researched and reported in heartbreaking detail by Caroline Moorehead, provides the depth and scope my fictional tale will not allow. As I cannot begin to convey the remarkable individual stories of these women, I highly recommend to you Ms. Moorehead's moving and important tribute.